The Tale of
Gold and Silence

also translated and introduced by Brian Stableford:
Anonymous: Sâr Dubnotal vs. Jack the Ripper; *Anthologies*: News from the Moon; The Germans on Venus; The Supreme Progress; The World Above the World; *Henri Allorge*: The Great Cataclysm; *Cyprien Bérard*: The Vampire Lord Ruthwen; *Richard Bessière*: The Gardens of the Apocalypse; *Albert Bleunard*: Ever Smaller; *Félix Bodin*: The Novel of the Future; *Alphonse Brown*: City of Glass; *André Caroff*: The Terror of Madame Atomos; *Félicien Champsaur*: The Human Arrow; *Charles Derennes*: The People of the Pole; *Renée Dunan*: Baal; *Henri Duvernois*: The Man Who Found Himself; *Achille Eyraud*: Voyage to Venus; *Henri Falk*: The Age of Lead; *Paul Féval*: Anne of the Isles; The Black Coats ('Salem Street; The Invisible Weapon; The Parisian Jungle; The Companions of the Treasure; Heart of Steel; The Cadet Gang; The Sword-Swallower); John Devil; Knightshade; Revenants; Vampire City; The Vampire Countess; The Wandering Jew's Daughter; *Paul Féval, fils*: Felifax, the Tiger-Man; *Octave Joncquel & Théo Varlet*: The Martian Epic; *Gustave Kahn*: The Tale of Gold and Silence; *Jean de La Hire*: The Nyctalope vs. Lucifer; The Nyctalope on Mars; Enter the Nyctalope; *Lamothe-Langon*: The Virgin Vampire; *Gabriel de Lautrec*: The Vengeance of the Oval Portrait; *Georges Le Faure & Henri de Graffigny*: The Extraordinary Adventures of a Russian Scientist Across the Solar System (2 vols.); *Gustave Le Rouge*: The Vampires of Mars; *Jules Lermina*: Panic in Paris; Mysteryville; The Secret of Zippelius; *José Moselli*: Illa's End; *Marie Nizet*: Captain Vampire; *Henri de Parville*: An Inhabitant of the Planet Mars; *Gaston de Pawlowski*: Journey to the Land of the 4th Dimension; *Georges Pellerin*: The World in 2000 Years; *P.-A. Ponson du Terrail*: The Vampire and the Devil's Son; *Maurice Renard*: The Blue Peril; Doctor Lerne; The Doctored Man; A Man Among the Microbes; The Master of Light; *Jean Richepin*: The Wing; *Albert Robida*: The Clock of the Centuries; The Adventures of Saturnin Farandoul; Chalet in the Sky; *J.-H. Rosny Aîné*: The Givreuse Enigma; The Mysterious Force; The Navigators of Space; Vamireh; The World of the Variants; The Young Vampire; *Marcel Rouff*: Journey to the Inverted World; *Han Ryner*: The Superhumans; *Jacques Spitz:* The Eye of Purgatory; *Kurt Steiner*: Ortog; *C.-F. Tiphaigne de la Roche*: Amilec; *Théo Varlet*: The Xenobiotic Invasion; *Paul Vibert*: The Mysterious Fluid; *Villiers de l'Isle-Adam*: The Scaffold; The Vampire Soul; *Philippe Ward & S. Miller*: The Song of Montségur.

The Tale of
Gold and Silence

by
Gustave Kahn

translated, annotated and introduced by
Brian Stableford

A Black Coat Press Book

Visit our website at www.blackcoatpress.com

ISBN 978-1-61227-063-0. First Printing. December 2011. Published by Black Coat Press, an imprint of Hollywood Comics.com, LLC, P.O. Box 17270, Encino, CA 91416. All rights reserved.
Printed in the United States of America.

Introduction

Le Conte de l'or et du silence, here translated as *The Tale of Gold and Silence*, was initially published in its entirety in Paris by the Societé du Mercure de France in 1898. The first six chapters—which include the first chapter of Part Two—had previously appeared in 1896 in *La Societé Nouvelle*. It is not obvious why the serial version was suspended, given that it did not conclude at a "natural break," but the likeliest explanation is that there was a pause in its improvisation. I say "improvisation" rather than "writing" because much of the book, especially these early chapters, is a patchwork that must have taken aboard a number of previously-written stories, poems and prose fragments, providing them with a narrative frame that sometimes seems cursory and is not altogether coherent.

Gustave Kahn was born in Metz in 1859 and educated in Paris. Although he published some critical pieces while still a student his literary career was interrupted thereafter by a four-years sojourn in North Africa; although he did submit some poetry to Parisian periodicals during that interim, it was not until 1886—having returned to Paris in 1885, perhaps with a considerable body of unpublished work in hand—that he began to publish poetry prolifically, initially in the first of several periodicals whose editorial staff he joined, *La Vogue*. In September 1886 Jean Moréas published "Le Symbolisme"—effectively the manifesto of the rapidly-burgeoning movement—in *Le Figaro*, and Kahn immediately joined forces with Moréas and Paul Adam to produce a showcase for it the weekly periodical *Le Symboliste*. The periodical did not last long, but the movement did, and Kahn remained at its heart, promoting himself as the pioneer and champion of *vers libre* [free verse], which he regarded as a form uniquely well-suited to symbolist expression. He subsequently occupied editorial positions on the staff of *La Revue Indépendante, La Revue Blanche* and the periodical that became the chief organ of the Symbolist Movement in the 1890s, *Le Mercure de France.*

Other examples were inevitably advanced to dispute the honor of being the first French writers to adopt *vers libre*, but the two most plausible—Kahn's close friend Jules Laforgue, and Arthur Rimbaud—had both been published under his auspices in *La Vogue*, so his leading role in its promotion is indisputable. Whether or not *vers libre* is uniquely appropriate to symbolism is similarly debatable, but it certainly caught on with several of the leading figures in the movement, and it formed a bridge of sorts between conventional Romantic and Parnassian rhymed verse and prose-poetry, which had been proclaimed by Joris-Karl Huysmans' Jean Des Essenites as the ideal format for the exercise of "Decadent style."

In the view of most critics of the 1880s and the bulk of the reading public there was no real distinction between the emergent schools of Decadence and Symbolism, and the two terms were bandied about rather indiscriminately, but the three editors of *Le Symboliste* did not care for the "Decadent" label, and instead of accepting it and inverting its pejorative implications, they tried to draw a distinction between their emphasis on the use of exotic language in the service of some kind of philosophical purpose and an affection for Decadent style for its own sake, as advocated by Théophile Gautier's doctrine of *l'art pour l'art.* Kahn's attempt to claim a special role for *vers libre* has to be seen in that context. Whether there was any real difference in the distinction remains a matter of opinion, but it had some success as a marketing ploy, and Kahn elaborated his discriminatory perspective with considerable depth in his seminal critical study *Symbolistes et décadents* (1902).

Kahn was also an important art critic and, in that capacity, a leading advocate of Impressionism, partly under the guidance of his friend Charles Henry, a mathematician and physiological psychologist who had published *Introduction à*

6

une esthétique scientifique [Introduction to Scientific Esthetics] in 1885. Kahn introduced Henry to the pages of *Le Symboliste* and used his ideas and discoveries regarding the physiology and psychology of perception to connect the literary and artistic schools. Just as the impressionism could be interpreted as an attempt to take a kind of psychological back-step, so that the artist could produce a suggestion of what the eye registered prior to the brain's synthesis of a more coherent, knowledge-based image, so symbolism, in the theories of Moréas, Kahn and Stéphane Mallarmé could be interpreted as an attempt to suspend a part of the brain's analytical process and tackle ideas in a more immediate form, prior to the intellectual sieve of interpretation and explanation.

In his manifesto, Moréas declared that Symbolism was inherently opposed to "plain meanings, declamations, false sentimentality and matter-of-fact description," all of which seemed to him to be overly conscious, and thus possessed of an apparent directness that was, in fact, misleading in its simplification and imposed coherency. According to Mallarmé, truth could only be approached indirectly, through the medium of symbols, because it was by nature evasive, if not unfathomable. According to Kahn, the purpose of symbolist art was to "objectify the subjective" and replace imaginative elements censored or tidied up by intellect to their true priority in the processes of perception and enquiry.

Opponents of Symbolism routinely charged its exponents with such alleged literary sins as making up words, deliberately using archaic terminology, distorting the meanings of words and generally tending toward incoherence, but all of these strategies were seen by the school's exponents as virtuous and necessary. Those writers who preferred the label Decadent to Symbolist committed all the same sins, for motives that were hard to distinguish if they could be distinguished at all, but tended to be more pugnacious in defense of them. The core of the collective ideology of the compound Movement was a reaction against the philosophy of Naturalism, although there was much more of an overlap between the seeming rivals than

7

might have been expected, with writers like Huysmans and Adam moving back and forth between the two, and literary titans like Gustave Flaubert and Anatole France functioning with equal ease and mastery in both modes.

The Symbolist opposition to vulgar naturalism drew writers naturally to topics drawn from folklore, legend and mythology, but there was nothing new in that, and the calculated primitivism of the manner in which they tried to grasp such substance extrapolated an entire Romantic tradition stretching all the way from the chivalric romances of Feudal times to the Romantic Movements of the late eighteenth and early nineteenth centuries, initially spearheaded in France by Charles Nodier and effortlessly extended into Decadence by Gautier. Symbolism had never been absent from such work and had very often been central to it, but the proto-psychological theories borrowed by Kahn from Charles Henry and formulated by Mallarmé did offer some potential for its transformation into a quest for a new kind of insight—a tentative precursor of the far more elaborate and determined quest undertaken by Carl Jung in his attempted analysis of "archetypal imagery." Much Symbolist prose—and *Le Conte de l'or et du silence* is a cardinal example—can be construed, with the aid of hindsight, as an exercise in the further development of, and an aspirant commentary on, the archetypal images subsequently categorized and explored by Jung.

Kahn's first three collection of poems, *Les Palais nomades* [Nomad Palaces], *Les Chansons d'amant* [Love Songs] (1891) and *Domaine de fée* [Realm of Enchantment] (1895)—all reprinted in the omnibus *Première poèmes* [Early Poems] (1897)—were devoted to his principal concern, the development of free verse, but the bulk of his publication was in periodicals until he began to publish books on a regular basis in 1896. It was in that year that his first novel, the baroque comedy *Le Roi fou* [The Mad King] appeared, although a substantial fraction of the text of *Le Conte de l'or et du silence* had probably been written earlier, and the fact that he published three novels in quick succession in 1898 suggests that he had probably built up a considerable backlog while struggling to get his career under way.

Although *Le Roi fou* certainly qualifies as a symbolist work, its literary method is not nearly as exotic or extravagant as that of *La Conte de l'or et du silence*, and its humor contrast quite sharply with the latter novel's earnest pretentiousness. Kahn's later novels, including *Les Petites âmes pressées* [Hurried Little Souls] (1898), *Le Cirque solaire* [The Solar Circus] (1898), *L'Adultère sentimental* [Sentimental Adultery] (1902), *L'Aube enamourée* [The Enamored Dawn] (1925), *Mourle* (1925) and *La Childerbert, roman romantique* [the title refers to the nickname of a building] (1926) are markedly less exotic than *Le Roi fou*, and he never returned to the kind of prose endeavor that he had undertaken in *Le Conte de l'or et du silence*, perhaps considering the work a failure as an artistic endeavor. His poetry, however, never faltered in its symbolist method, and he continued to address the themes touched on in *Le Conte de l'or et du silence* in *vers libre* with the same urgent passion that is displayed in the most impressive passages of the novel.

This apparent discrepancy reflects the fact that symbolism, as a literary *modus operandi*, is more easily adaptable to poetry than to prose, and more easily adaptable to brief "poems in prose" than to longer works. Moréas and Mallarmé restricted their symbolism almost exclusively to poetry, and although Paul Adam claimed to be writing symbolist novels in some profusion, it was not always obvious that the novels in question were much different from his earlier Naturalist endeavors. The leading novelists identified with the Decadent Movement—including Jean Lorrain, Rachilde, Catulle Mendès and Pierre Louÿs—often attracted that label as much for the deliberate perversity of their subject-matter as for their deployment of Decadent style, and it is noticeable that the prose "Bible" of the Movement, Joris-Karl Huysmans' *À rebours* (1884; tr. as *Against Nature* and *Against the Grain*), is more an extended character-study of a Decadent lifestyle than a novel.

This pattern extended as time went by. Remy de Gourmont's novels made far less use of symbolist technique than his short fiction, and could easily be seen as exercises in psychological neo-Naturalism in the same vein as the novels of the supposed chief exemplar of that school, Paul Bourget. Gourmont was, in any case, a much more precise and analytical employer of literary symbols than the Moréas-Kahn theory advocated, as was Anatole France when working in that vein. At the opposite end of the Symbolist spectrum, the deliberate recklessness displayed by Gourmont's sometime editorial collaborator Alfred Jarry in his own symbolist novels moved them decisively in the direction of surrealism, one of whose most important precursors Jarry became. Jules Laforgue never wrote a novel, but his short fiction moved flamboyantly in the same direction, extrapolating precedents set by Rimbaud and the satirical performance-pieces acted out in Le Chat Noir by the core members of Émile Goudeau's Hydropathes—which Kahn testified that Laforgue enjoyed enormously.

Within this spectrum, *Le Conte de l'or et du silence* occupies a location that is virtually unique. It is not only Gustave Kahn's most overtly and most extravagant symbolist novel, but one of the most overtly extravagant symbolist novels ever attempted, and it demonstrates in no uncertain terms why such attempts were plagued with enormous difficulty. Perhaps it does not qualify as a novel at all, given that it is such a disorderly patchwork with so many variegated intrusions, but if it does not, it is very difficult to specify what it is; it is far more than a random collection of tales. Indeed, Kahn was not otherwise given to seeming randomness is compiling short story collection, carefully organizing the contents of his three major collections under the categorizing titles *Contes hollandais* [Dutch Tales] (1903), *Contes juifs* [Jewish Tales] (1926) and *Vieil Orient, neuf Orient* [Old Orient, New Orient] (1928). *Le Conte de l'or et du silence* flies in the face of this orderliness by mingling mock-parables, Old Testament fantasies and visionary fantasies, and throwing in a couple of mock-folktales and an adventure story for good measure. The frame-traversing threads connecting up these disparate elements seem rather arbitrary at times, but are sufficiently robust to insist that there really is a connecting theme binding the whole together, however eccentrically.

Kahn's knowledge of and attitude to literary symbolism was inevitably colored by his Jewish ancestry, and it must have seemed natural enough to him to deploy symbolist methods in re-examinations of Old Testament mythology and the supposed modifications introduced by the subsequent reinterpretation of much of that mythology by the New Testament. He was not a devout Jew, however, and was prepared to take the view that all such symbolic myths could be fruitfully placed in a much wider context, taking in Classical mythology, all manner of folklore and the tradition of French Medieval romance, and also licensing the invention of entirely new mythologies to challenge or counterbalance allegedly-unfortunate aspects of existing ones. The core of his world-view, however, remained firmly rooted in the Old Testament, and the supposed wisdom of Solomon—as handed down, in the novel, to the Mage-King Balthazar.

There is no surprise, given its importance in the history of French literature, that Kahn should also have seized upon the Christian myth of the Wandering Jew in order to provide Balthazar with a sidekick and sounding-board. He was undoubtedly familiar, at least by reputation, with the use of the Wandering Jew in a frankly symbolic fashion in Eugène Sue's classic feuilleton serial *Le Juif errant* (1844-45; tr. as *The Wandering Jew*), and was probably aware that Alexandre Dumas had deliberately adopted the same figure as the central character of his intended masterpiece *Isaac Laquedem* (1853), although Dumas abandoned the work in disgust when it fell foul of Napoléon III's censors. He might even have been aware of Paul Féval's ideological reply to those Radical and

Republican tales, *La Fille de Juif errant* (1864).[1] We can, however, be certain that one work with which Kahn was definitely familiar, and which undoubtedly had an influence on *Le Conte de l'or et du silence*, was Edgar Quinet's epic drama *Ahasvérus* (1833), which uses its eponymous protagonist as an interested viewpoint with which to survey the entire history of the world, from its creation to the long aftermath of the Day of Judgment.

Kahn is not quite as ambitious as Quinet in organizing the stage on which his action is deployed, but he attacks the same enigmas with a similar intensity, and Part Two of *Le Conte de l'or et du silence* employs the same Medieval frame as the third act of Quinet's drama, with a similar bitterness of tone. The interpolation of an episode of Arthurian mythology into that part of Kahn's narrative, which might seem odd and awkward, is probably not unconnected to the fact that Quinet's other major exercise in mythical reinterpretation was *Merlin l'Enchanteur* [Merlin the Enchanter] (1860). The world-views of the two writers are markedly different in several respects, but a methodological kinship is obvious, as is an unsurprising commonalty of feeling, arising from the fact that when they take their lyrical examinations of the human condition to its furthest limit—a much further limit than any other nineteenth-century writer of extended *contes philosophiques* attempted to attain—they both discover a perspective that is exceedingly bleak. Kahn's particular bleakness is, of course, solidly licensed by the Old Testament, and in the most telling passages of his main story the tone of his lamentations often seems to be echoing *Ecclesiastes* and *Jeremiah*, although the alleviation of the *Song of Solomon* is not entirely absent.

In terms of parallels with English literature, the writer with whose work *Le Conte de l'or et du silence* has most in common is undoubtedly M. P. Shiel, who had a similar fondness for Old Testament mythology and language, and took a

---

[1] Tr. in a Black Coat Press edition as *The Wandering Jew's Daughter*, ISBN 978-1-932983-30-2.

similar delight in the construction of exotic rhapsodic prose. Shiel, who spent a good deal of time in Paris during the 1890s and was acquainted with several of the writers involved in the Symbolist/Decadent Movement, almost certainly met Kahn, and might conceivably have taken some inspiration from his work. Whether Kahn ever read Gabriel de Lautrec's translation of Shiel's *The Purple Cloud* is uncertain, but he was definitely acquainted with Lautrec, and surely read the most Shielian of his dream-tales, "La Terreur polaire" (tr. as "The Polar Terror"), which appeared in the *Mercure de France* in 1904. The parallels between Shiel's work and *Le Conte de l'or et silence* are, at any rate, sufficiently striking to give this translation a particular interest to admirers of Shiel, although it will offer some delight to all English lovers of the eccentricities of Decadent style.

This translation was made from the London Library's copy of the first edition of the full text, published by the Societé du Mercure de France. The expectable difficulties of translating a text that does not always aim for coherency were compounded in this instance by the fact that the printed text in question is strewn with errors, to such an extent that it is difficult to believe that it was ever proof-read. (I have run a cursory check of the first part of the text against the serialized version, and identical errors occur there, suggesting that the *Societé Nouvelle* text was used for type-setting the early pages of the book, without any attempt being made to correct it.)

The pattern of those errors that are not mere misprints strongly suggests that Kahn dictated the bulk of the text rather than writing it by hand and that he entrusted much of the work of punctuation and syntax to his amanuensis—or, more likely, amanuenses, given that some of the elements of the text were probably written a intervals of several years. It seems to me that Kahn's amanuenses did not always understand what he had said—or perhaps what their own shorthand signified—and that their work was then inadequately checked by the author.

Any attempt to "restore" a text suspected to be corrupt is bound to be presumptuous, and some of the alterations I have made in the interests of trying to assist certain passages make more sense might be mistaken, but I have done what I could to the best of my ability; I can only apologize for any passages that stubbornly retain their nonsensicality in spite of my attempts to work out what might have been meant.

Brian Stableford

THE TALE OF GOLD AND SILENCE

To Stéphane Mallarmé

Dear Master,

If this is the book of mine that I have decided to offer you, it is because it is the one that extracts the most from the sources of the pure idea and because its territory is the one in which I most closely frequent regions of which you are the prince.

At the debut of my literary life, you were kind enough to welcome my juvenile admiration; it is with the same sentiment, fortified, since you have permitted it, with affection that I offer you this Tale, delighted should you be indulgent toward it.

Gustave Kahn

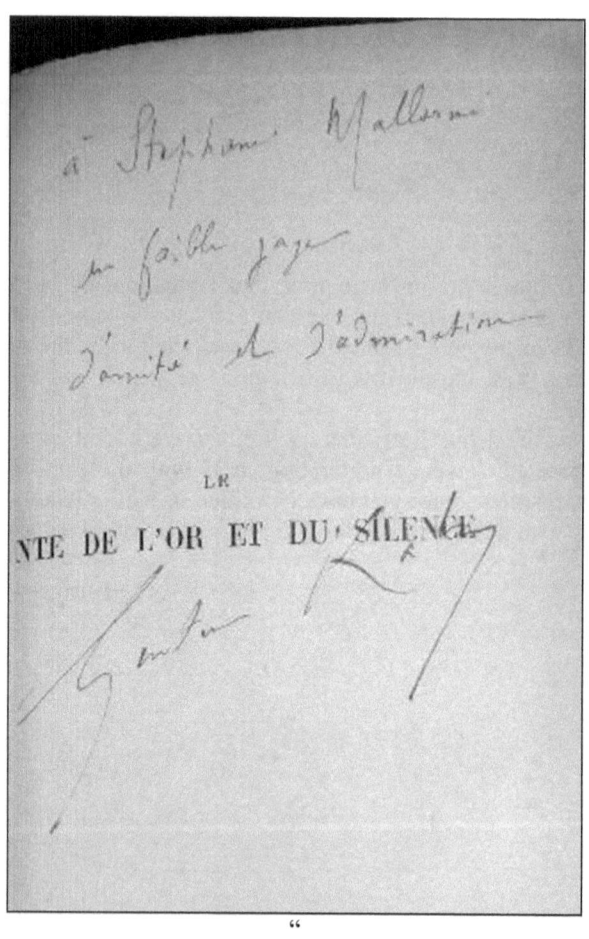

"To Stéphane Mallarmé:
*A weak testimony
of friendship and admiration
Gustave Kahn*"

Notice to the Reader

This book is a mythic and lyric tale.

The first part is set in a castle in the legendary land of Sheba,[2] in the first century of the Christian Era.

The second part is set in an imaginary Empire, through which one may imagine that the Meuse and the Rhine flow; the temporal setting of the action is around the fourteenth and fifteenth centuries.

The third part is set in the same locale as the first.

Some of the characters, representing ideas, are immortal or reincarnate. Thus, the mage-king Balthazar, in the first part, becomes Master Ezra in the second. Other characters, representing phenomena of the passions, behave according to the norms of legendary life.

---

[2] Kahn uses the Hebrew spelling (Saba) but the word is used in the main text almost exclusively to refer to the individual known in English literature as "the Queen of Sheba." I have similarly substituted the spellings made familiar in English by the King James Bible for other places and characters drawn from the Old Testament. The warrant for Kahn's frame-narrative is based on *Isaiah* 60:6, where the prophet predicts, in connection with the advent of the Messiah, that "all they from Sheba shall come: they shall bring gold and incense"—a reference construed by Christian commentators as an anticipation of the Mage-Kings' interaction with Jesus.

PART ONE

Chapter One
THE TWO CULTS

I

Late in the day, the old king soothed his ennui wordlessly, walking alone on his balustraded terrace, from which the vast expanse of the sea could be seen. The waves were blue, ornamented with white foam, and no ships ever passed by except, once a year and far out to sea, a flotilla laden with merchandise from Taprobane. The coarse mariners hastened past this commerce-free haven; their gross ships seemed to the king to resemble fragments of papyrus rolled by a clam and pleasant wind. That was all, for the year, until the same habitual and quasi-ritual seekers of gold appeared again on the clear threshold of the horizon, to constitute a futile white stain there.

The most frequent visitors to the gloomy king on his solitary terrace, where mosaics of small stone retraced the features of Theano, Mobed and Glyphtis—who was once Helen[3]—were the white swans and agile swallows for which bowls, jars and nests were periodically prepared.

In the marvelous silence of the Sun, and its golden powders on the white sand, the grains of which were amber, agate and lapis lazuli, the old king lived a very solitary life, and every day the black men of his bodyguard, unoccupied and otiose, played interminable games with blue and white pebbles. They only varied that occupation of interested relaxation to polish their weapons, made of the most beautiful metal, and to make sure that the serving-women had laundered the cloth of their tunics to the necessary whiteness.

---

[3] Presumably Helen of Troy.

And all the surrounding territory was as calm as the dream of its king. The ancient gift that he had made of all wealth to all the poor kept him and them safe from any invasion of thieves—and besides, the world had the Roman Empire at which to gnaw away.

For years now, the old king had not left his solitary palace, where his meditations focused more intently on his own mystery. His former ministers, each retired to some royal residence in which they exercised their tastes as they pleased, did not weary him with any questions, for similar rules regulated subjects haunted with the same desire: to live simply, to work very little, to dream incessantly. The only animation that stirred the petty kingdom, on King Balthazar's birthday, was the urgent and competitive choice of gifts of marvelous beasts, wine and vegetables to restock the contemplator's larder.

Inside the palace, almost all the rooms of which were permanently locked, a few pale servants muffled the sound of their footsteps on thick carpets and animal fleeces. They lived on tiptoe, and their wise speech was taciturn. Only one among them served and approached the king, and the lethargy of the old citadel of colored marble was uninterrupted, save for the occasional click of dice in the doorways.

The high vault of the church dedicated to the gods of chance and the unknown were abandoned, and the organs no longer accompanied hymns; only the servants sometimes murmured the ancient melodies rhythmic with infinite hope, as if they were old marching songs. Sometimes, a tremulous voice murmured:

> *It is from the giant flowers of the origins*
> *that it is necessary to demand the fading secret*
> *of the ambush from which souls trail*
> *from church to church, from portal to portal.*

or:

> *My soul has seen the chariot of God pass by,*

his right hand sowing seeds
over the world,
and his foresight adorns the world beneath the skies
with living flowers on the saddest walls
and gilds the fields and multiplies the oxen.
His will raises islands in the seas
which no human has ever fathomed,
in order to provide a refuge when bitter ills
have crushed old worlds beneath the heels of war.[4]

King Balthazar had nailed the doors of the churches shut and silenced the organs, and the God of his fief of the world of the Spirit was Silence.

Silence, radiant reparative force, slumber of life, brief glimpse of the mountains of faith

Silence, original to the beginning and the end, overwhelming law

Silence beneath the arpeggios of the Sun on serene coasts

Silence of the coraline cities of submarine depths

Silence of the time when, weary of its futile sleep, the Sun drapes itself, and the clots of its blood stain the quotidian and temporary crosses of the ether

Silence, promise of Erebus, and of the lairs of inspired seers

---

[4] Considering the meaning of these verses to be more important than their rhyme-schemes, I have translated them directly, without making any attempt to reproduce their poetic formalities. All of Hahn's *vers libre* is partially, but never entirely, rhymed, and sometimes exhibit a fugitive scansion, but translating it without rhyme or scansion does not pervert it unduly. The poetic sequence that follows, undistinguished by font or positional setting, similarly contains a few rhymes. I have reproduced its dearth of punctuation precisely, although I am not at all certain that it was fully intended, and I have taken the liberty of adjusting the punctuation of some of the subsequent poems and "songs," where greater orthodoxy seems to have been attempted.

Silence, sole word among the blind who dream the worlds

Silence, of which only the tortures of hunger draw the iron talons from the excoriated prophet

Silence, liturgy and panacea,

Silence, thou the hope all the days of the world, Silence, father of the night of our over-feverish and excessively ambulant dreams.

Silence, unique and necessary bed of Speech,

of the Speech of one who gets up to say the fundamental words, the only short words, that indicate the cult,

the cult of absolute silence.

Silence, god persecuted by tyrants and plebeians

God massacred since the dawn by the carts of rubbish-collectors

God starred with the bloody wounds of speech, impatient dense and ambitious, which the poor name the Word

Silence on the ultimate terrace of the world

That which the rising seas of the waves of the deluge has not reached

transporting words of love, words of glory and trumpetings of war

Thou holdest the strange and supreme cup,

The marvelous everyday philter against the gods of activity,

against the machines deified with glory or terror by famished crowds,

Thou holdest it without ever extending it

and it is necessary to scale the asperities

of all the somber paths of mortal checks,

in order, deprived of pride, to attempt therein

the supreme chance of happiness,

in thine incarnation, Silence.

And that final word, that final hymn, King Balthazar no longer communicated, for the adepts of his faith discovered it for themselves, and those to whom his advice might have been a beacon for life succumbed in their ardent gaiety, in inns, to the overexcitement of their strength, or sought repose in deceptive philters that were poisons, the futile ambushes of Azrael.

For the King, death is something for which it is necessary to wait. The ultimate lucidity of an absolutely calm soul can only attain its original word—to wit, the meaning of vague words exchanged during its brutal or amorous and charming conception—when, every other individual being set aside and all affections extinct, "for affections are merely ornaments of life, marching songs and the distant music of the traveling fair, and the music of two hectic lutes," the dying man sees coming, not the mirage of the avaricious Azrael, but the white specter that paints for humans every evening the truth of their ideal beneath their eyelids, and then, after the light descent of the black curtain, shows them the stars in sheaves upon the horizon, and then throws them a dream of hope in which pure nymphs sing with Paraclete voices in colonnades of fire and joy.

The absolute canticle of being, the pivots of which are the love of pure form and the voice, reflections of an *empyrean without dissonances*, cannot be attained by the body alone; the bushes of Horeb[5] only awaken when the fermented bushes have defeated the desires of interest, ambition and capture that carry humans away in their squares and their crossroads, behind their bed-curtains and in their heroisms; that is why Mobed the benevolent has spread the poppies of wine in the great churches of joy; but the scoriac hymn of felicity rings its changes with such stymphalic notes that the joy has quit the wine, conquered in any case by merchants, like gold, like dancing-girls, like the entire divine figuration of our planets.

Now Azrael, the evil minister of the Demiurge, has, alongside dolors, tempted mortal souls, and human beings

---

[5] Horeb was, in some versions of the story, the mountain in which Moses received the Ten Commandments, so the "awakening" in question is to possession by divine fire.

have exhausted, with their atavistic desires for power and gold, the gifts of drunkenness, profound amulets, symbols of the embrace of Pan, mute contemplations, solitary dominations amid the serious fictions of life, and humans have forgotten God, the silence that holds the cup without extending it, in favor of the noisy demons that unroll the gifts of evil, and speak their language, and thus persuade them.

II

The gentle pallor of night expanded over the violet Earth. The terrace where, beneath the maternal caress of night, the old contemplator of everything remained awake, allowed itself to be invaded by the avant-garde of darkness, and only in the distance, near the exit door, was the light of a torch gleaming. The perfumes of the divine night took flight from sleeping flowers, and nothing troubled the quietude of the resemblance, the austere daily consecration of the Silence, but the animated face of the Moon, pale with suffering, like the hollow eyes of a solemn vision of eternal misery. The gardens of the sky were devoid of the gigantic mirages profiled by worlds in birth, and the emotional human, now that the pallor was extending the gentle word of sleep over the hemisphere, was able to perceive the flowers of Eden, perhaps apparent, that the god of illusion projects in the illuminated Heavens.

The vesperal coolness of an autumn in the sultry zones brought, upon the soft fans of breezes, the great residues of the fresh perfumes of marine plants, and the opals of the altar of the god Silence radiating conflagrations of a joyful soul from the depths of the universal tabernacle.

This was the unique demonstration of that cult lost in the sands; it was necessary to flee the cities to perceive the magnificent grandeur of the mirage lavished by solar force, and the consoling peace that night poured out, those two clear appearances of the opaque fact of existence. In the corner of Ethiopia where King Balthazar reigned over a few peaceful sages, the sunlight lavished the shadows of apparitions upon the stroller,

24

as on the dazzling surroundings, the palaces and cupolas, but the evenings raised up the charm of slow avenues of meditation for him.

The King blessed all the corners of the horizon. He blessed with his palms of despair those who were agape before the new word, those whose ulcers were deceptively aggravating the old words of the world proffered before wooden masks and stone effigies. He blessed those who adored the book in the Ark, without knowing that its old counsels of blood and localized privation are the work of Azrael. He blessed the sons of Iblis who attack cities where bright-faced girls are walking in order to steal and sell them in ports where black kings, helmed in silver, await them impatiently. He blessed the conscienceless pirates who commit their souls to the stormy sea in order to bring girls as yellow as the rising Sun, whose tresses enclose the mystery of the birth of night, to markets where blond, pale man idly stroll. He blessed the people of the Archipelagoes, who days are spent mixing the divine wine with base products of naphtha, to augment its weight and sell it at a higher price.

He sympathized with the giants who precipitate themselves upon empty lands, whose former prosperity seduces them, crying: this is mine; and with the decimated who, from the fissures in the mountains, watch for an opportunity to surprise the thieves, when prosperity has rendered them defenseless, in a bed that is too soft and too large. He mourned for the cunning and deceitful folk who live in the great cities, and the faithful who weep and mourn for themselves in desert spaces, invoking the eternal Immanence because a vow of poverty and asceticism will exasperate their nerves and destroy their physical being.

This is the hour in which the Pontiff-King suffers for all the souls on Earth, for the miners and the mariners, the agile people of the cities and the feeble toilers in infertile fields, for the deserving hypocrites of false gods, the illuminates of charity, for everyone who speaks and moves, for everyone who amasses and calculates, for all those who do not know that what is necessary is to listen one day, in the bosom of profound silence, to that which one ought to say to oneself—a sensuality equal for the criminal and for the benefactor, since it is justice to which one listens, attenuation by days of repentance for the humble who know not, infinite praise for one in whom feeble enlightenment and habitual self-knowledge have allowed a few benevolent attributes of the taciturn world to flourish.

And if the people of the pale castle could hear the last hymns, their memories would be furnished with such refrains as:

> *Meditative indolence beneath the fronds of palms*
> *shows us the way to the good spring*
> *where the honey of life is never seasoned*
> *with the cruel gaze of the last scruple*
> *of those who do not know thy law.*
>
> *Thy law is to wait for the infinite dawn,*
> *that which sleeps over the sources of life*
> *awaiting the wise benevolent awakening.*
> *While beneath the festival stars and the trellises*
> *of wines of wisdom and forgiveness for all sins*
>
> *the fortunate sage of the benefits of silence*
> *will speak to the simplest, the infinite word;*
> *then the sage dressed in light and equipped*
> *with the dazzling procession of the humble*
> *will climb the hard ramps of capitals.*
>
> *And the weapons of those who gesticulate*
> *and the arrows that ornament the dusks*
> *of old people hardened to suffering*
> *will fall before the true word*
> *that will cause to germinate in all the intoxication*
> *of the sleeping world of noise*
> *the slow meditation of silence.*

O Silence, contemplative god of the world
who forbids offense,
O Silence who determines the virtues
among the solitary, in the headstrong universe
whose power reigns until death over the round
of caprices lost in the errors of ambience.

III

King Balthazar had retired; as soon as the heavy drape-ries fell back upon his icy footfalls, through a silence magni-fied by the distant growling of large dogs and the dull plaint of the sea, a shadow traversed the pale terrace. A man came for-ward, hunched, aged and pale, his eyes gleaming like silver in his basalt face. That servant, clad in a saffron tunic, was carry-ing a small torch.

He stopped in front of the image of Mobed, his eyes and lips reflecting one another in prayer. The effigy alone was illuminated, gleaming from top to bottom, shining in the night with a fugitive, isolated beauty, wading off the surrounding darkness. The overly large eyes in the thin face, too black within the pale face, the night-dark hair flowing in symmetric-al waves over the shoulders, seemed to testify to a feverish life, accentuated by the glints of gold in the pupils—and yet it was a effigy. Only the fact of having no relief attenuated the materialization of the idol, and he beauty of its features consti-tuted its entire prestige.

The old servant contemplated, and murmured:

She it was in the gardens of Gaza,[6]

---

[6] Gaza, where Samson was taken after his betrayal by Delilah, was one of the principal cities of the Philistines before falling to David. Among the principal deities worshiped by the Philistines was Astarte, a moon-goddess worshiped in numerous eastern Mediterranean cul-tures, often equated by later scholars with the Egyptian Isis and other

Her gaze burning like lamps.
When she appeared
the stones of the temple were sparkling
with lines of dancing-girls, flamboyant on the temple

steps

and the roses of the gardens of Eden flowered
at her supple tread beneath her ample cloak.

When her mantle fell
from shoulders of contemporary marble.
Those whose mask was the beauty
and the coaxing vice of spring
lifted up the immemorial flagstones
and the gems of the world's veins sparkled
on their breasts, their girdles and their turbans.

Her stature alone summoned hymns
in alternating savors by night, in the ruins
her gesture decorated the crumbled walls
where the dolorous ivy inclined its dark leaves
and the decor of the day where the spring wept
in the disjointed leaves; Astarte and her glories
scaling with the luxury of goddesses in celebration
the stepped firmaments toward the splendors of her

head.

She has raised up the strong beside torrents
and blessed the chariots of tribes on the march
in order that smiles burst forth in flecks of blood
on the lips of dark girls draped in white.
She multiplied the goats of the herd
and dulcified the grass they grazed with balms;
her voice smoothed the cradling lips of nurses,
and inflated the grave voices of priestesses

---

important goddesses; Kahn is fusing here with his fictitious primal
goddess Mobed.

when the heroes fought against the harsh giants.

Her hands, her fine golden hands,
her lips, her beautiful lips of balm
soothing after evenings of combat
her sons and her men.
Her caressing hands unlacing helmets,
her tender voice caressed the men
too weary of the broken blade and overlong road,
too weary in the face of fate.

Mobed, profound flower in the depths of the ravine
where the soul of life's evening stumbles,
you decorate on errant nights the gardens of enchant-
ment,
you console through the long day the stumbling slave.
It is your smile that the poor man divines
along the cool sashes of the wind.
They are your eyes, the beacon in the dark shadow
of those gardens of silence and diamonds,
that are the brief clouds, the vast sea and the eternal
eve.

And the old servant lost himself in his reverie. It dated from long ago, and its distant limbo was only reminiscent of harshness and misfortune, of shackled hands and hobbled feet; of slow-leading wounds striping his flesh before a kinder destiny, by the hand of conquest, had detached him from that heavy servitude in order that he might come under the benign domination of the king. The beast of burden and fatigue that he had been throughout the years of his youth hand then lain down in a fresher litter, and his function had been to follow Balthazar in his wanderings and serve him. He had accompanied him faithfully, his heart everpresent, and his soul too, haunted by a quest for gentleness and hesitant in its generosity. He loved the image of Mobed because those features had given form to his own disheveled and personally inaccessible dream, and he venerated it as a present and tangible promise—inanimate, but a promise nevertheless.

His appointed task at this hour was preparing for the King's evening meal, and soon, under the caress of the breeze, between enormous gently undulating torches, bruits and beverages, meat-dishes and cups were set out for the solitary meal that he had to serve.

AN ENCOUNTER IN THE PAST

On the table, an open pomegranate displayed its droplets of congealed blood in a silk of mat gold, enclosed in a solid red and yellow rind like a nomad's cloak; the down of figs recalling the nacreous coolness of a sacred wood, and the sun-tanned dates reminiscent of a golden grape in which the mist of a sunrise remained, no longer tempted the King.

From a turquoise-bellied jug the slave poured him a profound wine with golden gleams like a lake in the kind of paradise of which children are able to dream. At his gesture, the servant, standing until then, sat down on a mat and filled a goblet of violet glass for himself. That is a custom established by the wise Balthazar, and, at this hour, weary of the expectations which he is calculating for the future, he likes to revisit with the other man the dead hours of their life, according to the infantile wanderings of his fancy.

"Do you remember, Sire King, that journey which was interrupted, so many years ago? My memory often returns to it—not that its ups and downs were particularly notable, but it's undoubtedly the only time that we didn't arrive at a destination determined in advance, especially in those times of you maturity when you were seeking out the masters of wisdom, in order to learn from them and debate with them.

"Your friends Melchior and Gaspar were coming from their domains to an arranged rendezvous. It was usually at the junction of the eastern and western roads, close to a ravine that might shelter a caravan for the night, near the still-recent ruins of an old mercantile city. By night, the air still seemed to shimmer with the sonorous waves of the ancient words of So-lomon. Next to the fires of forest trees, which seemed to mir-ror the sunset, sitting on the ground in your white burnooses, all three of you had the semblance of statues in the face of the incorporeal image of Horeb, which appeared to Moses, or be-fore the mobile and ardent veil woven by the eternal Hours before the irreducible face of Isis.[7]

"Why, Master, did we not go further that day? Had we not chartered a numerous and well-laden caravan in order to go to Liban meet the man that people called the Doctor of Kindness?"

"Dares, having lived with me for so long, you sometimes evoke the moths that dance around an old dying lamp, of a memory that has only just revived in me. More than once, my two brothers in thought and I, before age froze us in our dis-tant palaces and out henceforth-distant souls, talked about those days, and the predictions that informed us of experience and destiny.

"We were going toward Liban; our course traversed the sands where our Ishmaelites celebrated our presence by send-ing their falcons to hunt birds in the sky and jousting with their long lances.

"It was in a place called El-Hissa. We arrived by way of a gentle slope on the crest of a hill, whose other faces fell sheer to a yellow plain with pale clumps of greenery. On the flank of one of those escarpments, at the level of the plain, we saw a seated woman who was clasping a child in the folds of her blue burnoose, and a man who seemed to be searching for something among the stones. Was he hunting a jerboa? At the sight of horsemen, he seemed to want to flee, but in the face of the impossibility and our friendly appeals to his probable mis-

---

[7] The capitalization of *Heures* [Hours] suggests that the reference is to the Greek Horae, goddesses of the seasons and time in general; their association with Isis is a further indication of Kahn's syncretism is absorbing all the ancient goddesses of the Mediterranean into Balthazar's eccentric Mobed-led trinity.

fortune, he stopped, and told us that his name was Joseph the Carpenter, and that he was fleeing toward Judea.

"You know that shepherds and goatherds look after hollow stones and cavities apt to retain the rainwater that falls therein; at such places, known to them, they are able to find a little water in the dry season, and for fear that the source of life might run dry, they cover up their hiding-places with stones. It was that aid and comfort for which the man was searching amid the rocks of the hill; the poor travelers were exhausted. They found water-skins and a tent in our camp.

"The young woman, whose name was Mary, was miraculously beautiful, even by comparison with the imperious face of that Mobed, the calm and meditative forehead of that Theano and the excited child-like candor of that Glyphtis. Pure and delicate features, harmoniously silky, in which the Hebraic curve of the nose was attenuated; profound eyes devoid of astonishment, sparkling like a drop of pure water on a calyx; hair covered with the habitual head-dress of her race; a lovely mouth; and throughout her person, an attitude of infinite respect toward all those around her, which raised her above them.

"Joseph had chosen the purest of the young woman of a village in Galilee. He still spoke to her as one touches a precious and fragile vase. In fact, on seeing a soul of nacre inspire her rare movements, and her eyes reflect a divine security, the idea of the possession to which women submit was dispelled; one understood that the carpenter was still surprised by the delights of marriage, and that he had forgotten them before the immaculate quality of that young face. He was a Believer before the revelation by beauty of stars, clouds and murmurs of the echo of the Word.

"The child was beautified by weakness and the caress of Mary's hands.

"Do you remember, Dares, that Herod reigned by violence? His harsh soul, besotted with dancing-girls and tortures, dismantled by the phantasms of his remorse on the nights of his lassitude, sometimes cracked with fear like its

32

infantile counterparts in the darkness of a cell. That soul was a labyrinth in which the superstitions of Asia and Rome were wandering, without being able to get out. He was a king of men, but not of his own nerves; terror struck him down with the sacred disease.

"On cowardly evenings, via his ears and his will, nursery tales commanded him to capital executions. The Asiatic tribes believed that an armed and naked child would preside in Heaven over the death of kings in the ashes of cities. The Romans prostrated themselves on hearing that before great tragedies, fire-spitting lions haunt the vicinity of the Capitol; that the old sibyls reappear, enormous silent specters, their hands lit up by torches, that she-wolves crazed by pregnancy come to bite emblematic statues, when the faces of the heroes fixed in the marble silently stream with tears; that on those evenings, monsters with staring eyes emerge from the rivers in waves of slime, foaming with wrath.

"At Passover, when the Hebrews come from every direction, in concord, to bow down to their God in Jerusalem, what extortionist, what mercenary, what charlatan historian of the sky would trouble that weak mind? Would they want to pile up dead bodies in rubble? Did some self-important individual, seized by folly, want, through Herod, to imitate the miracle of the children of Egypt, struck down in a night of anger, or was a new mode of condemnation necessary to amuse his cruelty? All the new-borns were to perish in a single night.

"Joseph was warned by one of the followers of the Master of Kindness. The latter, without knowing precisely what was being planned, had foreseen some horrible carnage, and their voices counseled the temporary exile and indicated refuges. But were the sages believed? If they were believed, there was hesitation regarding their advice. Joseph and Mary were alone in their candor in sensing the imminence of fatalities, and their love for their child was so inexhaustible that they resolved to flee even the shadow of danger and go away.

"The following days would have presented the mirror of Edenic epochs, so glad were they to have sheltered their offspring from the slightest squall. Their goal was Egypt, where, in the populous cities, a man might easily life by the work of his hands; besides which, Sadducees and Hellenes were able to live in peace there.

"Melchior, Gaspar and I thought that a child thus protected, whose father was all honest virility and mother all devotion, holy timidity and courage in the face of adversity, would be protected throughout his youth and led toward the highest foundations of the human soul. The loving miracle of his conservation presaged other miracles in his life, and we said so. As it is necessary to treat poor and unknown guests better than kings followed by starry standards and caparisoned camels, and not daring to offer these saints money, on the evening they camped with us we entertained them with music, singing and legends. Shepherds attracted by our fires came to rejoice with us. The night was admirable, and God's torches gently illuminated the surrounding terrain.

"The next day they left, a little richer in food supplies; our horsemen helped them to cross the arid sand; our progress was halted. It would have been painful for us to go through blood-stained Judea in order to discuss higher knowledge and virtue. We stayed together for a few days, and then went our separate ways.

"What became of them—Joseph the Carpenter, Mary, so beautiful and gentle, and their child, blessed by chance from the very beginning? I don't know. Shall we ever know? The unbridled couriers of destiny abound on all the world's roads, without ever meeting one another."

THE GUEST

The diaphanously oily waves of the dawn had invaded the colorless highways, and the calm mirror of the sea reflected gilded harvests in its glaucous grass. A perpendicular arrow came over its surface, tracing the long wake of a blade of solar silver.

The irradiated solitudes were deserted, and there was an ecumenical silence around the palace. Long ripples of water came to stroke the steps of opalescent marble where bubbles of foam were born and died. The depths of departure and arrival, all the way to the illusory wall of the horizon, seemed gathered like a pure festival décor that the first sound, the first footfall, the first chord, no matter how faint it might be, would break.

For a few minutes, there was a pure presence of light.

Then a voice sang from a tower:

The hands of the future, on another propitious day
open the battens of the silent temple
where the candles of our heart, toward the mystic gems
of the golden star, reflection of the red infinity,
melt and spread forth their human spices.[8]

The plain extends to the limits of our desires
and our footsteps toward piety and pity;
our eyes that decipher the future in the night
will still live that day in the face of beauty,
calming the dream anxious that it has gone astray
with the momentary presence of bright lyres.

Greetings to those here, greetings to those who watch
in the love of being gentle, tomorrow as yesterday
and decking their hearts with an hour of purity.
Greetings to those elsewhere; greetings to the old soul
who will come to retemper in the Sun-haunted palace
his body broken by wandering on treacherous paths.

---

[8] It is probable that a line has been omitted from this verse; in the original, the second line rhymes with the fourth, as in both the other verses, and the first with the last, as in the second but not the third, so the omitted line is presumably the fifth (which might have rhymed with the third, as in the third verse, or might not, as in the second).

Then human life flowed, starring the clear mirrors of silence with its cracks.

King Balthazar had returned, alone and meditative, to the large terrace where the daylight ornamented the faces of the superhuman frescoes with its splendors. Abruptly warned by prescience, the contemplated the monotonous sea and perceived a black line in its insensible swell; it was floating like a sturdy abandoned branch, but heading nevertheless for the coast, and the waves never covered it.

At closer range a boat appeared; closer still, and a man became discernible thereon. The latter, astonished, gazed at the vast façade toward which the erratic will of fate was driving him. He was neither steering to rowing; the boat was small and hollow, without ornaments, like that of the poorest fisherman. A large white beard covered the breast of the man, clad in a long dark robe without a glint of gold, silver or color. The boat ran aground against a marble step and a wave carried it away again, now rocking hesitantly, fluctuating at the slightest pressure of the waves. The man climbed the marble steps with a firm tread, holding an elongated casket of simple wood in both hands.

The Mage-King greeted him.

"Be welcome, guest who has arrived among us, surrounded by calm, by the perilous and mysterious path of torments. It is easy to discern that the will that floated you over the liquid crests, devoid of oars and deprived of a tiller, was sending you to me, or toward some more profound power to which I ought to furnish you with guides, along with the necessities of travel. Certainly, your venerable air and the tranquil maturity of your gaze imply that you are not one of those scoundrels whom human wrath casts adrift on the ocean in a boat without rigging. If, however, that is the case, and mercy has only descended upon you in the final moments of your life, be welcome nevertheless, for the sign of momentary mercy will have enlightened you. And if the rhythmic respiration of the waves alone drove you here, soul still weighed down by a shadow, be welcome still and accept the greeting to which the god Hazard has brought you. Whatever language your actions have spoken, be welcome."

And the guest replied: "I have come to you. The child that you encountered in the sands of Idumea, the son of Joseph and Mary, has died under torture. As you, the mages, had predicted, his childhood increased in splendor and in knowledge, and without the doctors he divined the human soul. His clear mind, scorning the ambiguities of commentary and the anniversaries of ritual, understood that humans are weak before the great eternity of the Gaze; and his soul attempted, first of all, never to hide behind the wrathful wind of unjust words, for the most remote hiding-places become sonorous with the frightened cries of the wounded conscience.

"When he knew himself limpid in virtue, innocent in mediation, heightened by certainty, he came to talk to the doctors. Some he charmed, others he confused, but doctors are too numerous in too many towns. Then, knowing the brief instant of the Ephemerae, he preferred that simple folk should be his neighbors and live according to his example. He explained to them the hope of the trembling creature before the resorbent totality, and the visions of harmonic silence in the total magnificence of the Word and Motion.

"His doctrine was one of resignation, frugality and forgiveness. He wanted tolls to be paid, publicans not to be hated, the dolorous to be freed and sins to be washed away, for why punish the unconscious plants that grow on the world's crust? And when his numerous following of fishermen, artisans, soldiers and merchants, renouncers of false ostentation, women with dark or gilded tresses, swollen with exuberant sap but henceforth ardent for the truth, arrived on a hill near a city it was without the splendor of worldly kings, without cymbals and acclamations, but, on the contrary, with the slow pensive manner, ornamented with gentle gaiety, of those who have nothing to repent. The infirm believed in him sufficiently to be cured by contact with him, and queens of the flesh abdicated their power at his feet. The valleys of Palestine were, for a time, the lost garden of still-innocent humankind; missionaries set forth to preach the simplicity of life to the peoples of distant shores.

"But when they were too numerous, because the divine work is only able to appear momentarily and the multiform host of phenomena must incessantly recover it, dissension burst forth among the newcomers to the army of faith, and it was they who furnished the weapons of false testimony to the resistant forces of domination by usury, fraud and the blade. They pretended to believe that he, who wanted the lucid crowns of human love, was some new aspirant to a diadem and the property of a citadel in the heart of a canton.

"And Jesus, the son of man—thus named by virtue of his filial love for that antique uncertainty, Man—was crucified between two bandit chiefs seized with weapons in hand, for the conquest of illusory gold. The blows of terror dispersed his partisans, and his friends left to propagate the truth by means of stories and, at need, the example of a pure life cut short by torture.

"I was not, at first, one of these who followed him. On his own advice, after he had melted my old heart with an aspiration toward virtue, I remained one of the powerful individuals of the city of Jerusalem, in order that no iniquity should emanate from the rights I exercised. The torments of savage joy that greeted the weary march of the just toward agony gave me a horror of the world, and I no longer wanted to do anything but supervise charity.

"When we were able to bury him, his body was still oozing drops of blood; I collected them and am bringing them to you, in accordance with the imperious order of my conscience, the voice that proclaims verity in dreams, and the exigencies of my footfalls on my route. I'm old; it's time to bring you the precious deposit. Receive it from the proud hands of one of those who perceived a slight ray of his truth; receive it from hands washed by contact with him—and now that my task of transmitting it to you is fulfilled, deign to let me spend the few minutes of my life in your shadow, for those faithful to the verity of Jesus no longer have a homeland. Your guest is no longer the envoy of eternal forces; he is poor Joseph of Arimathea.

"The vessel in which I collected the Incarnate's drops of blood in enclosed in this primitive casket; it's a vessel of coarse wood. It's as simple as the truth. Just as the Incarnate contained in the poverty of his body and soul the immense piers and desperate towers of the truth, so this coarse vessel contains the memory and testimony of his existence. Only men like those who detect in the son of man a power superior to that of the forces of nature, of which forms of metal are the effigy, will be able to experience the consolation that this vessel will bring, and deduce the eternal truth from such a legend of a single moment in time. It is to you, for my strength is failing, to you the old contemplator isolated in the face of the Profound Rationale of Silence, that the responsibility now belongs of conserving it, of testing its strengths, and of explaining the details to them of what they must discover in essence alone."

Then King Balthazar summoned the black slave in order that he might take the guest away for a few hours' rest. He gazed pensively at the vessel, and the profound sea, and the superhuman frescoes, still absorbed in the auroras of a new verity that was about to enlighten his eyes.

Chapter Two
THE DOCTOR OF KINDNESS

Joseph of Arimathea lived in the castle of King Baltha-zar. One day, on the terrace constructed to overlook the gardens, King Balthazar and Joseph watched the noisy activity of the birds and butterflies. In the cheerful gardens there were palm-trees whose fronds became silvery in the sunlight, po-megranate-trees whose flowers burst forth scarlet, delicate and slender olive-trees and a heavy brown curtain of cedars barring the horizon. Beneath the vertical sunlight, veils of gauze sown with powdered gold seemed to extend into the distance, the soft and aromatic vapors of the warm earth.

Joseph asked Balthazar what he knew about the Doctor of Kindness. Joseph knew him by reflection, through tales and a few words of Rabbi Hillel,[9] who had quite recently ornamented Jerusalem with the glare of his virtues.

"I knew him," the King said. "He was a child-like and profound soul. Hillel could have given an idea of him; at least, he echoed a part of his lustral benevolence, over the harsh city where gold is overly prized. But the Doctor of Kindness had entered long before Hillel into the knowledge of verities—or, if you prefer, plausible symbols. In reaching that point of intellectuality, Hillel had been hindered by the ardor with which the contemplation of his traditional God warmed him. A scribe may accumulate virtues, but he will nevertheless only become the best of scribes. The gifts that one perfects in the shade of temples never blossom into extraordinary flowers. It was in

---

[9] The prominent Pharisee Hillel the Elder (c110 B.C.-10 A.D.) was one of the most important sages of Judaism, and played a leading role in the organization of the Talmud. He advanced Aaron as a role model for human conduct, on account of his mildness, and preached a doctrine of kindness closely akin to the ideas attributed to Jesus. The Nehemiah with whom he is here alleged to have been acquainted appears, however, to be Kahn's invention.

the book of life that the Master of Kindness had stammered, spelled and then read.

"His name was Nehemiah; his father was a rich merchant, one of those that are escorted around markets in order that small item of advice might be obtained from him, a man of strict justice whom neighbors sometimes took for an arbiter. That man as eminent among the common run of the sages of Israel.

"In his early youth, Nehemiah was noted for the stocks of knowledge that he brought to school every day. He had a very pure upbringing in close proximity with his mother, and yet he confounded the doctors, for he studied the holy texts, he knew the songs, the glosses of the humble and the plaints of transients, fresh flowers in the golden meadows around the Book.

"Before he was fifteen years old he conceived a great disgust for what he knew and a bleak apprehension before the unknowns, only too well-traced and well-defined, that he still had to cover. He no longer studied the holy texts; he dreamed. He abandoned Hellenic philosophy, all decorated by lucid imaginations, the dances of bees, a shady quarry from which half-sculpted marble-clad white statues emerged, because he did not find there what he sought above all: a truth that might contain a happiness.

"He dreamed beside torrents, beside cedars, and lay down in the shade of fig-trees to see the scarlet of the Sun melt away and master the troubled face of the Moon. Then love, with which his heart was impregnated, became focused. Young people, when they love, repeat aubades to the aurora of desire and he morning of the flesh. He gave rhythm to his dolors, issue of the disparity between the desires of life and the facts of life, in numerous melancholies as broad as the sumptuous evenings of autumn.

"Then, weary of science and song, he set forth into the world. Already, his family no longer recognized him; he did not like to count gold; he did not like to run a careful and prideful eye over the lands over which his herds passed; he did not seek the ostentation of dignities, having bought them too easily. So he set forth into the world.

"And yet, there was great mourning that day in a palace in Jerusalem; a mother suffered all the torture and heartbreak, for the flesh of her flesh was going away, her son had changed into someone else, a stranger. And a father said nothing, for what could he say? The child that had been familiar to him had been transformed into some enigmatic judge—and that father, on seeing the numerous servants hand him their keys that evening and render him their accounts, suffered as if he were henceforth performing a futile formality. And the house was enclosed sooner by the darkness, for the lamp in the upper room where Nehemiah worked was not lit, and the two old people preferred that night hid their faces from one another, which grew older that evening.

"At first, Nehemiah followed military leaders. Often, during halts in the shadowless plain, lying down to refresh his limbs, his helmet unbuckled, he followed in the sky, sparkling with promise, dreams other than that of human grandeur. An ingenuous conqueror, he pursued the pillagers, with the attention that the timid pay to fawns, and one day, he found blood repugnant, and the dream of trumpets and lictors seemed stupid.

"Then free, he visited numerous cities, without conforming with the custom of ancient sages who headed first toward the temples, toward initiation, toward the maintainers of new truths, or those who dryly retain a creed powdered by the centuries. Instead, he listened in the marketplaces, the circuses, the theaters, the tribunals and the brothels—and an entire popular clamor roe up toward him; cries of suffering escaped from broad and low faces, and plaints from tragic masks, and the gesture of a dancing-girl was imploring—and in its ant-like swarming, amid the songs and torches, humankind bumped its head into walls as hard as they could be.

"He sought out thaumaturges, did not laugh at tales of the primitive miracles of sorcerers, and lent a willing ear to the fable of metempsychosis. He did not always disdain dice and

42

his virtue never claimed that abstinence shone upon him, as a certain sign. He was later accustomed to say that he had gained more insight into the human soul during nights of orgiastic religious festivity than in conversations with theologians. He listened to them avidly, however, and also to the rhetors, for, knowing from the thaumaturges how base and puerile the desires of the human soul really are, he learned from the latter with what external appearances one may decorate the sterile agitation toward unreal goods. Finally, weary of ports of call, mimes and philosophies, he returned to his own land.

"He was even less recognizable than before; his indifference to everything that agitated his city was too entire. The people of his home town only had clear ideas about commerce, clear passions for the construction of enormous palaces with cupolas of precious metal. The few minutes that remained free to them, the minutes of luxury, the minutes of meditation, they occupied in turning over from every angle the external idea of God, in order to discover a more ostentatious fashion of marking the extent to which they were penetrated by it. Some simplified the rites, which became slow and grave gestures; others complicated them with sudden appeals and repetitions of florid and theatrical celebrations; a few—the most profound—argued as to whether God was a force, an essence or a power; and on the terraces and the benches of shady gardens, in the evening, white-beards let slip gentle and headstrong axioms. But no one cared about his own soul.

"When everyone saw that Nehemiah definitely did not want to be a merchant, a judge, a pontiff or an army leader, he was disdained. He would have been scorned, if it had not been evident that his father would leave him considerable wealth. In the town, he was the unexpected specter of Inactivity.

"As Nehemiah felt this muted reprobation, without being afflicted by it, he often went away on brief journeys. This time, he did not go to the sumptuous cities of the horizon, to the great smoky intersections of the confluences of rivers. He sought out empty river-banks, bare plains or isolated mountains. Sometimes he stopped at nomads' encampments and conversed with them. He loved discovering how the legends of the past had been fashioned in those simple minds on which a magnificent pomp descends every evening: the sentiment of the extent and the impersonal, the sentiment of a brief conclusion before the perpetual recommencement.

"More often, however, he wandered alone, and his march sometimes hesitated in meditative halts. The rumor spread quickly that, slightly mad, he conversed with the void and imagined singular apparitions. In truth, during these peregrinations, he was seeking a comfortable place to dwell. He found it on Mount Liban.

"There was a house on an elevated but narrow plateau, like a straight bar on the horizon, tall and spacious, ringed by strong walls, flanked by a high tower. Behind those broad walls and bronze gates, one could defend oneself against an enemy. From the top of the tower, the Mediterranean mists were visible in the far distance, beyond the fields of Judea and the sands—the endless sands.

"To the right of the castle yawned an abrupt ravine; on descending into it by means of a goat-track one soon lost sight of the castle entirely, in spite of is proximity. It was a vast blue hole; there, the walls of luxuriant vegetation reduced the appearance of the world to a sort of funnel, above which nothing could be seen but the play of the clouds and beating wings.

"To the left of the castle was another ravine, much broader, also descending abruptly. Within it there was the debris of a temple dedicated to some unknown faith. The capitals of columns still offered a few lotus petals, the walls stripped of their cladding were primitive and devoid of memorial signs. A profound crypt opened therein, and there, by torchlight, one could see very ancient frescoes similar to those placed on this terrace, facing the sea, by one of my ancestors.

"The Master of Kindness settled there; he had found his place. The alternating curse of life and death having instituted him as master of his wealth, he transported it there and surrounded himself, in order to protect them and protect himself, with a company of slaves, whom he liberated, and bound them to him more firmly by his generosity. The nomads who knew him, who had recourse to his science as a physician and his arbitration in quarrels, often came to deploy their bronzed complexions at the foot of his hill, to wash their dazzling linen beside the springs and to count the new-born kids. Their chiefs came to the tower to gaze at the blue plaque of the sea and the blond powder of the sand—and the Doctor of Kindness lived like the master of those powerful tribes.

"He reigned over that corner of the Earth by virtue of science and wealth, consequent with one of his ideas, which was that supreme power over humans is the only thing that ought to be bought, that being the universal explanation for the existence of gold, but that it is then necessary to know how to use the power acquired by ordinary means, and that science is the sole means of conserving and preserving it.

"The causes required to fix a man in one location of the world or another—which are all as similar as sectors of shadow—are often very slight. These are a few of the reasons that decided him. Firstly, the crypt and its decoration led him to believe that someone had already lived there whose rare and little-divulged ideas were in accord with the results of his own enquiries regarding the world. Secondly, he was glad that the house was defendable, for a sage, once he has refused to admit the vital collaboration of towns and their conditions, needs to arm himself for his defense. Thirdly, the deserted ravine, a quiet brushwood-lines hollow beneath the naked sky appeared to him to be a salutary refuge for meditation. There, he had the symbol of the human house, a fortress, an ancient temple and a retreat.

"When he was powerful, his renown for wisdom, denied by the pontiffs and magistrates, grew among the young dreamers and those who studied the arcane of reasons for being. He welcomed visitors. The majority remained with him in his fortress. Others only stayed there for a few months, and departed graver and wiser, with greater certainty written in their faces.

"He often taught by means of parables. I will give you an example."

I. THE ARK

On the evening of the day when David, full of the delight of glory, danced before the ark, after which Michal had reproached him for the vulgarity of his triumph and he had replied to him,[10] he consulted the sage Eliah, whose advice he often sought. Eliah was clever and prudent, brave enough and vigorous enough to be counted among the king's peers, and the monarch valued him in the council, for Eliah had often understood his maneuvers clearly, and deduced his objectives and the motives for some of his actions. The word of Eliah was precise and rare; if he has not left a famous name beside those of Jacob, Abishai, Asahel and Benaiah, it is because he was primarily a friend of the king in difficult days, and subsequently set aside the pomp of his triumphs.

Eliah admitted that he had not understood. "The love," he said, "that you have for the people, after having spread benefits so wide, preserving their savings, and protecting their harvests against foreign invaders, leads you to prefer a simple glory and a mere passage through the loving crowd, to the splendors of a despot enclosed in his palace, whose face is sometimes glimpsed through the fissures in the wall of the lances and golden shields of his guards—but I cannot see, Sire, any other motive for your behavior today."

And David said: "Eliah, the trumpets with the slow and gilded fanfares, the drums whose grave tone marks the fall of the instant into the past and the music of harps extend like the necks of joyous birds, stretching a spring-like smile, a music adequate to our brief felicities, the processions of guards who are the assertion of our power, and that crowd of dignitaries, the incarnation of the multiple facets of the people, and my own presence, which is the clarified mind of the race, are not

---

[10] cf 2 *Samuel* 6:13-16.

too much to accompany the universal symbol along the roads. Know that the ark is the universal symbol because, entirely constructed as it is of the most precious wood, which so much piety has encrusted with so many gems, and never opened, it is empty.

"The profound sense of our first legislator forbade its ornamentation with figures and forms designed to reveal that. It is in our minds, by virtue of example and instruction, that the verities that our ancestors judged best for us are inscribed. The shining and empty ark signifies the miser's casket, whether, after loading it for a lifetime, he finds it open and empty one evening, or, full and resonant with metal, it remains no less futile and sterile. It also signifies what the temple ought to be, a bare enclosure without idols.

"The temple ought not to be the abode of God, the temple is the place where one seeks him; priests and saints ought ask for him in their conscience, and the resemblance they extract therefrom they ought to show to everyone; but God has no complete form or description. Just as he is, so he constructs himself at every moment, and by virtue of that his will changes; it cannot, therefore, be codified. The law of the passing moment is not that of the moment to come.

"The ever-closed ark also symbolizes the closed aspect of the night, the profound night that hides its stars in a mantle of cloud. Night is not the hymn of silence, it is merely the moment of silence. It is necessary that, under the fatigue that the Sun pours out every day, weary of earning bread, men sleep, or at least fall silent in their dreams, in order that the thoughts of the discoverers of God can rise up toward him. They can only configure his essence when their eyes are enveloped by the invisible.

"The ark also symbolizes, by its form, the white tombs that stand in the plains. What would you see if you penetrated their sealed vaults? From oblivion, rusty weapons, blades engraved with old characters, the dust of laws, orders and powers. If the ark contained anything, would it not also be a tomb of dead desire? That is why the ark is empty.

"One day, years from now, the temple of the Israelites will stand on the highest hill. It will be like the ark made of wood, clad in precious stone and rich metals; it will be ornamented with immobilized wealth, a tax levied on the ambitions of believers. The likeness of God will not be represented there, but representations of hopeful anticipation will be seen; they will be patient oxen, the image of the contemplative oxen that will support the bowl that ought one day to be filled with divine benediction, the pure wave, contact with which gives purity. Statues will also represent the form we attribute to cherubim; they will be there to represent our desire for the ideal and our hopes.

"That temple will only be commenced in years to come, because it will require years for the conscience of Israel, relieved of the memory of murderous battles, defensive struggles and civil wars, to recover.

"A people can only contemplate itself in souls that have become limpid again, just as one can only see one's face in a pool without ripples. Then only, with my consent, will the tribes build that temple and the figures of anticipation and hope with it; they will line the walls with long golden palms, solid and symmetrical, which will be the affirmation of their belief—a belief that is a hope solidified, and nothing more.

"Then, on feast-days, amid those ornaments, attempting to imagine what their illusions will become, amid the shrill songs rising up to appeal to God, the clarions calling upon the Heavens or announcing he hope of the majestic arrival, amid the harps whose music will be like the cooing of amorous doves, after the voices of cantors summarizing the words of pontiffs, they will sing themselves with their own particular emphasis, and their prayers will be the very image of their souls.

"They will have their palms of hope, still living and green, in their hands, bearing the premises of hope and faith, and perhaps, in the mobile element of their voices, their palms and their desire, something will be manifest of that which we await, we who are about to raise a signal of permanent appeal on the highest place, since our arms are tired of being extended toward the divine horizon.

"Those dances, those songs, will be the same as my song and my dance today. I sang and danced before the ark today, as the soul of the crowd, in its name and in its place; I represented their hope and their young belief, and the bounds of delight of auroral betrothals that inflate their ignorant hearts. Being the king, I had to be, today, the crowd.

"When the temple is built, it will be a square enclosing a casket: a square full of hopeful voices around an empty casket; and the prayers and hymns will be the echo of my song and my dance today. That is the symbol that I need to leave to humankind; that is my monument, the portrait of my dream and its certainties, such as I want my sons in Israel to see it, and delimit it.

"But look at the true verity: down there, beneath its tent of white cloth, like a ewe washed for the alarm or a young woman's new veils, is the holy ark; to its right and left the flames of resin torches curl and spring up; unreal red tints pass over the temporary abode. A little while ago, the arrows of the setting Sun came to awaken its gems like a sudden burst of light and hope, a beam of contemplative joy, a white blade of radiant faith. And yet, there is nothing there but stones, wood and white veils, which are beginning to flap in the nocturnal wind. And that last burst of light, which the people and the Levites interpreted as a magical promise of clear dawns, for us, should we not see as the flaming blade of the Cherub at the gates of the garden of Eden?

"Soon, this evening, between the torches that are the common sign of delight and mourning, their psalms will declare an echo of their joy once again to their visible God. Do you not read in that song in the night, and those flapping veils and hesitant torches, the universe, and consciousness flapping in a floss of uncertainty at hazard, but nevertheless submissive to a law, unknown to them, unknown to the wind and unknown to us, but which exists? And is not my psalm, like their more naïve one, an interrogation? And if we sing in the mode

49

of certainty, is it not like humans who are afraid in the night attempting to summon up their courage?

Look, Eliah, at the insensible ark and the advancing night—and think of my psalm, Eliah, and my dance. Every day, under the Sun, I have sung and danced, the brightness and the movement imparting a rhythm to the play of my illusion, and now, before the voracious and still-young night, I shiver like an old man. My father's field is too large; there is no limit to it, no light shines there in the darkness and no one can show me the road to it. The field is too vast and the darkness too intense. I'm shivering, Eliah."

"As am I," replied the sage Eliah.

II

"One day," Joseph said, then, "While passing through the land of Sarras, I had a dream, or vision—for the contours of my dream, if it was a dream, were so clear that my soul considered it as a real moment of my life, or as a monitory from the powers on high.

"David's ark was before me; it sparkled with an inner light, as if a joyful fire were displaying its red gleams through spars that had become diaphanous. It thus attained a festival color more exquisite than all the gleams of gemstones—and then it opened.

"I saw within it a man clad in red; the fiery splendors that streamed so thickly that they had seemed immobile through the walls of the ark tinted him all over with the incandescence of the setting Sun, but his eyes were as calm and blue as the sea. Five angels surrounded him with a burning transparency; their wings were pure flame and their white faces were afflicted; each of them was holding one of the instruments of Jesus' martyrdom—the bloody cross, the nails, the crown of thorns, the scourges and a spear—and the blood on all the objects was trickling. And their voices said: 'The man who has submitted to the hardest and the most derisorily unjust death will awaken to judge others; he has plumbed the abysms of dolor and the entire Earth is soiled thereby.' The entire ark was a red furnace.

"Then the angels, weeping, seized the man clad in red and nailed him to the cross. He did not resemble Jesus. His bones cried out, and his blood ran from the spear-wound, and a voice said: 'Behold the emblem of the ark; this has happened to one just man, and it will happen to other just men, and they will take out their pain on those of the bitter word, on those of the voice of salvation.'

"Then the ark seemed broader and taller. It was as vast as a country. Its ignescent walls seemed as distant as the luminous background of a landscape. I saw forests, meadows, rivers, the indented walls of cities, and people dressed in gold cloth huddled together and singing—when suddenly, at a point within that festival landscape, the lugubrious apparatus of the cross and the martyr reappeared. And the men adorned with pure joy, the gentle women and the quiet children, who had been rejoicing before, fled, vanishing like a mist. That superb nature filled up with soldiers with bestial faces, and they remained there, drinking and gambling with dice, whereas the cross and the envoys from on high had already disappeared.

"Then a tall, white-haired, well-dressed old man emerged from the ark. The ark was behind him now, like gray stone and ivory; it was as tall as a temple and the man was in front of the temple's portico.

"And the voice said: 'Behold the son of David, the depository of secrets and futures. He has marched for a long time through the crypts of God, and that is why you see him for the first time.'

"But the tall old man was immediately seized by the turbulent arms of a crowd. Every time he died under torture, however, another appeared, to suffer the same fate. Some were nailed to the same cross, others drifted in galleys devoid of oars or sails, and were seen to run aground on peaceful desert islands—but suddenly, those islands were invaded by furious crowds, and their tortures recommenced.

"Finally, as dusk descended upon the landscape, which had almost become a vision of the world in winter, one of these white-haired old men appeared to me, surrounded by a few young men who were listening to him respectfully. As if invisible, they passed through the turbulence of the murderous crowd, which spread out along the banks of a river, shouting. They went into a house of petty appearance, which was immediately lighted in all its windows, and something like a joyful concert was heard. Then darkness fell upon my eyes and my soul.

"And in that dream I saw the promise that there will one day exist a house of faith and happiness, not large and multiple like the world, enveloping it with its immense walls, but a frail dwelling in a valley of dreams, far from howling packs and armed bands."

"Joseph," said the King, "Would you like me to tell you another of the apologues of the Master of Kindness? Perhaps it will give you a response to your vision."

THE NATAL HOUSE

A young man had left his city, his father and his mother—not that he did not love them, but his soul contained all the crazy flames of curiosity and aspiration. He had formed an image of the world according to the tales of travelers who had returned to their hearths long before—which is to say that they were embellished. He believed that at the gates of cities, wise old men, touched by his fatigue, would interrupt their conversations to give him good advice, and that adventurous young men like himself would help him to discover everything about their corner of the Earth.

He saw himself thus associated with all experiences and all the songs of youth, and believed that tresses would be unbound for a stranger who knew tales from far away and had seen other climes.

His route was long and no part of his hope was satisfied. The old men sitting at the gates of cities questioned him thoroughly, asking his name, his age and his origin, and then shook their heads and proclaimed the benefits of stability in the natal house, deploring before him ancient misfortunes whose victims he did not know. The young people were impassioned by their own adventures, some absorbed by hatred of the local tyrant, others living in a great desire for travel and fortune; the latter sometimes accompanied him as for as a bend in the road, but that was all. And the young women laughed together at the spring, no longer astonished by one more passer-by; so many of them disappeared before their large eyes, among the caravans that went through the city without stopping.

Sometimes a tax-collector, alone in his tollbooth, entertained our young man for a little longer, but that was to hear fresh news. Everyone demanded a little of that from him, but no one gave him any—and to his saddened mind, the foreign earth seemed monotonous. As he clung stubbornly to his chimera, however, he continued on his way, with the result that one day, he found himself direly impoverished, exceedingly weary and a long way—a very long way—from home.

He also fell ill, and one evening, exhausted, the fell down by the roadside. It was a road almost devoid of trees, and the sky above his head, palely violet, was impregnated with such total calm and such negative nonchalance, and the silence of the place was so deep, that the young man had the impression that he was going to die there, alone and far from any human assistance.

As the invincible somnolence overwhelmed him, he seemed to see—and did indeed see with the eyes of his soul—a peri.[11] The merciful goddess wanted to know the cause of his distress.

---

[11] The use of the term *péri* [peri—the Arabic equivalent of a female spirit, or fairy] is a deliberate echo of Antoine Galland's classic assembly of Arabian folklore, *Les Mille-et-une nuits* [The Thousand-and-One Nights] which was so popular in France that the "Galland method" became a recognized way of organizing texts, and a godsend

"Oh," he said, "if only I might return to my father's house. It is in my native land, beside the tranquil river, where the clear water passes over white pebbles; there grow the reeds that I cut, as tall as my childish stature, and where I poured out my confused and ignorant songs. White room where I played on the carpet, which I always saw as high and colossal; fountain in the interior garden, always filtered by the minutes of the maternal smile; maternal house, original basin of the springs of my life; high window from which I discovered for the first time the red, yellow and brown caravans of the infinite plain; fig tree with the first-rate figs, in whose shade I often slept; the little harden all, the first obstacle I was able to overcome—you live on, silent friends whose advice I did not understand, perhaps awaiting the one who wanted to go wandering and would like to become one of you again, and participate in your static calm. Doubtless, today, my father has asked the criers and guides returned from afar whether they have seen me."

And the merciful peri enabled him to see his father's house once again, in spirit.

They both departed, and the road was beautiful—much more beautiful than it had ever seemed to the young man when he was traveling it at first, even with the joys of adventure.

The landscapes recognized him. A tree said: "He's far less sad than he was a little while ago, and his tread is lighter; he's undoubtedly returning to his father's house, having got his wish, and the person who is accompanying him is very beautiful."

A stream that was making a mill-wheel turn tuned its song to his footsteps, joyfully, and the young man realized that it was possible, with that clear accompaniment, to accomplished thousands of joyful strides.

Night rang very numerous silvery bells; they were the peris who were going to visit one another in seductive apparel.

---

to improvisers like Kahn, who wanted to bind pre-existing texts into some sort of whole.

Their hair is the color of the fraternal night; on their foreheads they bear the lucid amber color of the plumes of celestial fire that seem to humans to be shooting stars. Their dresses are of every beautiful color, but they pass by so quickly that mortals only see white veils, which they mistake for little clouds; at close range, however, they are exquisite robes whose fabric is made of pearly grains—and to run from one celestial terrace to another they launch themselves forth of exceedingly rapid little horses, which furrow space with their wings, as iridescent as those of the butterflies of the realm of gods and genies. Bells suspended from their necks emit a harmonic confusion of clear notes, infinitely.

On fine evenings, the peris visit one another, or occupy themselves with helping a human in his misery, or, or devote themselves to embellishing flowers and young women, whose features they retouch while asleep, by presenting them with dreams of happiness, or spread long trails of perfume through the world, which drift the following day, idly circulating over the Earth, astonishing with their unexpectedness and complexity the humans who are able to perceive them, without fixing them clearly in memory.

Our young man, his eyes open to all that joyous enchantment, followed his protectress ardently, even though, intoxicated by the perfumed course, he could no longer remember the objective of their journey—and he was very surprised when, in the evening of the city still lit up by a few torches and tambourines, he perceived his father's house, black and enormous. Only one window was lit, so meagerly that it seemed a crack in the wall, and that mass of masonry was so gray, mute and enclosed that he felt a chill in his heart.

"Oh, Peri, kind Peri, is that really my natal house?"

At that moment, in the only lighted room, he saw his brothers. Thanks to the peri, he could hear them; they were calculating the use that they would make of their future fortune. Their father's fortune would surely be divided into three parts, since one of them had left and not returned.

55

"However," said the eldest, "I can certainly oppose that. Our brother wasn't one of us; he didn't understand the language of our hearth; so far as we are concerned, he was born a stranger. And such is the opinion of our father—but our mother will defend him. Anyway, he's undoubtedly dead."

That was certainly their desire, but, because they were young and their senses still keen, they had a vague notion of some divine presence, and separated without formulating their thought.

The peri then took him into the room where his aged parents were sleeping, and thanks to her, he visited their dream. He saw himself there, still small and frail, amid all the things that he loved and had once seemed to him to be so large, but as if diminished, dried-out and frayed—and his father and mother saw him too. They both spoke about him often.

The father said: "Infinite justice will bring him back to us; I shall be clement, but he must immediately, not humiliate himself, but take his place at our counters and in our labors."

And the mother said: "Infinite generosity will bring him back to me; when he comes back I shall heal his wounds and make sure that, for at least three full days, his father will not force him to lend himself to his labors—but he will resume them; feeble as I am, I shall demanded that of him."

And their dream filled with slow minutiae, hollow-eyed cares. Examining crevasses in the walls, laborious ants ran in all directions.

"Let's go," said the young man. "Let's go."

As soon as he pronounced those words, he found himself alone on the bend in the distant road where he had fallen down. The sky was brighter and the dawn indulgent. A great calm penetrated the marrow of his bones, like the gentle, still half-broken awakening that follows the fatigues of a long and difficult journey.

He got up and went on his way, into more distant lands. As he knew old chronicles, he told their tales; as he knew songs, he sang them; as he had beautiful handwriting worthy of ancient manuscripts, he applied his calligraphy to documents or copied exemplars of poets for rich people who liked to display books—and he made a living. It transpired that during these years the young man became a man, and, if the cares of his existence were diminished by that, the uncertainties and troubles of his soul became heavier.

One summer's day, the countryside was scorched by the terrible aspect of the Sun, and he distant hills smoked at the summit like a white fire of mists, and the paving stones of the town, as white as chalk, burned the feet like bricks hated in a Turkish bath. He went in search of a shady corner in one of the side-lanes of a bazaar.

It was so hot, although the alleyways were cooled by their high vaults, and little black slaves were pouring trickles of perfumed water on to the ground, that all the merchants were asleep on their cushions, without keep watch on their open coffers full of colored scarves and silk mantles, and carpets embroidered with marvelous golden birds, and leaving their caskets rippling with the fires of precious stones wide open. Although their sleep was heavy, their tranquility and security were complete, for the boldest of thieves would not cross the ring of torrid streets that surrounded the bazaar.

Our man sat down on the threshold of a humble shop selling paltry foodstuffs and cheap beverages, and went to sleep. No sound vibrated in the covered streets of the bazaar, save for the words of dreams, and the black slave responsible for sprinkling yielded to fatigue and went to sleep.

The man's dream told him that his temples were going gray, and that he was even further away than the day when he thought he had visited his father's house, his birthplace. It seemed to him that it was sinking, but very slowly, sliding not through the streets but into the gray mirror of a lake.

He thought he heard a vague sound of weeping, and the peri of the former vision reappeared to him, who knew wrinkles, still cheerful and light-hearted in her immortal youth—and as he wanted to see his father's house, she took him away so that he might see it via the mind's eyes.

The road glittered like a furnace; where he had seen trees, the area was cleared, and further way, near clumps of woodland, teams of woodcutters were asleep beside their axes. The stream that made the mill-wheel turn accompanied him again with its song, so lively that one might have believed, and even desired, that one could take thousands upon thousands of strides to the enthusiastic accompaniment to its laughter—but the man understood that the stream was so cheerful because it recommenced the same circuit indefinitely, and that its apparent gaiety was only movement.

The atmosphere was still. The peris did not show themselves in that raw daylight, in which only the leaders of caravans stayed awake, waiting in the shade of walls until it was time to get under way again.

The natal house seemed even grayer to him; once, a few flowers had appeared at the barred windows; now heavy shutters supplemented the stone in the upper part of the house. Down below, his brothers were supervising slaves, counting money, filling orders.

Alone in the interior courtyard the father was now dreaming alone, and thinking: "Those, by their presence, and the other, by his absence, have rendered me more solitary than death."

The old man understood that he was worn out, that the best of his dreams now looked forward to a sealed tomb, devoid of care, devoid of hope, devoid of regret, devoid of confidence and devoid of movement.

Things no longer had any of their natal appearance. They were old and sullen, attentive to the avaricious dreams of three new masters. The old man's head was slumped on his breast. The things around him did not recognize him, and he had forgotten them. Momentarily, he had the presentiment of a divine presence, but as he was very old, and his thoughts often followed the same course, he thought he saw Azrael and shivered from head to toe.

And the traveler's heart ached. "Let's go," he said. "I see, dear goddess, that there is no natal house for a man, but only a banal corner of a city that is everywhere the same, that only a child naively believes that he is discovering. And I see that a man soon forgets the tree that he had planted himself, if it does not produce basketfuls of fruit every season. My father's fig-tree is desiccated, and its bark is hollowed out, and my father is growing old beside the fig-tree like a decrepit, exfoliated tree. There is nothing beautiful in human life but the memory of some dream that fills us with joy and even that is the memory of the beginning of a dream. Oh, when you came to find me in my near-mortal fatigue, when I perceived your eyes, which are divans for a god, and the ebony forest of your hear, and the scintillating plume of your eternal youth, I thought I was seeing the battens of Heaven opening, in order that beauty and truth could explain to me what the dream of happiness as, and the meaning to the dogged pursuit of life. And the bells of beautiful adventure rang out for me—but it was only the consolation and remedy of a single day. Peri, beautiful Peri, is there no longer any happiness?"

And the Peri replied: "Your rose-bushes are flowering again, and I like your misfortune enough to save you from it. My love, made of pity for the children who weep at ground level will save you. In a land that I know, where the dawn is perfumed and the evening full of fans, we shall live; the water of the profound spring will make you forget who you were, and I shall be your beloved and loving guardian, and only smiles will illuminate your face, for, no longer recalling suffering, you will no longer remember your life.

"Would you like to come with me to the land without mirrors; the noisy springs there are invisible, the valley resounds throughout with an indolent concert, and the shady corners are so profound that one might sleep for years without perceiving a hint of the sky between the trees..."

"But what about you? Won't you be losing anything?"

"I will be like a dream enchained for long years yet, before your breath expires in blessing me. The matrix of my mortal love will deprive me of my wings, but later, ennobled by a regret and a dolor, I shall joyfully travel through the air again in quest of some new unfortunate. As generous as the evening breeze, momentarily captured, I shall come back beautiful, like the free and errant evening breeze."

And the man replied: "That will be my whole life, then—the murmur of the stream that I can hear, cheerful and rhythmic because it is scarcely larger than the breadth of the basin in my father's house? I prefer my troubles and cares. Let's go."

And he woke up in front of the humble shop in the market.

The next day he left that city. As he knew old chronicles and new songs, and could draft documents, he made a living. When he grew very old he stopped in a humble side-street of an even more distant city, and awaited the final slumber in a low room. He wished that the Peri would return to him, to show him one more time he perfumed Heavens and his father's house, but he was so tired that when she brightened the air he shivered from head to toe, as if he had seen Azrael.

When one has traveled too far one can no longer see one's father's house, one's natal house, ever again.

"But another lesson might brighten our solitude," said Joseph. "And you, Sire, do you think the same as the Doctor of Kindness?"

"I will tell you the faith of my old age," said the King, "but before then, the Sun is setting and my old slave Dares will set food on our table. Perhaps he will tell you his life-story, and you will find therein some echo of things that astonish you here."

Chapter Three
DARES

"To the south, well to the south of the castle," Balthazar said, "beyond the fields, the flowers and rice-paddies, beyond the sands that are excessively mobile in the swirling of violent winds, lands commence that are defended against penetration, so it's said, by thick tangled forests and overly shallow lakes, where monsters crawl in the mud of the shores.

"Old tales relate that those who contrived a passage thereinto would find themselves within a circle of high hills formed from colossal statures. Suspended on the breasts of these granite forms were silver necklaces whose plates were engraved with the meaning of the future. To put a hand on these necklaces, however, it was necessary to climb the unstable and fractured pedestals of the statues, and if the stones of the pedestal shifted, the stone statue crushed the unfortunate seeker of destiny as it fell.

"The old counsels retained by tradition told that the route was traced by white ossuaries, for many caravans had been destroyed there by the wind and fire of the sky, far from wells and verdure. The ancient sayings warned people to avoid the vast ruins of long-deserted cities, their stones crumbling away, one by one, in the immense silence, until the stagnation of the ruins buried them under the perpetual thrust of tall weeds.

"In those ruins, it was said, the extenuated voices of ancient sorcerers whispered faintly, and singular gods were manifest, shadowy tresses curling above excessively profound gazes. Unknown plants distilled poisons with no antidotes. Furthermore, those plains were the abode of giants, as tall and broad as towers, who stopped armies and devoured their prisoners. It was a land of incessant miracles, and I wanted to attempt its uncertainties.

"It did not take long to reach the first ossuary on the road of oracles. We entered the empire of a harsh sun—not the

61

nurse who swells the grapes and warms the wheat, but a bitter tyrant whose blades prohibit the horizon. Beside crumbling dunes of sand, with forms reminiscent of giant mastiffs, skeletons lay, and there was nothing as funereal as that solitude and those vestiges of death beneath the ardent and cloudless sky.

"There was no sign other than that memory of tragic death in all that isolation; its implacable message was the idea of limitation; solely by the force of existence, unrolling a shroud of sand, sick beneath the luminous hammer, the landscape indicated every deterrence, every failure, every abandonment—and my cavaliers hesitated. The land, studded with the appearances of monsters, uniform in the color of the sand, oscillated endlessly in hostile powdery flames. There was not a blade of grass, not even the shadow of the wings of a hawk, and no other voice than ours, which died away by mutual accord—and we marched thus for ten days, drinking the water that our camels carried and killing the sheep of our flock.

"The eleventh day displayed before my eyes an entire city with vivid waters; men were building, draped women bearing jars, and heaps of green and gold seemed to be gardens of orange-trees. Full of hope and anxiety, we headed for that distant city; but it seemed to retreat before us incessantly, and when the Sun was not so high above the horizon, the hopeful décor vanished. Late in the day, however, we halted near a small stream flowing beneath coarse grass.

"Fatigue had overtaken my cavaliers—fatigue caused by the loss of their chimera of discovering a beautiful city of shade and perfumes; fatigue determined by a measure of fear. Who had deployed before our eyes the city of promises, only to withdraw it, as if into the folds of a cloak? Were they true, then, the old tremulous legends, and was the southern land a realm of redoubtable spirits, architects of despair and disillusion? And what new torture would be imagined tomorrow by the malevolent djinn?

"No one, apart from myself, had any other explanation for the sudden elevation of the cupolas into the azure and their abrupt disappearance; and even I, attained by the contagion of my men's dream, with all their fever of anxiety, was not far from believing, when the hour of weary slumber came, that powerful giants were closing the defended territory. For we had seen that city!

"Was it an image momentarily set before our eyes by the subtle mirrors of the Empyrean? Was it a sign and an encouragement, or ought I to believe that a deceptive city glimpsed in the morning will always collapse that evening in the gloomy dusk?

"According to the sages of the men with yellow complexions, who come in light ships to pillage and devastate the florid cities and opulent ports of our seas, the divine world covers the terrestrial world like a delicate and mobile arborescence—and the spirits of evil are powerful enough sometimes to prevent perception of the blue and serene Heavens, the refuge of providences, save through a gap in thick branches. The ray of sunlight is seized by the demon of fevers, which straddles it and makes use of its rapidity to propagate death. On the shores of rivers, spirits give rise to pestilences, so that the boats the glide thereon pass before terrified villages on the banks, filled with decomposing cadavers. They are the ones who cause the sleeping pilot to fall from his bench and lead the vessel on to the reef, and even pirates dread the southern land at whose frontier we had arrived.

"The night spread forth its violet tints. The men of my retinue, grouped by their horses, were conversing in low voices and the lips were repeated those nursery tales, so powerful that they return, with their procession of naïve fears, at the anguishing moments when one dreads everything unknown. The water that sings and the water that dances; the trees with the fruits of eternal life, guarded by formidable chimerical lions; the hero raised up by the gods to destroy the trap set by the evil demiurge; the young hero whose shield predicts with its polished steel the dangers his master will run; the hero who triumphs because he has taken pity on an old and crippled woman, who reveals herself to be a beautiful and powerful

63

fairy and can give him a talisman—all of that was circulating in their tales.

"They entertained one another with tales of great rings of iron that a foot trips over in uncultivated lands; a trapdoor opens and the privileged individual descends into the realm of marvels. Sometimes there is the forgotten treasure of an ancient king and the magical ornaments that give supreme power, sometimes a loud noise is heard originating in the bowels of the Earth, which is that of the redoubtable forges where the divine dwarfs fabricate precious metals, gold and colossal stones, of which the slightest splinter, the tiniest fragment, will recompense the audacious adventurer if he can conceal himself prudently. And the lull of the legend, the heredity of all the tales babbled by all the ancestors, was bedding them down them in softness and sleep, when the man on watch uttered a cry that brought us all running.

"A strangely beautiful woman, with powerful magnetic eyes in a thin, dark face and a double wave of black hair covering her shoulders, wearing a helmeted and armored, had suddenly emerged from the ground in front of him. He had not been able to cry out nor make any movement while the magnetic eyes were drinking his strength and his courage, and the tall form had gazed at him for a moment, as if to see clearly who these new occupants of her familiar ground were. The face of the apparition had remained severe, almost terrible, and the man's knees had trembled, knocking into one another, causing him to kneel down involuntarily. The vision had immediately disappeared; his strength had returned, and he had called out.

"The superstitious cavaliers started searching; they took inventory of the ground, expecting with a terror full of hope that their feet might encounter one of those iron rings by means of which the trapdoor opens that invites a descent into the realm of dreams. It was in vain.

"I wanted to keep watch during the night on the place from which the apparition had surged. Nothing came; I heard nothing more than the weary sleep of my companions, the glimmer of words in their dreams and the sound of the immensity of the plain, comparable to that of a calm sea, and saw nothing but the twinkling of starts, punctuated by the sudden brief blaze of shooting stars.

"My mind searched until daybreak, wondering what the mysterious apparition could have been: a glimpse of a goddess, or a chimera analogous to that of the distant city glimpsed under the burden of the Sun; the puerile dream of a man or a warning from the guardian of horizons to halt the march toward forbidden discoveries there.

"The next day, we set off again. Sometimes, distant violet-tinted hillocks among the sands seemed to be watching over our passage, and then long narrow ravines barred the route. Heaths of light ashy grass extended, bushes crawling along the ground in acute clumps, from which we built our evening fires. There was no trace of humankind, nor of animal life, save for a few insects, or the circling flight of some great bird in the distance.

"The power of the Sun became harsher, the water-holes became a little more frequent; in the evening, next to a stream flowing over a stony bed, we unsaddled our weary horses and unloaded our camels. Lassitude was written in every face, and the words 'go back' circulated among my companions. Go back, go back before we had lost the memory of our route; fear gripped us at the thought of wandering for a long time in plains without issue.

"Finally, one morning, as we resumed our march, we perceived horsemen in the distance. We hailed them, but they fled; we pursued them, but their speedier horses escaped ours, already weary. Soon, we perceived nothing more than the cloud of dust that their flight raised.

"For several days we sensed that we were being watched from dawn onwards. My companions were no longer murmuring; to reach these people was to know—to know *something*, since the old explorers' texts were mistaken and we had perceived neither tangled forests nor shallow lakes nor giants as tall as towers casting shadows around their cemetery, and the distant city had only been an irony of the gods.

"Finally, in a heavy midday, while we were nearly falling asleep as we progressed, we saw the horsemen again, in large numbers, coming toward us, and arrows notified us of their hostility. Hazard gave us victory; then, their thick curtain having dissipated, we perceived their herds drawing away rapidly in disorder, the women shaken by the trot of donkeys, the dogs baying and the frightened camels running across the plain. That was our trophy, and we liberated prisoners who had been enchained or shackled.

"All those we had vanquished maintained a grim silence; the women wept and talked, but no one understood their language. Only Dares, on hearing our language, spoke in terms of gratitude and welcome. He was brought to me and he told me his story while we made camp after having buried our enemies, holding on to our booty until I was able to formulate a plan.

"Dares had been captured while very young, near a big city, about which he knew nothing except that ivy covered the breaches in its wall and that those walls were full of the songs and fluttering of birds and the hum of insects, He had a memory of loving faces associated with is earliest awakenings. He remembered having seen, a long time ago, a profound barge, a glaucous river in which leaves as large as shields had hundred the prow of the boat. His terrors reminded him of enormous beasts swimming after the vessel, against which the pillagers, his masters, had to defend themselves.

"When he grew older, however, he recalled carrying burdens in a spacious city, with small low houses the color of thatch, and whips sometimes began to lacerate his shoulders. Then he was made to row on the sea; the voyages were long, without anything to be seen but playful dolphins or ferocious sharks. When the crews finally reached land, they sought to lie in ambush in deep inlets that sheltered all the ships and concealed their presence from the land. The masters then chained their slaves to their oarsmen's benches; a party of them set forth and soon returned, rich with spoils and captives. Then they set off again across the vast sea in order to return to the spacious city with the low houses.

"One day, that city was attacked; black hordes pillaged there for several days, killing the inhabitants and taking away those they spared, leading them into slavery in their wilderness. It was these new masters that we had just defeated.

"I questioned Dares about the marvels of the southern land; he seemed to understand, after explanations, since he had come from far away in the south. He knew very little. There too, in the land from which he came, tales were told of a distant country guarded by sands and forests, of routes marked by ossuaries, but it was far way—very far away. No one among the masters of the deserts had ever attempted to go there.

"I spoke to him about the city that had fled before us and the apparition of the warrior woman. He told me that, far away, there was an abandoned and devastated city that everyone avoided, because it was thought to be inhabited by demons. The pillagers that we had defeated did not go near it, deterred by superstitious terror. He had heard it said that sometimes, in the night, mysterious forms emerged from the ground, but he knew no more, the fatigue of his evenings having always been too heavy."

THE RUINS

"One evening, after a long march, we reached the deserted city, the sleeping city to which Dares knew the way. It appeared to us lying beneath a pale light, propped up beside bright waters. Our companions camped some distance away. I took Dares with me, in haste to penetrate those alleys of dead stone.

"Winged griffins reared up on the thresholds of temples; paved streets sank into a horizon of columns, and the neat faint light of the stars displayed infinite gray perspectives. Basins had been invaded by a thrusting vegetation; the air was warm, s at the moment before a storm, and perfumed, as if the incense of ancient cults were still burning in the depths of some temple, as if the empty city had remained an odorant offering to some primitive god, and sparse floating music were passing beneath the lunar light. Then a more vivacious perfume of roses reigned; or footsteps rang too loud in the silence, inviolate for so many years.

"The monuments were low and squat in their architecture. Their walls were ornamented with repeated emblems: weighing-scales, axes, eagles and lions were engraved in hard granite—and the stone was also imprinted with the vertigo of that noiseless place. The Moon, having initially trailed a light veil the color of steel over the city, which rendered the details of the immense hypogeum strangely clear, had allowed itself to be ringed by a large black cloud, and appeared in the sky like a captive, like a white princess palpitating amid the wings of evil angels who were carrying her away.

"A lightning-flash appeared, like a gigantic owl beating its wings, another fluttered in the sky like butterfly wings; they followed one another, their meanders combining, as if in a joyful race. They were javelins suddenly launched, one after another, from the depths of the invisible toward a single target, and the majestic cry of thunder resounded, the modulations of its howl broadening, like a monster growing enormous and tortuous hindquarters; the voice of eternal caverns covered the entire city with its bellowing, after the gaze of the lightning had shown everything to our eyes in the bosom of its flamboyant menace.

"The bright flashes hurtled down like the thrusts of the simoom. In that irradiation, large drops of rain fell like pearls, like long lines of diamond broken by the wind, like brilliant fatalities lavished uselessly upon the desert. The gentle forces that had previously seemed to envelop the city had fled beneath the empery of growling powers, and the stars had dispersed before the maws of gulfs. The lightning blinked its amethyst fire again; I saw something like an overturned cart go by and crash into oblivion, columns trembling and capitals tumbling.

"Four clouds of a mild and milky hue displayed themselves, seeming spirits of peace come to calm the musicians of terrible organs; an oscillation of the entire cloud-mass carried them away and the lightning triumphed in seven consecutive furrows of light, in the midst of which, in a pale halo, blazed something like an eye of violet fire.

"Suddenly, Dares cried: 'Look! It's her, it's really her!'

"Personally, I saw nothing. 'Look!' he repeated, in a low voice, his face dull and the color of gold, the color of thirst-quenching fruits, the color of liberating metal, the color of the bright tunics worn by the Hours driving the chariots of destiny.

"'Look!' replied a voice, its hair undulating like the waves of the sea: the sea that builds the new foundations of future lands beneath its rhythmically mobile waves.

"'Look!' cried Dares, his red lips the color of scarlet mantles, the color of blood that spurts forth in battles, the color of large flowers at the turnings in the paths of bitterness. 'There are her eyes, her eyes that smile in a mist, her eyes of sadness, her inexhaustible eyes, her incurable eyes, her pitying eyes, her angry eyes, her eyes reflecting the Heavens.'

"'Her expectant eyes,' the voice resumed, 'for since the world scintillates before her, her eyes are unable to become either joyful or desperate; her eyes are hopeful, as her hair is an appeal, the sweet heroine of time.'

"Dares prostrated himself. 'Mobed, Mobed, before I saw you I awaited your contemplation with all my prescience. Mobed, eternal goddess, cry of the dawn, adieu of the night, beacon of ships, repose of our fatigues, if I had seen your victorious face, how much lighter would my fatigue have been when I rowed upon the infinite seas, throughout a life that did not know that it would one day serve for anything else; how I would longed for sleep to see the dawn of your smile awaken beneath my closed eyelids, O Mobed with the eyes of hope. And now your face, in the nacreous light, becomes as white as the promise, as white as pure snow, in which the sufferer that I am will be able to write is new history, his new legend, his new hope. O Mobed of hope and clarity, so near and so far away!'

"And the voice replied: 'It is She, of the first times. She descended among the tribes, and the heroes came to deposit their weapons at her white feet. With the daughters of the priests she traveled the pastures, and taught them the arts, and the tribe hat she visited flourished. On the day of misfortune, when the enemy roamed the plains where the great monsters menaced humans, her face reddened with wrath, and she led the men into combat. A reflection of the divinity, she is a goddess. She existed before the God of armies; she was the goddess of beauty and attraction; it is to reproduce her fleeting vision that the rude herdsmen attempted to engrave stone or wood. It was to summon her that the youths strung lyres and hollowed out flutes. She is the universal soul constructed from the desires of all of young humanity. She rides in lunar reflections, gilds herself with solar rays; it is her shadow that passes through the great woods. It is her tresses that hide the sky of cities, her movements that the great wild beasts imitate, and her smile that is copied by the summer. The halo of the lightning is the bistre of her pupils and the lightning-flash is her anger thundering through space. O warrior woman, O sage of olden times, O goddess who was beside the cradle of humankind, it is for a reflection of her indifferent beauty that men kill one another; it is to raise temples to her that they build cities. It is because of her long absences, because of the rarity of her apparitions, that dolor appeared.'

"And Dares went on: 'Key to my enigma, center of my fibers, O my entire heart bursting with joy, reflection of hopeful dreams, source of paradise divined, Mobed, be generous and unveil yourself.'

"The violence of the tempest calmed down, with corners of the horizon still ablaze; the sky became blue and white again, and the black cloud was expelled earthwards. At the summit of the black cloud, ephemeral fires persisted, but already, at ground level, a white light tinted with blue was rising up, silvering the walls of the angry cloud; and in a livid region, in a wide band of bruised and weary color, the star reappeared.

"Bluish silver in hue, it slowly drew out of an archipelago of little clouds; enormous lizard-like forms accompanied it, and then a large white aureole, ornamented with greenish lances, surrounded it—and the storm was no more, in its diminished fires, than a quivering of white lights on the horizon.

"The prostrate Dares was still stammering his hymn, but the alternating voice was no longer replying. I was surprised that he had not perceived any of the scourging of the universe by the enormous squall, but no more than he was when I affirmed that I had not seen the apparition.

"'But you heard the distant voice?'

"'Yes, but as a echo of yours.'

"'She was there before my eyes, tall and almost colossal, and her eyes bathed me.'

"'Did you know that she existed, this goddess Mobed?'

"'No, and yet I recognized her; a thousand signs dormant in my memory were revealed. On seeing her, I seemed to be moving through the garden of a palace forgotten since infancy, and I thought that statues came to life in order to say: *we knew his distant ancestors; he came into our flower-beds; he was very small and played with garlands too heavy for his hands; he knew us well, but perhaps he has forgotten us.*'

"Noises and footsteps became audible, so precise that I thought I would faint as the marvel approached; the voice awoke such profound echoes that the truth of the apparition was affirmed before my mind's eye. It was a few of our companions, bearing torches, who had come into the ruins in spite of my prohibition.

"'Sire King,' said one of them, 'troubling mysteries have drawn us out of the camp. We have seen the haughty face, the envoy of the gods, that stood up before our sentinel. She gave us a sign to follow her toward these ruins, and we have seen an entire circus of colonnades light up, and a long line of multicolored fairies dancing with sidereal plumes on their foreheads. Music and light sprang forth from every stone, and the

71

great veiled apparition presided. We stopped, surprised, delighted and afraid, and the dances continued; tall apparitions clad in scarlet mantles passed by lightly, not far away from us, but when we tried to take one step more, the entire vision disappeared as I a single hop, and resumed capering further away. It has just vanished, after guiding us here. Let us go back, Sire King, let us return to your kingdom, to the land of your fathers. Let us leave this land of illusions and marvels. Do you not fear the hatred of these forgotten temples, the wrath of their disdainful gods? Will not the sands be hostile to us tomorrow? Will not the demons of error deceive us in order to lure us into noxious swamps and the tombs of sand that will become our ossuaries? And having died so far from our own people, we shall be no more than a trace for some new conqueror of the unknown, the sign of an excursion that perhaps no one will ever see. Let us go back, Sire King, let us go back.'

"As I hesitated, a pale light appeared at the top of a stairway that had only a few steps. A tall old man in a linen robe called out to me: 'Sire, if you have come as far as the deserted and forgotten city, it is because you needed to come. If you have passed through the zones of death, it is because you needed to know. It is to you that the ancient memories, and the labor of this soil and those who sleep within it, are to be revealed. You are the son in spirit of the old Mage-Kings who built here long ago, when the sun of virtue and knowledge shone vertically above this city. Come with me; come in, but come in alone.'"

THE PRIEST OF MOBED

"'There are, Sire King,' said the old man, 'no inaccessible countries guarded by the ill-will of the gods, closed lands whose gates are guarded by angels with flaming swords, shores where monsters crawl before excessively thick forests—but there are lands that die, forgotten mantles with which the gods drape tombs, of desiccated trees and withered flowers. Humans are not masters of their own duration, but they are masters of their gods and the duration of their cults; of that they are the masters because of that they are the makers.

"'The city in which you find this almost-empty palace was great and opulent when the cities you know were, like humble songbirds, fearful under all the threats and gods of hostile men. Its power commanded fleets and armies, its science created the fidelities and cults that were imposed by the fleets and the armies. You have not yet seen here that which you need to see. You have seen the storm and the thunderbolts that, in effect, manifest themselves; you have recognized them, for you know them. You have not seen the face to which the prayers of your slave rose up, for your over-complicated soul only sensed therein a play of shadows beneath the diffuse nocturnal light; you have not seen the celebrations and the dances that your cavaliers have perceived, because for you they were the fires of the lightning drawing away in space. You are no longer, Sire, one of those who believe; you are one of those who create faith, credence, legend—truth, since it is. Listen, therefore, to the counsel and the tradition of the priest of Mobed. I am the last of her priests.

"'If the people of this land, like all other peoples in the same phase of their existence, adored gross idols as the principle of things, and then the mysterious sense of terrestrial terrors, and then the forces that tamed them, they soon came to a stronger conception of it, and they adored their means of struggle and salvation. On these walls you see weighing-scales, axes, eagles of lions. The scales symbolize the foresight that before action simultaneously weighed their strength and the dangers. The rapid axes are the evocation of their decision in council, which was, in their eyes, true wisdom. The eagles signify the respected sages who could scrutinize the solar rays with a calm eye, the idea of the force that enchains those of superstition and error. The lions are the men of action who defend the city.

"'For a long time, thanks to their cult, which ensured the predominance of the age, these peoples progressed powerfully and without terror. Priests explained the verity of life to the young men, and the qualities of the man were those of the gods that one might assimilate by will-power. The processions of our festivals thus displayed, not idols but heroes, fair-minded judges and poets. For if the heroes fight and the sage decides in council, the poet is the organizer of festivals, which are the cult and the education of the city.

"'The poet, in our ancient and legendary prosperity, sang in the public square on the threshold of the temple. His art was to occupy and rally minds to him, for voices come from the anxiety and poor advice of the empty hour. He grouped the choirs of young men and young women, and rendered ideas tangible by means of song, for it is through pleasure that knowledge must first acquire a soul. And if you do not see a special emblem on these walls that symbolizes the poet, it is because he must be able to be equal to anything, and contain the great aspects of real virtues, at least sufficiently to excite any adept. The groups of our young people who went forth to found a distant fatherland for the use of ours departed under their guidance.

"'Those colonies did not stop at river deltas, estuaries or the nearest point of the land to the sea. In the depths of new regions, they had to create cities similar to this one, sufficiently guarded against foreign influence for all the virtues whose seeds they brought to have time to grow to an entire adult fruition, before a mixture with less pure cultures could compromise them.

"'What became of the hundred cities whose founders departed from this soil? Scattered stones in the depths of forests doubtless astonish the pilgrims of the unknown in the most distant parts of the world; perhaps, in a few cities that attribute their angular stone to an uncertain hero, balances signify human pauses, axes the power that may punish, eagles and lions the monstrous footsteps of conquerors amid ruins and rubble.

74

Fires of violence glow behind the insignia of all calm meditations.

"'Even here the meaning of the law was obliterated, and instead of adoring the qualities of human being, people came to bow down before those who were scarcely clad therein, and the heroes, adoring themselves, obliged worship and obedience, whence came tyrannies and discords-and he city was no longer strong enough to defend itself against the peoples that its wealth attracted, and these walls saw the vanquishers.

"'Now, it happened that the poets had refused to worship force, and even courage, or even virtue; among the human qualities they venerated beauty above all others, and exclusively the beauty of women who live according to the celestial rites of the Moon, whose eyes are the color of dawn or night, whose breasts fill with sap, as if nature were born therefrom. The qualities of human being, the sovereign virtues that are the gods, strive to adorn woman, as a sign that she is the reflection of the beyond that is merciful to us. In the hero's action, the ardent poet saw nothing but the latent natural effort produced by the loins of woman, and by the accumulation of thoughts that might have remained silent, and more precisely, all the voices of nature and all the created harmonies circulating in her, some of them crystallizing out and a hero surging forth. If one takes care to render them stronger, will they not fight alongside combatants?

"'And our wars proved the veracity of our poets' words. Mobed was a woman, undoubtedly the most beautiful and strongest of all, who was able to pick up the weapons that men had dropped. She rebuilt the walls and the cult for a time, and for her recompense the people deified her memory.

"'For a long time, in their difficult hours, they invested their hope in Mobed and appealed to her, but no one any longer spoke to the heroines who did not know it in the sacred language of old, and the people had to disappear, the time of brambles having arrived for the city—and so much admiration and prayer created the goddess you see here.'

"And the priest unveiled a large fresco.

"'Such is the apparition that your companions have seen—and really seen, for she has lived in the memory of humans and she lives in their presentiments. The reflection of an immense belief, she can exteriorize herself; her form doubtless floats between Heaven and Earth when she wishes, when it is necessary for her to show once again her triumphant beauty and the stars of her eyes. Familiar with this image, I do not know whether I have never seen her outside this place or whether I see her everywhere.

"'This fresco in which her features are traced you will take away, stone by stone; this faithful representation contains all her wisdom and all the intelligence of an ancient people, from whom you have certainly inherited a little of your blood, since your will has driven you to search in this dust.

"'Go, leave me without saying any more to me.'

"And when I attempted to persuade him to follow me, he said: 'Go; I must speak no more. Henceforth, I am a mute tomb.'"

As Dares, according to his custom, had crouched down on his sleeping-mats not far from King Balthazar and Joseph of Arimathea, the King said to him: "Dares, tell our guest one of your stories. He has never heard you speak at length, and perhaps, during the time I have been taking about you, he might have formed the desire."

And when Joseph of Arimathea nodded approvingly, the old slave began.

THE MADMAN IN THE FOREST

There was once a great forest near the sea; it had as many leaves and as many birds' nests as the sea has waves; it had as many lovely clearings, with beds of moss and carpets of grass, as the sea had cheerful isles; as many fawns bounded through it as gilded fishes lived in the marine expanse; as many springs filtered though it as little red and green stars were reflected in the mirror of the Ocean. It also possessed many agile lizards with ruby eyes and bodies of emerald, which slid between the stones and roots, and thousands of wings fluttering, and thousands of throats singing beneath the green domes of its trees; there was also a bird that talked and a pious hermit who listened to it.

There was no road through the great forest. There were thousands of little paths that ran like the streams to the river—the river that descends to the sea. The little paths ran, ran into flowers and then wound around to seek a better route; they ran into the rots of giant trees and then fled to find a better route; and sometimes, they hid themselves beneath dense thickets where only hares could follow them, and then they ran to nestle in the reeds on the edge of springs, and divide in two and follow one another. There were a thousand little paths in the shade of the great forest.

There were a thousand mirrors of the shade of the great forest: round mirrors, in which water awaited the delicate flight of butterflies and the ablutions of small birds; long mirrors, in which one could see oneself while walking, for the entire length of a confession, a speech or a song; unexpected mirrors, increasing in size under the long grass. There were a thousand mirrors on the floor of the great forest, but no one knew about them, for there was no road under so much shade, and only a thousand little paths led there, which it was necessary to know by heart, and which it was necessary to have loved before going in there, for the people of the neighboring lands stopped at the narrow edge. What good is there in going where no road leads?

There was a madman in the great forest; he watched out for the dawn there; he knew the moonlight there. He gamboled around and whistled his trills beside the hermit who listened to the talking bird. What did it matter to him what the beautiful bird said? He was agile, he was joyful, he danced all day long; although he could not fly, he could climb into the treetops. What did the pious hermit matter to him? The madman had scarcely more concern for thought than the agile birds; he always picked up their most magnificent feathers with which to adorn himself, and his crown was always woven from the freshest and rarest flowers.

The madman was not without some knowledge; he could find his way along all the little paths; he knew all the hedges; he called the wary roe-deer, and they followed him; he charmed little birds, which hopped on to his shoulder. He knew that the plain at the edge of the forest was bare, and that the frightful towers of stone in the distance were much less beautiful than the shade of the forest. He knew all the slopes by which the forest descended toward the sea and he lay down for hours on end watching the little clouds putting on new dresses, or watching the white hem of foam as the growling anger of the waves broke, and he laughed and he laughed, and then, with a bound, came back to pester the hermit or sing in the forest.

And as the hermit, absorbed in meditation, scarcely ever left the tree-hut from which he could just perceive a clearing, so absorbed in himself that he did not watch the animals playing, nor the beautiful sunsets inundating the foliage with gold, unaware of the numerous mirrors and the thousand little paths, the madman was the king of the great forest. The madman was the child of the great forest, for he did not know where he came from and did not worry about it. The forest clothed him with leaves, nourished him with fruits and berries; he slept there between two branches. He was perhaps fifteen years old, perhaps twenty, and did not care either way. Life in the great forest was good to him.

One day, from high above the sea, the madman saw a beautiful, rapidly-moving ship, spick and span with white sails and glorious with scarlet ones, and the men on the masts were so sumptuously dressed that one might have taken them for statues of light—statues of sunlight, the color of noon.

The ship came toward the shore, and men got down from it, so numerous that the madman took fright. At any rate, when they arrived he jumped into a thicket, from which he watched them. Nimble hinds, also curious, were grazing not far away. He saw one of them suddenly fall down, its mouth flecked with foam and blood, and only jut had time to run away, for the men from the ship came running.

When he came back to spy on them, he saw some of them, armed with axes, clearing the green thicket. Their fires, fed with twigs, were blazing beneath great copper bowls; he saw that the hind, and other animals too, had been butchered. He fled, and that day, the madman was sad in his forest.

For many days, the forest resounded with loud noises; the trees bled, the roe-deer fled. Other ships came racing over the sea, and a large manor was gradually constructed, with walls and living hedges—and the axes of armed men scintillated at the gates. The poor madman was sad in his forest; he withdrew to the darkest ravines, where he was afraid that he might be taken by surprise and afraid that people might come to chase him away.

He consulted the talking bird, the beautiful bird with the vermilion, saffron and azure plumage and the white throat with the silky feathers.

"Beautiful bird, tell me what our danger is?"

But the bird was proud.

"You disdained me when you were king of the forest; you whistled when I talked to the hermit. You disdained me; you shall know nothing. I shall go to the castle; I shall be given a fine welcome there. I shall perch on the shoulder of the lady and I shall talk and talk to her! She already knows that there is a wicked madman in the forest."

And the madman addressed himself to the wise hermit.

"Oh, poor madman, you know the path to my hut of branches well; for a long time you have been coming to disturb my prayers and my contemplation with your hare-like races and your fawn-like bounding. However, I shall tell you this: never go to the strangers' manor; your heart will bleed later in consequence."

Whereupon the madman went there at top speed.

Through a hedge of rose-bushes, he saw a young woman dressed in white, with long hair the color of autumn clouds, amid the yellow leaves. She was throwing scraps to large greyhounds with white pelts, dancing before her ring-laden hands. It was the first time the madman had seen such a spectacle, and his heart was rent by a thousand cuts in consequence, and swelled with impatience at not being able to see her at closer range. But a young man came who was carrying a golden crown, wearing a long sword, and approached in order to kiss the lady's lips—and the madman could not bear it, and fled at top speed.

But he came back; strong is the glue of a beautiful gaze.

And the beauty said: "Stay with me, Prince; I'm so lonely when you leave; my hours drain way so slowly then, and everything bores and irritates me. Put off your annoying duties and stay. We can go into the trees over there, to see behind their shady curtain what marvels they reveal, or—don't be annoyed—we can stay in your palace of marble and fountains, and count the roses at the same time as our kisses."

"Yes, Glyphtis, I'll stay one more day, but the shadow of evening will remind me of the dawn that will one day take me away from you, from your arms. However, although I must go away for a little while, since I'm constrained by the summons of my sovereign, I'll come back to you soon."

"Alas, Prince, those who go over the sea do not know when they will return."

"The route is marked for me over the sea."

"But what about the pilots? What about the sirens?"

"My ship is solid."

"And the reefs hard."

"But it isn't far!"

"Do you know that for sure?"

"When the force of Eros brought us here, our sails were inflated by all the powers of the Earth and the sea. Our ship floated at the slightest movement of the oarsmen."

"But when you leave…and what if you never return?"

"What if I never return? You're joking. What would you do?"

"I'd go to find the madman, the madman in the forest."

And the queen laughed, with pearly youth; she laughed so prettily that the madman's feelings were hurt again, for the prince also laughed, and his love was further augmented.

From the crown of a cedar, the poor madman saw the ship with large scarlet sails leave one day. And as that made him joyful, he heard the talking bird.

"Ah! Look at the handsome lover with his festival crown and his luxurious loincloth. Ah! Won't he have a lovely belt of new bark, some day? That will really suit someone who pretends to the wealth of a king's son. Ha ha ha!"

And as he got down from the cedar, he saw the hermit, who said to him: "King's son, where are you going to war, then?"

"Why king's son?" replied the poor madman.

"You're scarcely a king's son, but might become one, to your great misfortune."

When the madman came to the palace, he slipped into the hedges, in order to avoid the gaze of the archers. When he was close to the large garden, and perceived his Lady, the madman started trembling, and large tears ran down his cheeks. The queen had raised her pure snow-white face toward him—but her eyes were cold and staring, and her body was like a statue, expectant. The queen's soul had gone away, doubtless over the sea, with the ship with the large sails.

Then the madman took up his flute and launched into his song, copied from the dawn chorus—and the queen, believing that some bird was nearby, raised her eyes toward the tall trees, and then lowered them toward the shadow at her feet and looked into the hedges—but she did not see the madman of the forest.

When he approached her, however, pale-faced and emotional, she perceived him, and fled, laughing. She had become light-hearted and cheerful again, and full of smiles.

She went back into the palace and went up to a turret, and then to another, and then to another—and the poor madman ran back and forth. On each turret she displayed her laughing teeth and inflated bosom, and the poor madman ran back and forth; then so quickly did he show herself, laughing, on each turret, that the poor bewildered madman fled. He fled into the forest, and from all the turrets pale women laughed, with harsh gaiety.

Oh, how he wept, the poor madman—but when he came back to the rose-bush in which he suffered, he saw ships with scarlet sails appear, and ships with white ails. And the prince who loved the lovely Glyphtis got down—but the other ship disembarked men-at-arms and a king's son. So the two princes fought, and the first was killed.

All the horror of bloodshed, which he saw for the first time, pierced the madman, but not as much as the welcome Glyphtis gave to the victor, for she came to him and gave him her heart: her heart, with a confident gesture of her two hands; one might have thought them doves in the hands of a butcher; her heart, with her neck inclined on the shoulder of the new-comer and her forehead offered to his lips; her heart, with her eyes, which filled with a languid auroral mist while she looked at that face for the first time, beneath the helmet; her heart, with her figure, which bent back supply, and her knees, which became unsteady beneath her white dress and her plaited hair, which she untied.

And as they both headed for the castle, she noticed the horrified madman. Then clinging closely to the captain to whom her soul had gone, she favored him one again with her puerile rippling laughter.

She had laughed at him and the manor was closed. New men-at-arms were guarding its walls.

"Madam, madman," said the talking bird, "you must make yourself a helmet out of the flower-bells that grow in the forest, and make arrows from reeds, and fashion a large bow out of a long rush and a good archer out of a poor madman. Ha ha ha!"

"Son of a king," said the hermit, "why are you so sad? You don't sing; you don't whistle. Are there no more ripe berries in the forest?"

"To be a king's son would be no cure for my unhappiness. Tell me, Hermit, what is that great manor over there, near the sea, where the beauty scintillates who had rendered me madder than before? Do you know her? Her face is as profound as the mirrors of the forest, but how much whiter and more delicate. All the clouds in the sky pass around her eyes. Their pupils are tranquil stars, her neck is the stem of a milk-filled reed. She passes among the flowers and laughs on the turrets of the great new manor that was recently built, and the galleys come to her, drawn by sails, from far out to sea, like sea-birds."

"And the madman of the land, like a timid child," screeched the talking bird. "The madman of the forest, as toward the birds' nests...oh, wretched madman, who does not know what he is saying!"

Then the songbirds—the nightingales, the beautiful birds that only knew how to sing their breath in a few notes, the breath that is their entire being—came flocking around the poor madman from everywhere and, in order to console him, sang like his flute, which summarized their songs of love at dawn.

The madman picked up his flute, and the fawns and hinds came to lick his hands, and vigorous birds that the madman had never seen made as if to hurl themselves at the talking bird, which was obliged to fly off at top speed to the castle—and for one sweet hour the madman told the forest and the timid couriers of its feathered tribe the mystery of his soul, parallel to theirs; and the forest was in religious celebration, all those petty souls adoring Tenderness.

"Poor madman with the warm heart of a little bird," said the hermit, "beware of the manor with the beautiful smiles. Listen: this is not the first time that a tower has been constructed for Glyphtis. For a long time there has been talk of the golden hemp of her hair, and of her beautiful eyes, in which all forests and all rivers are painted, and of all her beauty, so new, O poor madman, to you.

"She was born many years ago—so uncertain in number that no one knows whether she emerged from the world's first spring—and since that time, she is the one who seeks out young princes with pointed beards, the one who mourns the old discrowned kings in their deserted palaces.

"There was one very old king, so old, so white and so tremulous that he was carried every morning to a large glass window from which he could gaze at the horizon. His horizons were the green hills of the sea's wrath or the calm carpet of its indolence, and the old king never spoke. He had lost his sons, whom he had sent on difficult journeys to consult the oracle, and what he demanded of the gods was whether he would ever again see Glyphtis, who had been the loving wrath of his youth. He sent away his daughters, because he did not want any feminine image to trouble the image that he retained beneath his eyelids. And the very old king died in despair.

"There was a young shepherd who saw Glyphtis in a splendid court, the most ardent knights seeking to obtain her smiles, her husband the king ruling the elite of cities. He loved her and she loved him, for her fate is to love incessantly. He took her to his home town, and his home town burned for a long time, for the king and his knights came to capture it after a long siege, and the shepherd's entire race sank into the dark past.

"Glyphtis comes, sees and disappears; the gods steal her away in a storm, and then send her back to us more beautiful than before, and that beauty is the mask of their wrath. She descends from thrones to follow pirates; she leaves the pirate for the triumphant admiral, and the admiral for the young princes who hide in lost lands—but what land remains unknown that she lights up? Madman, madman, hope that armed ships will come to take her away from here. Flee into the depths of the forest, far from the castle, far from her smile, and sing or dance or weep—but flee."

"I can't," the madman replied.

One day, however, the beautiful manor was attacked by foul and hairy enemies who had also come to conquer the youthful, smiling face, and their vigor overcame the last handsome prince and his loyal servants; and the manor was set ablaze like a resin torch, and it black smoke rose up into the Heavens, as strange and twisted as an angry ripe, like a charred arm still imploring, like the first clouds of the eternal night over the blaze of the last dusk of the Sun.

Glyphtis fled through the hedges of rose-bushes, utterly terrified. She perceived the eyes of the kneeling madman, shining like embers, and his hands, trembling with emotion, reaching toward her own face and hands. As she was no longer laughing, he took her in his arms and bounded into the green thickets.

"Madman, madman," said the talking bird, "your retreat will soon be discovered. Oh, the handsome ardent madman, the hurdles and whips are ready for you. Ha ha ha!"

But Glyphtis implored, so tenderly: "Let my friend hide me close to his pools, in his castle of leaves and his squirrels' turrets."

And the bird followed them without saying any more, and the hermit, seeing them pass by, gave them his bread.

Then they wandered along the thousand paths, far away, so very far! Glyphtis looked at herself in all the mirrors. The flight of hinds and fawns and the rustling of undergrowth warmed them about the approach of enemies. Then, soon wearied, the barbarians left, and the madman became the king of the forest again.

Grass and trees are growing once again beside the sea; little pathways run there, and the creepers follow them. The hedges of rose-bushes have become gigantic and closed the approach from the sea with a thick curtain. And the madman gambols beside Glyphtis in the heart of clearings. They sit down together on the shady beds of moss.

The Madman is the king's son, since he is the victor and Glyphtis does not know how to get out of the forest. For there is no road, but only little winding paths, which escape and disappear beneath her feet when she is alone; for the talking bird does not want to tell her when ships are prowling not far from the shore, and the hermit amuses himself with his grumbling and his well-intentioned exhortations, as the worthy madman does with his flute and is whistling, and also with his muscular arms.

Furthermore, he listens to the beautiful tales she tells him, about great manors far away, kings surrounded by a thousand guardsmen, pontiffs whose gestures halt armies. She sees him suffering slightly at these tales of the great wide world, and perhaps she imagines that he will take her back one day to the civilized world—but the madman, who is becoming wiser with every passing day, leans over her.

"The forest is beautiful," he says.

She can make no reply but: "Yes."

Chapter Four
THEANO

Because it feared sages and scorned the inspired, the crowd hunted them down, exiled them and killed them. It appealed, with its billowing voice, to those who butchered oxen and sheep, those who caused fermented beverages to flow, those who stocked their granaries in seasons of abundance in order to profit therefrom in years of famine. It addressed itself to those who endured unjust justice in order that they might color its actions. And the leaders of the common people armed those who labored for others, those who extracted at from the arid shore, those who rowed on the sea for a meager wage, and promised them a golden age if they would pillage the palaces of the sages with them. They fattened themselves on the hope that those who disdained public functions and business must have stored up immense riches and that their cellars would disgorge gold and silver. When they had finished killing, and pillaged the little that they could, cruel and boastful soldiers rose up in their midst, who seduced and pressured them, and the men of violence suffered.

There is no safe haven for the man who lives according to his conscience and the true law; the sages, however, do not all die. If their lamps are broken by the fists of the strong, the parchment upon which they wrote will later be read, and the tablets that they filled.

All science is in the desire for science, all intelligence in the study of intelligence, all virtue is loving one's own intelligence within universal intelligence. The primordial obscurity and the chaos in which formless creatures crept were not abolished by a posterior and superior structure of humankind and the universe; they still exist in base souls absorbed by the functions of living.

And the crowd will always seize the taciturn and gentle contemplator, to beat him with staves or put him to death. The ignorant soothsayer will prescribe the crime, and the most fortunate among the men of ideas will drag their disinherited lives into the wider world.

It was in that fashion, miraculously saved from the firsts and stones of a populace and offended by the sarcasm of a numerous crowd, that Theano the Savant, who lived and died like a man, came to die here. The men of her city detested her for her beauty, because it was illuminated by a gleam of intelligence more powerful than those of other women and her large dark eyes sparkled with a durable drop of Heaven, because her beauty was distant from the pleasantness of those who spun yarn and also those who displayed themselves indolently before the young merchants. They hated her because they could not understand her, or, in addition to the elevation of her mind, she was various. She explained at length to young men who sought the truth the origins and early history of the universe, then sang about the sufferings endured by the Titan and the beauty of the one whose smile was born from the sea in a nacreous dawn.

"When the ancestors sang," she said, "the Immortals were haunting the light foliage and circulating in the clouds, and the caress of the breeze inflated with tenderness beneath the stars was their meditation and the allure of their bounty. Their wrath thundered in the storm and their benevolence gave the trees to the countryside, and the wheat; and everything became godly by virtue of having appeared. At first, human beings lying beneath the hand of the gods dreamed of the sources of happiness and rejoiced in seeing them masters of the fire that warmed them and the herds that nourished them; they prayed to them during the long years of wandering and thanked them for the comfortable city. Then, as storms are more frequent than days of albuminous purity, and misfortune visits houses, humbly demanding hospitality and fleeing surreptitiously amid outbursts of tears, more often than the happiness that arrives to the sound of flutes and cheerful bells, they feared them. O heavy terror of the man whose chimera might be dispersed like wisps of straw by an arbitrary fit of

88

divine wrath, to every corner of the horizon! O terror of the man cannot live without the invisible witness and who hears the raucous approach of the Eumenides in the dark night, in search of sin in the sleeping city!

"The gods born of humans are beginning to disappear. Jupiter is the son of Minerva, the goddess of Intelligence, the star-studded ornament of our mirage. It is Minerva who built him before our eyes, a colossal statue whose forehead touched the fronton of the tallest temple, as a symbol of the enormous idol that the immensity of our terrors and the exiguity of our science are able to construct. It is a helpless rower weeping in the storm who sees disheveled Neptune rise up, a coward hampered by his shield in the obscure wood who dreams that Diana is firing arrows, and hears in the oak-trees agitated by the wind the formidable howling of Mars.

"There are no gods and goddesses but Beauty—let it be told again that she is born in the nacreous dawn of the sea— and Wisdom—let it be told again that she protected the subtle Ulysses—for it is necessary to dream aloud, so that others who listen to us might also dream, but dream of joy and not of terror. Listen to the fabulous voice of Marsyas; if someone runs through the wood so swiftly that people hear of it in every city, it is him, for he is the wood itself, its birds, its leaping beasts and the agility of shepherds, and their sing.

"Tear up your robes of terror! You are only imploring specious stones. Tear up your robes of terror, for no one is watching over your actions with a jealous eye; the crystal sky studded with golden stars is empty and devoid of any gaze. Only your mind goes forth to bump into the solid cupola. Live in contemplation, live in the mind. The minutes of the mind are fecund and happiness is born within yourselves. Let the shining processions pass by, with baskets of odorous flowers reposing on pretty leads, and the decorated carts, and the joyful priests, for all religion is there. It is a hymn to certain days. Tear up your robes of terror!

"There is no god or goddess but Birth, Death and Mind. You do not die, you finish and depart again in the bounding course of atoms, and live in accordance with recommenced curiosity. The fields of death are bright and gilded, they are those of knowledge. There is no Tartarus, nor judges at its threshold; there is no Lethe or Elysian Fields. Live and die in order to learn, to walk the paths of the knowledge that does not descend into the abyss but climbs in white hills toward the blue infinity. The soul, with its benevolent fire, enlightens you, envelops you, guides you: the inextinguishable lamp of the enduring soul remains alone and identical.

"What does it matter to you that it is not always the same, that it does not remember the journeys you undertook in your city, the insults of the stupid, the vexations of the rich, the enemy's blades, your hunger or the appeasement of your hunger, if you awaken to another dawn without and memory of yesterday? Death will be the benevolent guide leading you to another facet of the world.

"Never fear; live in life, since within that moment your intelligence lives among perfumed dawns and ephemeral dusks; never despair. Eternity is a clepsydra, which empties and is renewed, and it is always the same sans; never hope and never be sad; you may discover the same flowers tomorrow, with a heart so much warmer that they appear more beautiful.

"The world is a screen on which one sees the moment pass in jeweled robes, veiled with regret; remain there. Your movements and travels are the sole cause of suffering. Honor beauty. Thought ought to move calmly in the ether as a trireme cuts through the white foam. Proteus must always resume his true form and become an evasive and pensive old man again—Proteus, the human soul in the innumerable liquid drops of existence.

"There is no chance; there is no specific destiny; there is a universe that is dying and coming into being at every instant. Await therefore, calmly, the instant that appears to you more agreeable or more severe..."

The scribe does not know anything more about the woman who came to die here, except that she did not pray to the gods of her nation, and yet celeb rated them in her verses as statues in the gardens of her race. She was beautiful, savant and persecuted...

HAGAR

Joseph of Arimathea lowered the parchment that he had unrolled, in which old annals displayed the ancient gold of vanished lives, and he murmured: "Mobed, Glyphtis, Theano."[12]

King Balthazar advanced through the narrow and high-ceilinged galley, and the long pleats of his orange robe, ornamented pectorally with bluish solver designs, slid over the white marble flagstones. He stopped beside a basin into which a brief jet of perfumed water trickled.

Having set down the manuscript, Joseph said to him: "Sire, since archives and legends depict them, were Mobed, Glyphtis and Theano living beings?"

"Living beings, forms, appearances, tales—it's all one. What does it matter whether they lived, or whether the splendid mantle of an enchantment of glory was thrown upon their shoulders? The poet who carries myths and fables in his brain and the race that carries them in its loins, invent nothing that is impossible. They remember or they predict; they create, describing in advance by the indication of life that they give to great hearts, but every poetic invention is latent in the Earth, so it lives. Imagine the intellectual world as a vast meadow; the green surfaces as are great as the Earth, and the same flowers grow everywhere therein; the pollen is the same and the same wind bears it away.

"Oh, if we knew everything—and I'm not talking about the laws of the universe, remote laws that retreat even further

---

[12] Of these three names, Theano is the only one that Kahn did not invent; it is that of the most famous female philosopher of the Pythagorean school, sometimes identified as the wife or daughter of its legendary founder. Several letters attributed to her—almost certainly falsely—survived into modern times, giving some hint as to her ideas.

as soon as we reach out toward any certainty, but only the memories of human beings, that which has happened and been thought; the melancholies of the Northern barbarians beside their grey rivers, which flow in blackened waves through their vast forests, and their cries of joy beside cups of foaming ales; and the nonchalant dreams of the fisher of the Persian Sea; that which the calm stars say to him, and that which the rippling waves murmur to him; and the promises that their own minds, extended and enlightened by the sky, make to the deprived and starving solitary dwellers in the highest Asian summits; and the words of the Chaldeans on the high towers nearest to the stars; and the infinity of the words of sadness of the great nomads of the deserts of the South; and that which the sages of Greece and Palestine have not said, and all the suffering and all the love and all the legends—oh, if we only knew!

"On the green meadow of the world, at enormous distances, the same plant germinates and deploys its ephemeral beauty, its instinctive beauty, which will recommence tomorrow and is hence eternal beauty. A herdsman, a poor man or a young woman, picks the common flower, the pretty and vulgar flower; they carry it away, and what does it matter what vase they place it in: a clay jar, a copper pot, a wooden vessel or one of pearly glass? And if the son of the king of kings passes before the young woman's window, and takes away the plant that was, for a moment, the confidant of modesty and charming hesitation, the plant may wither and another will grow. It is one verse more in the young woman's song. The son of the king has passed by. And if the herdsman loves the young woman whose eyes burn on seeing the mantlet of the king's son, that is one more line of the song. It is the same song in the palaces of the North, the furnaces of the desert, the liquid gems of blessed shores; and the dolor amid the diversity of languages speaks everywhere in accordance with the same sad and beautiful modulation, ephemeral but eternal since it exists simultaneously and everywhere.

"It is from to the same spindles that the treads of life and dreams, moments and death are unwound. In fables, the guardians of forgetfulness, the numerators of death, are forever old, never having been young, but seeresses, and those who sing beside torrents, enjoy eternal youth and beauty. The wise and the weak have agreed, confusedly, in thinking that perhaps ages have elapsed without trace, and their enigma resides in these guardians, always hundreds of years old; but the recommenced spring lives and flourishes, we know not when, for how many ardent suns we do not know, and we all sing, and will sing more loudly than the little birds at dawn. Travel the great meadow and you will hear nothing there but alternating cries of fear and certainty; that is the echo of the noise of peoples you hear, and sages are little children before a black wall."

"But the song is also an annunciation," said Joseph.

"At every moment, since nothing has arrived before the eyes of the world. But listen to the possible origin of the myth of Mobed, the warrior woman for some, the most beautiful for others, the totality of womanhood for many of those here, who is their sister in every epoch, a spirit, while Ghyphtis and Theano come to them so variously in the thousands of mouths that repeat their names on Mediterranean shores—unless all three are merely the reflection of some dispersed cult even more ancient than our most audacious fables.

"In the great green meadow lived King Abraham, with warriors and flocks, and when his tribes came to some new land of the great meadow to build their huts of branches, one might have thought, the next day, that a marvelous forest had sprung up. King Abraham knew justice, tamed wild beasts and defeated rebels, and no one defended the part he had conquered better against the barbarians of the North and the pirates of the South.

"When King Abraham was still very young, his father, who was powerful in a great city nearly the ancient cradle of humankind, had sent him far away, with his servants, the sons of his former servants whim he no longer wanted to feed, for the city within its dry stone walls had become too narrow.

"Abraham augmented his people with slaves who moaned under heavy iron collars; he took them from miserly cities and diminished nomadic tribes of their number. He called poor people to the renown of his justice, as well as mild-mannered populations fleeing from galloping hordes. From the as-yet-pure dawn to the bloody sunset, Abraham offered to the Unknown his people's prayers of hope and expectation, and he listened to the gentle advice of three night until the Unknown had spoken to him.

"You know that an embassy from his aged father Tharah, who lived in the cities of Chaldea, had brought him a wife, the most beautiful that he had fund among the daughters of his race. Dark and pale and tall, Sarah knew the travails of women better than anyone else. She became queen beside the king, but no lineage emerged from her and Abraham became desperate.

"And his people said: 'We shall not be a great people, like the races that surround us; we shall never send our sons abroad, under the command of our king, to edict our laws and found a people in our image in the distant plains. The Elohim made humans in their image; the image of the human closest to the Elohim, the king, ought to guide the tribe, the image of the people, into the distance. Our people will not be able to engender a filial people; our people has not been chosen by the Lord and we shall not the founder of numerous and sovereign races.'

"Abraham thought as they did. He thought, dolorously, that his laws and his symbols would remain limited to one corner of the universe, and that the wisdom of pastor kings would die with him. As he loved Sarah, who was for him the only residue, and also the evident sign of the house of his father and his ancestors, He despaired without acing, and he loved Sarah, for her beauty as well as the memories she evoked.

"It happened that among the liberated slaves there was a very beautiful young woman, who was named Hagar.[13] The dull bronze of her complexion made her dark phosphorescent eyes stand out; her, as lustrous as onyx, was beautiful when she bound it into a crown, and abundant when she loosed it, like the foliage of a willow tree, and the men said; 'Queen Sarah is not the most beautiful woman in the camp. She is as splendid as the cold Moon in a calm sky, or as a ripe fruit, but she is the daughter of the Sun and her eyes warm like a flamboyant noon.'

"And Abraham shared the enthusiasm of his men, to the extent that he refused her to the best of his warriors, and had a son, Ishmael by her. But Queen Sarah threatened to go back to the cities of Chaldea. 'I shall take with me,' she said, 'the memory of your race and the link of the ancestral chain that connects you to the Elohim; and it will be said that you were not able to abide by the law and justice, and you will be cut off from the past, and your people will be a new horde, without laws and without rights in the great green meadow.'

"'A people does not only live in the past, Sarah,' Abrahams replied. 'Perhaps it is only a migration that plants the laws and faith of a fatherland elsewhere than in its cradle. You have not given me the son who could lead the son of my men to distant lands and unknown seas, and the other has been sanctified by life.'

"'In that case,' said Sarah, 'I do not want to wait for him to come of age, to bear your name and your laws elsewhere; let him depart immediately, and she with him to guide him; let them depart alone.'

"And King Abraham, still dominated by the memory of the long years of his first love, allowed it.

"Hagar went into the desert, and a few men followed her. Dire fatigue decimated them; many returned to Abraham's

---

[13] cf *Genesis* 16-17, which offers a very different account of the events narrated this story.

camps, for it was humiliating to them that a woman should seem to have the power of supreme command.

"Hagar wandered in the desert. She suffered hunger; she suffered thirst; she suffered fear when the voices of large wild beasts reverberated in the solitudes; at meager oases, among the water-holes, she found populations still in their infancy; she taught them the arts she knew, and they protected her. She was a queen; she was a captive; her flights prepared her triumphs; her triumphs succumbed to the conspiracies of avarice and cunning, and she was often obliged to flee far from burning tents, carrying her son in her arms—and little Ishmael smiled at her abundant tears and ran his fingers through her beautiful black tresses. Her beauty often saved her life, when she appeared tall and upright between the fires of nomads to ask them for bread and shelter, and they prostrated themselves at first as before an apparition.

"Finally, Ishmael grew up to become a war-chief, and his people grew to be numerous; he reigned by conquest and by science, and Hagar fought beside him in battles. She promulgated wise laws, and the memory of her great beauty lived among the peoples.

"None of the old men had been able to forget the charm of her first appearance and the serenity of her first words, and when she died, her memory was deified and became parallel to that of a victorious Isis. She was the mother of races of splendor and courage, the vanquishing horses of which only stopped at the ocean waves, and when the Sun rises, it is her victorious face that sets the pale and charming Moon to flight."

GOD AND GODDESSES

"All that," said Joseph of Arimathea, "In the murmur of human beings; personally, I have seen the dawn of the divine."

"A dawn of kindness," the king continued, "but a human dawn"

"The angels of marvel predicted the birth; harps resounded on the eve of the annunciation."

"In the parvis of the temple the angels of light manifested themselves to the wife of Manoah.[14] The celestial promise flared up before the eyes of Hannah,[15] and both of them remained in prayer throughout their quiet lives before the miraculous guests of their wombs. That was also, at the time, the dawn of the divine. The man of the promise has often come, Incarnated, only to die without having spoken. Delilah killed the strong, and when Samuel got to his feet in the dwelling of the Pythoness, it was to harsh exile that he returned, not the tomb."

"In your thinking, Sire, your science, which is your cult, why do feminine forms rose up immortal and almost divine, and why are the men of the past no more, in your eyes, than sages?"

"The divine," the king replied, "is a cult accumulated by long prayer and long contemplation. Since the world of thought resides in men and woman alike, why has humankind not embodied itself in its goddesses? Is not beauty the immediately sensible form of the divine, and does not womanhood contain as many of the possibilities of suffering that complete it? The same moment, relived since the world has existed, has been recounted for as long as there has been speech. The same facts never tire of being. The entire network of joy, pain, hatred and love that passes, in the eyes of mere mortals, for the profound contemplation of the world, is contained in women as much as in men, more intensely and more rapidly. They hear the fanfares of victory and the lugubrious moans of mourning at the same moment; they think and they act, wholly given to impulsion. They draw nearer to the way through existence. They determine with a word the orientation of the road that is often so hard to fix in the sands. In the physical word,

***

[14] cf *Judges* 13.
[15] cf I *Samuel* 1-2.

97

men act and women listen. In the moral world, women act and men contemplate.

"To primitive humankind, therefore, the forms of goddesses were necessary. The god of men, the announced Messiah, has never come; he has been constructed slowly from those who arrive and die, leaving behind a babble more profound than those previously heard. It is in them and in those of us in whom their brief lives multiply by meditation and study—which is to say, the mental beauty of men—that God has been constructed. To the amiable seers, destined to a hard death, he remains a sign, and we are the ones who open our souls entirely to their essence.

"Thousands of tabernacles are waiting with an empty pedestal for the statue, a *tabula rasa* for the book, and festivals have already been ready for a long time for the rustle of the truth—but who has seen anything there but a reflection? And the conquest of the truth is so infinitely arduous that the great emissaries of consciousness have let it filter through our fingers like droplets of pale water.

"The man from the banks of the Jordan, whose voice thundered over Palestine, the lustral prophet who only remained on the frontiers of the world to lead more disciples to poverty and toward the silence of the desert, whose head was cut off—what remains of his thought? And what of Jesus, who remains, in addition to the tears of women, our sadness and consciousness of forgiveness? The Son of Man stirs the universe, like a shower of rain. Drops shine momentarily on all the leaves and flowers, then everything dries out and the same appearance as before returns. Many drops have designed mobile and temporary spheres on lakes, rivers and the ocean. A fine cloud passé over, full of blessed forbearance; the Earth is refreshed; then the ardent Sun becomes master again: a golden disk, a disk of glory and ostentation, a disk flamboyant with passion, with its lesson of violent and daily desire."

"What are we to do, then?" asked Joseph of Arimathea.

"Wait. If you keep your eyes fixed on the future, without looking at anything but the appearance of the enigma, the life of the Earth and human beings will seem motionless to you, and you will become sad because the not-yet belied effort of humans on Earth has no other end but watching the same ray of sunlight cut out the same expanse of shadow on the same wall. If you look behind you, hope will come to you by roads traveled.

"Oh, if only days of audacity were not followed by years of exhaustion, if humans did not hesitate so frequently before the tall grass of unexplored heaths! The wooden vessel that you have brought me takes its place among the elements of our cult, since it represents a prescience and a dolor, and it will doubtless long be its most precious object, since it is the most recent and signifies so many accumulated ideas—also because it emanates from the most instinctive of the heroes of virtue, and also because everything leads to the belief, by the very reason of his recent existence, that for a long time, no other will rise up in the radiance of life that we will be able to touch our thought.

"But Joseph, it is like the ark—a casket, a sign—and you can only explain it to me in terms of the beautiful melancholy that grips you when you contemplate it."

Dares came in.

"Sire, a traveler has come by way of the sands to present himself at the castle. He is very weary, very poor in appearance; his eyes are hollow, his long black hair is mingled with silvery undergrowth."

"We will see him," said the king.

And to the presence of the ser and the saint that they were, Dares introduced a man. At that moment a ray of sunlight penetrated the high-ceilinged gallery, so intense and charged with celestial vigor that Joseph of Arimathea's wooden vessel, deposited on the pedestal on an altar, seemed to catch fire, with a fixed and powdery blaze.

Chapter Five
AHASVERUS

"Be welcome," said the king. "Stranger, you can tell us your name or not, as you like. Our will and our law merely demand that you leave the castle, when it pleases you, less sad and better endowed with good fortune than when you entered it."

"I am Ahasverus," the man replied, "a poor artisan from Jerusalem."

"And how do you come to be here?"

"I was banished."

"Where have you come from more recently?"

"The broad desert."

"And where are you going?"

"I don't know and I hardly care."

"I didn't know you in Jerusalem. I'm Joseph of Arimathea."

"It's hardly likely that someone as powerful as you would remember having seen a poor wretch like me."

"Drink," said Balthazar. He held out a cup to the man, who emptied it in a single draught. His aquiline features brightened beneath his thick hair, and his hand trembled slightly, as if with pleasure, and his temples throbbed with the flow of the source of life. His hands were large, bony and hard, and when he put the metal goblet down his entire frame seemed tall and strong. His face was the color of raw copper, and his feet were bare. A long brown tunic and old cloak covered him.

"I've seen you often, Lord Joseph, and your palace in the vines. I've seen you going hunting on your handsome white horse with brass harness, with your white falcon on your wrist, and your retinue of servants, more magnificent than you in their costumes and weaponry. I've seen you come back joyful when, wearied by work, I was about to watch the Sun set, as red as blood, over the city."

"Where did you live?"

"You hardly even passed that way: in the street that leads to the charnel-house, the rubbish dump and the site of public executions, a street soiled by the neighborhood of the kennels of the poor and miserable courtesans, on stony ground where trees don't grow, where the dregs of the city went to chat by the fountain in the evening."

"What was your work?" asked Balthazar.

"Anything and everything. I helped masons, I was something of a carpenter, something of a smith—any work that brought me a windfall that would give me a few handfuls of flour or a little bottle of wine. It's not good to be poor in Israel."

"Why were you banished?"

"Don't you know, Lord Joseph? I heard talk, in fact, that Caiaphas had imprisoned you. Who knows anything, though, about a nobody like me? Or perhaps Pilate had already opened your cell-door. I was banished without being told the reason. I was threatened with torture if I stayed—which, to tell the truth, I had no desire to do. What does it matter, when one's unfortunate? I believe that it was for not opening my door to Jesus, who was going up to Calvary, or not having offered him a place on my bench. I didn't act out of harshness, but all the condensed pass in front of my house and when one must die, it's as well to make haste…it lessens the misery."

"I would have thought," said Joseph, "that the priests would have congratulated you."

"Yes, some of them—they're quite hard. With all my heart, I'd trade the years of misery that remain to me not to have done it. Why did I refuse…at the first impulse? I was hard man in a hard city…and then, it all happened, in spite of its apparent slowness, so quickly…and remember, among all that howling...

"'He wants to be king of the Jews, he wants to be Caesar's slave…oh, the descendant of David…call your gibbo-

101

rim,[16] son of David…protégé of God, bring down angels to flagellate us and open our skulls with the hooves of their winged horses…that's what it would take for us to believe you…where are your miracles, you who brought Lazarus back to life, when the tempting opportunity for a resurrection presented itself for you to…Lazarus was a nonentity…it's the Magdalen who…' And cries, a storm of cries, as there is every time someone is led to death."

"You didn't recognize him?"

"Who, Jesus?"

"Yes, Jesus, the gentle savior."

"No! The hatred unleashed on him by the dogs that escort all those passing funerals is always the same, and I'd seen so many, and heard the great voices of the poor. It was in the ditches of the palace that they were buried in the thick mortal sand, or in the depths of that well-trodden cave to which free men are dragged in obscure wood after death and washed. There are poisons…

"We were hardly ever shown heroes in our street being led to the cross, or we were told that they were thieves. Yes, I've seen brave men captured on the far side of the Jordan, sold by Arab guides, deceived by Herod's emissaries, whom God confuses with putrid murderers, but when they were led to Jerusalem, wounded, tied to camels like split bales because their blood was running, there was talk, above all, of their thefts and depredations. Many had left because the publican ruined them, some of who had robbed the publican—or had done even worse."

"Ahasverus, you weren't astonished to hear Joseph of Arimathea call Jesus the gentle savior?"

"No, he was his friend—and then, perhaps I've seen something."

"Thanks to what?"

"To the shadow of death over the city, and to not having understood anything, not having seen anything, known any-

---

[16] A Hebrew word usually translated as "mighty ones"

thing, to having rested that day, and doubtless many days before, in the company of souls more frail and more profound than my own, tormented and harshly chastised, without my being able to do anything—and it was nothing—but let him rest on my step. That's my concern in my new distress, no worse than the old, my only distress.

"I saw those who were weeping beside his body, desolate in their hearts, and the women who were with him were beautiful in nobility and filial suffering; the Pharisees mocking him were fertile in anecdotes, but they looked like ferrets—those whom the little people met, at least—by comparison with Jesus' friends. They carried his body away piously. As for Iscariot, I think they killed him. A short time after that death, people were saying—they were Galileans who were talking— that the death of Jesus was a crime greater than any before it, that because of that crime we'd see the old misfortunes again, and that the Hebrews would be dispersed, as before, by the conqueror's scourge—and many poor folk came to pay their respects and weep at the site of the torture...

"The priests began to talk differently; to hear them, they had been deceived, and only ought to have banished Jesus, the gentle, who had only made one mistake, that of consorting with the meanest inhabitants of the city, being otherwise a learned man, sometimes favored with divine communications. They no longer feared him, but they feared the Galileans who had made so many friends by their kindness, and promises of eternal ecstasy for anyone who followed their teachings. I was harshly reproached for having refused him my bench, for having closed my door on him. I was already unhappy about it.

"Ultimately, as you can imagine, nobody reproached Caiaphas or the powerful men of the Sanhedrin; none of those who had committed the murder were caused any anxiety, but they were happy to aim their hatred at me and banish me, as they were able to banish the carpenter who cut the wood for the cross, the metalworkers who had fabricated the nails and the fathers of the Roman soldiers who mounted guard on the torture-victims, as they did every day. And exile pleased me, because I had already banished my city and my race from my soul.

"I was too unhappy to love a city; traveling harshly now, not wanting to stop anywhere for long, anxious no longer to belong to any homeland, no longer to act collectively, no longer to be deceive collectively, I'm going in search of new distresses, all less injurious than the sight of the white lie of a city. Would you care to give me another cup? I'm weary, in spite of my strength."

As he drank, he continued: "Lord, this wine is the happy current of life; it's warm and it's brief; the pleasure it gives is as short as that of a glad thought, or the hope of a pleasant dream. Wine is almost as impalpable as the truth that flees from us, leaving us with a pulpy sensation in our fingers. One has seized it entirely, as a hope, and also abandoned it entirely, but one doesn't detest it, any more than the hope, and one wants to seize the charmer once again who sings in a palace beneath the skull, even one as hard as mine—that of Ahasverus, the poor workman of Jerusalem. And I've walked so far, for so many days, Lord, that I beg you to give me leave for a little rest. I'll leave tomorrow, and you'll have finished with the sight of a poor wretch."

"Ahasverus," said Balthazar, "Since you have come so far from Jerusalem, have you encountered any Jews on your route?"

"Yes, Lord, a few. They're preaching the new faith, and the new incarnation of Javeh. To listen to them, Moses was nothing but a small boy; they're beginning again. A Hebrew is a man who preaches the new faith. They've never done anything but that, and when their faith in Javeh seemed too ancient, they were sometimes idolaters. In my time, I too have sculpted Baals, crudely, for rich amateurs to put in the corner of their garden. But you can hear them chirping the new faith at every crossroads in the world, until the time when the gentiles reduced them to silence, until their bodies and the pyres evaporate with the firewood in golden flames in a puff of smoke. They always require a puff of smoke. They preach courageously, and heaps of stones serve at the same time as their tombs and as indicators to recognize the road. But they preach very courageously. They're beginning again—it's the sign of the race."

SOLOMON'S SHIP

Ahasverus did not leave the castle as soon as he had said he would, for the king's ingenious hospitality retained him for some time under the pretext of small tasks involving wood or iron. For the greater part of the day Ahasverus worked doggedly; then, in the evening, he sat up late talking to Dares. The black slave liked the wanderer and he had wanted to get to know him better in order to be surer of curing his sadness— because, for the worthy slave, not to be entirely happy was to suffer from the most profound pain.

To distract him, he told him his most marvelous stories. "Do you know," he said to him one day, "the story of King Solomon's ship?" And when Ahasverus, laughing, admitted to being unaware of it, Dares said to him: "For someone— someone like you—who intends to extend his life over long and multiple roads, it's necessary to know it. It's true, and useful.

"When Solomon had constructed the immense temple of which his son David had dreamed, in which thirteen thousand pillars of cedar sustained the domes whose golden strips presented in their curves all the noble words inspired by the Elohim, and where the marvelous lamp was suspended under which the simplest priest, transfigured by the light, seemed an omnipotent king, he wondered whether he had done enough for the praise of his God to be proclaimed over the entire Earth.

"He walked around the temple and was satisfied. The joy of the faithful filled the parvis with their admiring cries and their greatest respect when, through the forest of cedar pillars, they glimpsed the pontiff's massive silver chair facing the king's golden throne, and the marvelous carpet that was unrolled toward the sanctuary so that the king and the pontiff might kneel before the doors of the tabernacle before it opened contented him. He gazed at the palms on the walls, the bronze wings that seemed to be bearing prayers away, the large brazen oxen that sustained the vessels of purification; he went along the exterior terraces and climbed up the towers; he saw with pleasure all the familiar birds for which nests had been constructed, in order that their fluttering and calling might appear to continue in the infinite Heavens the enthusiastic words of women happy in their piety. He saw the pool consecrated to water so clear that, in spite of its depth, one could decipher on the bed of marble brightly-colored mosaics that were the names of God the Creator—and yet, when he went back to the palace at the slow pace of his chariot, he was worried, and felt that his homage to the Most High was incomplete.

"Nothing, however, was missing from the superb temple, and its hill surpassed the highest in the land of faith. Choirs sang the praises of Javeh with a voice so melodious that the captive kings and the hosts of Solomon dedicated to other religions felt the God of Israel embracing them in the silvery flow of loving sound, and some were converted when, to the most gentle rhythm, as tender as a bride's response, the doors slid open before the bright white gleam—like frozen lightning—of the sanctuary.

"Oh, in those times, it is said, the delights of Israel rang out in admirable songs, tambourines measured the serene joy of Palestine like that of the young and beautiful spouse of a triumphant god, and the peoples in their islands, in their deserts, beyond their rivers, enamored, jealously watched its beauty pass by on the golden chariot with ruby wheels.

"Nonchalant Sion extended her hand toward its baskets, and there were steaming vintages and gaieties loud with song in the stony roads, marriages in the high places, and thousands of donkeys laden with goatskins climbing up to the towns. Sion extended her hand toward its ports, and beneath its feet, emptying the galleys, she heaped up the scarlet bales; the great idols gilded in yellow lands; those of the blacks that are in crudely-worked wood but whose eyes are carbuncles, the nipples of the goddesses rubies and their necklaces of all kinds of splendid gems, assembled at hazard; and also the idols of the Hyperboreans, of ill-shaped wood but clad in the most beautiful soft white or blue-tinted fleeces of unknown animals. And between hers feet, piles of perfumed wood were stacked, so abundantly that the poorest house in Sion contained the aromas of odorant earths.

"On feast-days Sion decked herself in the most beautiful linen fabrics that could be found anywhere in the world, and she raised above her head, in order that the peoples might be charmed thereby, colored scarves as luminous as the stars. Then she smiled with her entire face, and all the wives of her master Solomon, the most of handsome of Javeh's sons..."

"An ancient dream," said Ahasverus. "Sion has shrunk within its boundaries, and although the temple, so beautiful, still embellishes the city, it's not the marvel that you believe..."

"I'm recounting the beauties of the true Temple," said Dares. "The one that Solomon built for himself as much as for Javeh—did he not think of himself as the reflection of benevolent Javeh? The one that you've seen, humans rebuilt, only humans..."

"But men tested by exile and misfortune," Ahasverus replied. "And is it not beautiful, that temple in which the pillars are suffering, the palms obstinate in their hope—yes, perhaps more beautiful, and yet less, than the bare halls in which the Hebrews of the exiles assembled in order not to forget their language and their law."

"For you, the solitary wanderer—but is one not closer to eternal forces when one can see their temple illuminated every day and their statues..."

"No, the fixed image of a divinity encumbers me. I prefer to listen to the temple being built within me."

"However," said Dares, "that wasn't the opinion of King David or King Solomon. They were powerful, and sons of the

Elohim, and you're only a poor devil—that creates a difference in ideas. Personally, I'm just a slave. I accept the thoughts of the powerful and believe them to be true, because they're more beautiful and florid. Those who carry an amulet are more content than people who, like you, seek the desert in the cities and swimming-pools in the desert."

"Very well. So what did Solomon's temple lack?"

"That which the King sought for a long time. He consulted the pontiffs, the sages, the judges; all of them were happy with their enriched tiara. He asked the opinion of shrewd merchants; all of them told him that the world's summer was in flower. He consulted ordinary people; they were delighted by being able to sleep peacefully next to the basin or the fountain, rolled up in their cloaks, without cries of panic ever signaling the arrival on the horizon of marauders on lean horses bent on rapid depredation. He informed the ladies of the palace about his anxieties; they were astonished by his singular concern, and their only response was to point to the effulgent cupolas and he colossal towers, and the terraces of the city that extended like a joyous lawn at the feet of the temple and the palace.

"One day, when King Solomon was wandering some distance from his house of pleasure in Gilead, celebrated for its great shadows and its colossal golden apples, he had abandoned the straight and shady route; he saw that he was in a region that did not seem familiar, and far from all the lustrous beauty of his kingdom. It was like a gorge between hills of gray stone, scaled by clumps of gorse and thyme, and hawks were circling above it.

"There, he saw a beautiful Ishmaelite girl coming toward him, singing and dancing, thrusting out her red-clad bosom, with castanets in her fingers. She had the features of those tribes which wander in the heart of the Arabian deserts, to which are attributed to gifts of prescience and deciphering the meaning of birdsong and the forms of clouds. Many of them lived within the confines of the land of Midian.

"And the young woman said to him: 'Greetings to the well-beloved, greetings to the anxious man...' Then she fled, laughing.

"The king went after her, but the capricious young woman passed through the large clumps of vegetation very nimbly and leapt over the stony bed of the dry stream. Finally, she deigned to sit down on a boulder, and then Solomon was able to approach her. He asked her what she had meant.

"'Well-beloved,' she said, 'you are by all Israel, for you are King Solomon; anxious you are, for you are searching for what the temple lacks, and no one can tell you—and the daughter of Ishmael does not want to tell you. Guess if you can.'

"Beside her, two large, superb and supple lilies were bending over. She tore up one of them and threw it into the air; the wind caught it, and it spun around, and was soon out of sight—and while the king reflected, the Ishmaelite fled again, without him being able to follow her.

"Solomon searched his wisdom. It seemed to him that the wild lily was the Ishmaelite herself, and the disappearance of the flower her flight toward the arid hills. One of the lilies remained on its stem; did that signify that the two flowers needed to be separated, that another had to grow in place of the one that had been torn up? And his thought never ceased to indentify the wild lilies with the slender, strong and beautiful girl.

"He left the cedars of Gilead again and returned to the rocky gorge, without seeing anyone there henceforth, and he was disappointed by that when, one day, on the terrace of his palace, the young woman appeared directly in front of him— and the King asked her, emotionally, to stay in Gilead.

"'If I accepted, Lord, you would soon send me away. How can a powerful King allow himself to be charmed for more than a minute by a rock-flower? And I would always think that it is in order to know the key to the enigma that you tell me that you love me. Powerful King, I'm going away— seek on your own.' And she disappeared.

"The king remained thoughtful. He felt strongly that all this had as much to do with the temple as with himself. 'If I, who am accustomed to the most marvelous perfumes, have felt so much pleasure in respiring the scent of these wild lilies momentarily,' he said to himself, 'if I, who am almost sated, light up with such joy at the approach of the wandering girl, and the aridity of that soil delights me, the master of domains and palaces...'

"He thought that Javeh might similarly appreciate being momentarily distanced from the luxury prepares for him, that the god of infinite space and the gulfs where matter ends might find the most sumptuous assemblages of marble and gold paltry and unworthy of him—and this is what he did, obedient to his meditation:

"He had a ship constructed, of the most magnificent wood, and decorated it soberly in the softest fabrics; in the heart of the ship a kind of closed pavilion was built, and there King Solomon placed one of the crowns and one of the swords bequeathed to him by David. The external sides of the hull were painted green, which signifies hope, the internal sides scarlet, which radiates glory. The poop, the prow and the masts were hung with the most beautiful garlands of resistant and spontaneous flowers that grow near the sea. Inside the pavilion, next to David's sword and crown, Solomon had engraved on a golden plaque: *The ship, the sword and the crown are destined for the Lord's new elect; they will be his most humble witnesses with regard to the people of the Earth.*

"Then, before a small number of his principal officers—those to whom he revealed his thoughts—the ship was launched on to the sea, without any mariner aboard. It cut through the waves with the ease of a swan on a river, and soon disappeared into the light mist on the horizon.

"And Solomon said to his people: "The Eternal now has his two temples: the one on the hill of Sion that will speak to him of our love, his strength, his will and our contemplation of his benefits; and that consecrated ship, which is going toward him by way of the caprices of horizons, homage to his unexplored form, to what is perhaps his secondary, but existent, form, Chance.'"

And the smiling Ahasverus said to Dares: "Happy old man in whom the golden tales of the ancestors live, like a tree in rich soil."

PASSOVER

As the days of Passover approached, Ahasverus asked King Balthazar for permission to leave. "Sire King," he said, "I have tarried to long in your gracious company, and remorse will not permit me to be one of the fortunate individuals of his world. The evolution of Ahasverus is not a matter of taking part in festivals that he no longer understands, and I do not wish, Sire King, other than in solitary suffering, to grasp the meaning of those festivals, which I used to celebrate passively. Permit poor Ahasverus, Sire King, to accomplish the destiny inscribed in all his dreams, and to march, since that is the desire of every fiber of his being. In acting thus, I believe, I am obedient to objectives superior to me."

"My only desire, Ahasverus, is that you leave with a little joy—and, if possible, to diminish your imminent fatigue. Would you like a ship to take you to whichever distant shore you please, and to leave here with a little gold? Would you like a caravan to accompany you across the sands? When you arrive at a rich city, or an abundant land, you can send it back, conserving from its cargo whatever you think necessary."

"Thank you, Sire King," said Ahasverus. "I want to march alone, and leave by the landward route. I shall go toward the meager pasturage, the desolate gorges and the poor tribes. There I shall find out, more easily than in great cities, whether my soul, which you have refreshed, will continue to enjoy new life."

"At least accept a good horse, which will lessen your initial fatigue..."

"I accept it," said Ahasverus, "in order to get away more rapidly from human beings, and your domains. I do not want

111

to see anyone for a long time, in order not to spoil the exquisite impression of pause and rest that I am carrying away from
your hospitality. Having arrived in another region, as soon as I
encounter a handsome young man who still believes that traveling more rapidly means arriving sooner, I'll make a gift of
your horse to his young impatience."

"Go," said the King, "and be happy. Dares will escort
you through the gardens."

And Ahasverus took his leave of the King and Joseph of
Arimathea.

"Old friend," Ahasverus said to Dares, when they arrived
at the limits of the garden, where a young groom was already
holding the bridle of a horse, "I no longer have my former life,
of the time when I was stern and hard and preoccupied with a
thousand trivia, like this bronze ring. I give it to you; it will no
longer remind me of the old man that I was and it will remind
you of the respite that I have fund in your stories and your
songs. May your life be long and may the peace of your soul
be the inexhaustible gentle fountain of the lilt of your song, in
which you weave the pleasure of living, listening and gazing,
as a clever man bends wicker for baskets that will be filled
with fruits. Take it, and farewell. No, don't give me anything
in exchange; I don't want to possess anything except myself.
Adieu."

And Ahasverus leapt on to his horse—and, with a few
bounds, drew away.

On the day of Passover, trumpets sounded from every
turret toward the clear and infinite sky. On the day before, the
servants had stripped the gardens of their abundant ornamentation, and the walls of the castle were carefully embraced by an
embalmed reflection of the sunlight. The terrace and the steps
of the staircase that descended toward the sea were ennobled
with red roses, like the blood of the Sun, and white and yellow
roses like the fires of the dawn. Amid the green assembly of
branches, large flowers in ivory flesh tones respired near those
that one might have thought adorned with the magnificent
robes of queens. Heaps of flowers as red as lips were asso-

112

ciated with those of flowers with hearts as velvety as eyes. Incense fumed in enormous bronze vases amid the warmest of breezes, and the white seabirds wheeling in the sky resembled winged flowers.

In the topmost room of the palace, tables were being prepared for the feast; the best-loved subjects of the king and his oldest servants were to take their places there beside him. Before sitting down to it, the King and the residents of the castle went to meet those who were arriving by the landward route. Their horses were decorated with sparkling white plumes and broad cloths in which golden designs were woven. Majestic old men and vigorous young ones left them in the hands of black grooms with light helmets and dull silver damascened corselets, then came together; feathers topped their turbans, ornamented with carbuncles and topazes, and chimerical lotus-blossoms and other dream-like flowers shone upon their long, brightly-colored robes.

Chiefs of the desert tribes, sterner and more bronzed than the others, mingled with them, draped in their monochrome mantles, relieved only by the gems of their fasteners. Enormous elephants arrived at a slow place along a broad path tiled in marble, and women in long white veils trimmed with gold got down therefrom, light sparkling crowns circling their heads; they did not unveil themselves until they reached the portico under which King Balthazar awaited them.

Then, from the road of the sands, came processions of camels, ostentatiously laden with bells, which stretched out their necks, mounted by nomads in tight tunics, bearing lances and polished bucklers that the Sun made into mirrors, or led by hand by slaves on foot, swinging the heavy paired coffers with which each was burdened, offerings from the people to the King.

And the castle, so grave and silent, the castle inhabited by taciturn old men, awoke, entirely given over to the joyful laughter of its guests and the pomp of their arrival. Around the old King, venerable in his long white costume bordered with scarlet, with a scintillating tiara on his head, over his abundant white hair, and a necklace of unparalleled gemstones, incandescent with white fire, on his breast, young women now crowded, laughing and respectful, their veils thrown back over their shoulders, allowing the sight of their silvery, orange and white robes, with superficial displays of chimerical flowers in radiant colors, violet lotus-blossoms and mauve flowers with coralline stems, and girdles with multicolored fringes, and, above all, their lightly bronzed faces with long black arched eyebrows and tresses the color of celebratory night, and their eyes.

Dares was occupied with the children that had been brought to King Balthazar in order that he might bless them, and all their questions, all their gaiety and all their polite babble flowed around him. His eyes were moist with joy in his black face, and the little ones surrounded him wherever he went, like living ivy mingled with colored flowers stirring on a windy day around a pillar of basalt.

It was Passover, and this year, the King, who had not celebrated it for a long time, had invited his principal subjects far in advance.

After the feast, when the young women and the children had dispersed into the gardens, the young men had returned to their horses and many of the guests had already taken the roads to their own countries again, King Balthazar said to the sages of his realm:

"I asked you to come, my friends, with your sons and daughters around you, in order to see you one more time—the last—for presentiments have warned me of my imminent end or transformation. I have asked you to come on this day of celebration, the only one that I have maintained a little more joyful in this castle, where the organs have fallen silent and the vaults of prayer are closed, in order to associate myself one more time with the joy of renascent life, for if some people think that this feast signifies the exodus of the people of Shem from the hands of the conqueror, a notion familiar to some branches of our race, I think that Passover signifies the renewal of life, the triumph of life over death. It is the eternal subject of human rejoicing, the feast that gives rise, when the promises of spring burst forth before the days of the blaze of the Sun over the Earth, to the joy of feeling still alive, forever giving life to what the hymns you sing elsewhere signify. It is for that coincidence of an awakening of more vivid flowers with the resurrection of all the minutes that unroll in the universe that Passover was chosen, and I admit that young intelligences perceive in the perennial nature of the feast a promise of eternal Forces, since the Forces disengage life and charm simultaneously.

"But the desire of the old King is to gaze at youth and hear an echo of his own before disappearing. Whether I die tomorrow or live on for many years, this castle is closed to any arrival from without; this will soon die, alive or dead; I am walling myself up in the definitive silence. Doubtless my friends the Mage-Kings are, like me, preparing in their palaces for the coming of Azrael; the snow on our heads designates us for dissolution in nothingness, and other men and other thoughts are being born, which ought not to encounter us in their route. Go, and let sunset find you far from this castle, which, like me, is entering its winter, never to emerge again, and may your memories of me be kind."

Then he withdrew, and everyone left the castle, with hushed voices.

On the evening of that day, King Balthazar and Joseph, with Dares close at hand, were leaning on the terrace and watching the sea; they were listening to the sound of the waves dying beneath the livid light of the Moon. Neither Dares not Joseph troubled the solemn sadness of the King.

"I shall be extinguished soon," said Balthazar. "Toward what rebirth shall I go? Oh, how limited the science of the Priest-Kings is..."

"Jesus," said Joseph, "tell us that all the dead will be resuscitated one day."

"And will those be resuscitated who made themselves of their moment, their hour amid the world? What will become of them? It is really the same faith, the new and the old, with the same uncertainties—and you, Dares, what will become of you?"

"I scarcely expect to survive you," the slave replied. "Oh, if one could choose...."

"And what would you choose?"

"I would like to be born knowing all the songs, and understanding them all."

"Perhaps that will be your lot," said Balthazar. "Fill three cups for us."

Dares filled them—but because he was weary after the long day, his movements were slower, as if imprinted with the distant fatigue that had now returned to the face of the King.

"I drink," said the latter, "to the unknown of eternal force, to the power, determined in advance, of their will, to the new forces that might be born of the necessities of destiny."

Suddenly, a profound and soft voice was heard, which said: "Joseph, Joseph."

And Joseph of Arimathea replied: "Here I am."

"Come, and bring with you the wooden vessel that you brought."

Joseph went away to look for it.

The night had become clear and milky; they could make out a ship at the bottom of the stairway, and a bright white form at the prow.

"Mobed, of the ruins of the city of the past!" murmured Balthazar. "Can you see, Dares?"

But Dares replied: "I see nothing but a broad reflection of moonlight on the ship." Then, however, he cried: "Oh! It's the ship of King Solomon, come to seek the Elect!"

Joseph had come back on to the terrace. The voice continued: "Joseph and King Balthazar must both come aboard the ship, which will take them where destiny must take them. Obey the divine voice immediately."

Balthazar replied: "May I not bring my faithful Dares?"

"No."

And Balthazar said to Dares: "It's necessary that some-one waits for me in this castle, where I have spent my entire life, and to which I shall return to die. Wait for me, my broth-er."

They both embraced Dares, and then went down. Imme-diately, the ship shot out to sea. A large white form was still at the prow—the one that Balthazar had recognized—but at that moment Balthazar was gazing exclusively at the feebly-lit castle, in order that he might still see his faithful servant, and Joseph prostrated himself before the wooden vessel, which was glowing beneath a beacon.

The ship continued on its way.

When Dares was alone, he took one of the lamps and went, as he did every evening, to consider the image of the goddess Mobed.

His lips were already mumbling a prayer when he sud-denly saw her glowing, as if with an interior fire. She seemed splendid and dazzling for a moment, and then the fire abruptly went out, crackling, and the stones of the mosaics fell apart, as if rebounding.

Dares fell backwards and died, while the little lamp shat-tered.

And the night became blacker and deeper, thickening around the castle as if it were invading it and burying it.

PART TWO

Chapter One
MASTER EZRA

The great city extends its low houses along the river. There are numerous boats beside the stone quay. The tortuous network of streets winds around the cathedral, whose granite, as pink as the living flesh of a salmon, reaches up toward the sky. Good people are talking outside its doors. Hoofbeats ring out. Children run toward the snow. In the square, a harper comes forward and sings, and nearby, a strolling player in Arab dress leads a bear walking on its hind legs.

The great city with the bright face is mirrored in the great river that descends from the mountains and soon, as if having finished its work, which is to bathe the great city, it will spread out into the fields in a thousand small rivulets and steams, which flow to the sea. The red-legged storks perch on the rooftops, and the wool-clad citizens go past a leather-belted almoner. They are cheerful, although of stern appearance, for the valor of the new emperor has dissipated the perils of war—and it has cost them so much to fund wars! And the other enemy, disease, has also been repelled; it had rendered the entire province, and the narrow streets of the city, livid. If the arms of the young men struggled against the enemy, the arms of the old men served to carry stretchers.

The province and the great city are breathing again; the mule-trains laden with bales are coming back on market-days, the gold of men of war clinks in the taverns, and in the pure air, from which the miasmas of the plague have been exiled by the long prayers of clergymen, the cathedral bells sound as cheerful as windfalls of silver, joyful and liberated. The interregnum of evil is past, and here comes the dawn of the kingdom of God.

As the setting Sun shines at the level of the hills, the great globe of fire is surrounded by long scarlet veils; magnificent angels seem still to be holding it in their hands of flame. A human would not be able to look the Heavens in the face if they were not veiled by all the pale distance of the horizon. They are headed for the distant portals where guards equipped with living and rippling golden shields await them, guards clad in scarlet like the kings of the Earth, placed there to form an escort for the star returning to its divine palaces.

The hill that the Sun has gilded retains the blessing of fertility, and above it, the sky dresses once again in a tender and profound blue, with pale tints, like an immaterial lake full of smiles, which pipes dreams, and whose waves are still warmed by the thousand gleams of all treasures. Cherubs in golden robes still streak across it, holding at bay the monsters of dream impatient to reign in their turn and to veil the avenues of the stars from humankind.

In the streets of the great city, a kind of profound peace has spread. See how the smoke of hearth-fires and cooking-fires is emerging from a thousand chimneys, and the lamps shine orange, reddened in the dying daylight! They will scintillate, serenely golden yellow, gilded like power, to protect calm and repose behind firmly-closed doors against the uncertainty and anxiety of the dusk.

Meanwhile, the everyday festival of the evening meal is renewing human strength everywhere, the beverage of labor, the bread of becoming, the gold of time, the flesh of thought. And immense lines of gold still divide up the sky, like bridges over the abyss for the messengers of infinity, before the night triumphs over the entire Earth.

Here is night over the great city. The river almost falls silent, save for a melancholy hum like a turning wheel near the pillars of the bridges that incessantly and indifferently divide the flow. The lantern of some heavy barge keeps watch motionlessly, like a cat's eye.

The light of the Moon is reflected from the water like a broken white staff. Amid the celestial solitude one might think it a long shape scattered in the still-virgin night, and its fingers, more beautiful for being free of the rings of the world and the day, playing with the clouds. The imponderable ocean of ether rolls its transparent waves; the stars are grains of sand in that sea, where black and blue ravines yawn, as profound as the total shadow of silence.

The Face of solitude and necessity appears pale and indistinct in the mediocre fires of the Moon, and its body stretches as if to bar all hope. The sky is a bottomless sea beyond its appearance of a closed wall, and here come clouds, troubled as on days of whit hail, and clouds blacker than the enigmas of destiny, and the entire face of the sphinx smiles amid the ballets of the gems of tiny scattered worlds, and the Milky Way, a happy and illusory valley, brightens like the return from a festival, with joyous lights in the hands of enigmatic passers-by, going who knows where, if not beyond and higher.

The houses around the cathedral are asleep behind their iron chains; a ray of moonlight slides over the Saint George in the doorway. The houses on the river's edge are asleep; lapping waves come to break against their leafy storage-sheds, whose steps bathe in the river near the market. The houses in the main square are asleep; gilded statues, the emblems of their façades, the decorative ships of the roofs and the eagles of the imperial house are bathed by the same diffuse shadow as the colossal bell-tower where the bronze copper with the crimson loincloth comes mechanically to strike the hour on the pure silver bell; and in the pools of water in the inlets of the promenade, the swans, their heads tucked under their wings—pale ashen veils in that shroud of delicate mystery—are asleep, like the great city, its towers, its river and its people.

In a small square, where the solemn tranquility seems to bear down even more on two cedars doubtless brought back from the crusades, a tranquility further enhanced by the slow trickle of a fountain into its marble basin—a trickle so slow that it seems to be counting the minutes of eternity—a ray of moonlight prolongs its vigil, as thin as a line. Rapid footsteps traverse the square toward that house, and the metal knocker sounds against the door, continued by a raucous, forceful barking, growling like a threat and a lamentation.

A window opens, and a man advances on to the wooden balcony, who demands: "What do you want with me?"

"It's me, Seigneur Ezra—my son's illness is worse."

"I'm coming—wait there."

Ezra the physician emerges from his house. A large gray dog squeezes past his legs and bounds into the square, then turns to look at its master, ears pricked, unsure which way to go. It comes back to sniff the woman who is standing nearby. A servant emerges in his turn carrying a lantern, and the door closes with a grave bronze sound that stirs up echoes—and Ezra follows the woman, the dog sniffing the walls. The servant, informed of the route in advance, precedes them.

They go along winding streets. A tiny light vacillates beneath a pious image; a rat makes off; beneath a windshield, a resinous torch held in an iron bracket finally goes out, casting twisted shadows over the wall. A square opens up, enormous and black, and they go along the wall of the imperial palace; in front of the first portico, at intervals, eight metal horses rear up, lifting bronze warriors with javelins in hand very high. A guard, with an axe over his shoulder, approaches them in order to recognize them and let them pass. They fall back into the network of streets, traversing the great empty bridge in the middle of which beggars are asleep at the foot of a tall calvary, and then they go through narrower streets with harsh cobbles, of small and meager houses, until the woman has them enter an exceedingly poor dwelling.

A tiny light was burning there. A young man was lying on a low bed; a tall and slender young brunette girl got up and said to the woman: "He hasn't budged."

Ezra went to him; the women lit another, brighter lamp.

Ezra made him swallow brown drops of a liquid he had brought, and said to the women: "I'll wait."

"Go to bed, Rizpah," said the woman to the girl. "I'll help Seigneur Ezra, if he needs anything."

Ezra sat down in an oak armchair next to the bed. The woman sat on a stool nearby.

Long dolor had hollowed out the surrounds of her eyelids, and they seemed like shells for the dull and weary eyes. Unkempt grey hair emerged from a black headscarf. Her parchment-like cheeks, her retracted lips, her forehead—in the idle of which a vein protruded—her long black dress, her fleshless hands, and her upper body, attentively titled forward on the lookout for any word from the invalid or the physician, dressed her with a tragic appearance of anticipation; every minute at that bedside seemed decisive to her, and perhaps irreparable. She was small and she was old, and infirmity, pain and extreme fatigue seemed to be her clothing and her flesh. The poverty of her abode was as evident as its antiquity and related to its antiquity; from the low gray joists of the ceiling hung dried herbs and a few copper jars; the sole fireplace was empty and there were only two stools in addition to her own.

The gray dog lay down at its master's feet, and Ezra asked: "What was he doing when the fever took hold of him again?"

"He was reading," the old woman replied.

"What?"

"This," she said. "He often reads it." She held out an old leather-bound book with copper-clad corners to the physician.

Ezra started reading it.

THE BOOK OF LANCELOT

The castle of the Lady of the Lake was hidden among the trees of the forest of Briosque. In front of the forest a great lake barred the way; as marvelous as it was profound, and mortal to any enemy, it drew away from those who were expected at the manor and allowed them to reach the high, strong door.

There lived young Lancelot,[17] whose mother, the pious Hélène, of the family of Joseph of Arimathea, had grown up amid the great disasters of her husband Ban, king of Benoïc, vanquished by King Claudas. Forced out of all his castles, King Ban, having no one to attend to him, his queen and his son but a single groom, had stopped at the extreme limit of the forest; the torpor of death had taken hold of him and his heart broke.

Queen Hélène had despaired to such an extent over his poor body that she had momentarily forgotten her infant son Lancelot, whom she had left with the horses a short distance away. The faithful groom, haggard with grief, had knelt down not far from his master's body and the unfortunate mother came back to find her son in the arms of a beautiful damsel who, as she approached, sank silently with the child into the waters of the lake, which became a closed mirror and an insurmountable barrier to the queen's dolor. Then she fainted, only to wake in a cloister, where the abbess begged her, since she was quite alone and had endured so much, to remain. She it is whom the histories name the Queen of Great Sorrows, and every day she went to pray beside the lake where her son had been stolen from her.

From the castle, so near and yet so far away, on the side opposite the one defended by the lake, the forest and heath extended marvelously, and the orchards were rich in the fruits of the Fortunate Isles, like those of Bretagne and Boulogne. There the young Lancelot grew up, amid the games and the amiable advice of damsels, without any man intervening except to reach him to bend a bow, mount a horse and handle

---

[17] The version of the story of Lancelot reproduced here differs in some minor respects from the one that is most familiar to English and American readers, thanks to Thomas Malory. The details are mostly drawn from the group of 12th century romances nowadays known as the *Vulgate Cycle*, especially its version of *Merlin*, supposedly based on an earlier romance—only fragments of which survive—by Robert de Boron. I have retained Kahn's spelling of the various names rather than substituting those familiar to English readers.

double-edged and pointed swords. No one told him his name, his rank or his native land.

Alone, the Lady of the Lake educated him accorded to her science. She had been loved by the prophet Merlin, when the seer already sensed the veils of old age extending occasionally before his eyes. She had extracted his science from him, and, as everyone knows, by the malice of clumped bushes and errant honeysuckle, rose-bushes with a hundred scarlet roses, and all the capricious creepers, encircled the resting-place from which Merlin could no longer escape, nor want to, for all those flowers were the beauties of his beloved, and the braches her gestures, and the garlanded creepers, which grew all the way from the earth to the treetops in order to dart a floret against the glass roof of his pavilion, her ruses.

Merlin had said to her: "Lady, it is perhaps as well, and my old age is the cause of my accepting gladly to live between your fingers. Far from taking pleasure, as before, in astonishing people with my rapid voyages and meriting their credence with my true prophecies, I would prefer, as you know, to grow old with my head on your knees, and I thank you for this curtain of nature that hides me, since it is yours and your true semblance, natural ribbons of magnificent cunning.

"Lady Viviane, you have only slightly anticipated my great desire to live some indefinite dream, amid repose and perfumes, for my task is done. I have no more messages for kings, since Artus is enthroned in glory. But do what I have told you; when the child of the Queen of Great Sorrows is strong and comes of age, send him to King Artus, and by his side he will find his life mapped out. In the meantime, teach him strength and grace, and see that every morning he finds a crown of fresh roses on his pillow, without ever knowing where they come from, in order that his mind does not close to the simple comprehension of marvels that so many men have lost. That will permit him, later, to follow his predestination, which would be effaced if his first steps brought him into collision with reason."

Lady Viviane obeyed. Gradually, she accustomed herself to thinking that, by giving the young man the best upbringing in the world, and adorning him with virtues, she would atone for a little of the wrong that she had done to humans by removing their prophet Merlin from them, and that the child would be the pledge of her redemption.

As soon as he was grown up, before the first fevers of love had varied his blood, she sent him forth to the court of Artus—and not without chagrin, for Lancelot was exceedingly handsome: long-haired, with large eyes as green as the marine expanse and the expanse of the new leaves of spring and incarnadine lips, tall and well-built, with a supple and strong tread. She loved him otherwise than one loves a child, but she was afraid that his taste for adventure might take him far away from her, leaving her with bad memories. She preferred lowering the barriers herself to letting him break them, and Merlin's obscure words regarding Lancelot's predestination had troubled her. Then again, she would have suffered if the young man, after an intoxication of years, had looked at her one morning with the surprise of having seen her thus for such a long time. The enchantress Viviane therefore let him go, and watched over him in his perils.

Ezra read the pages of the familiar old romance, and there were fine weapons, valiant deeds, heartbroken knights, well-fought tourneys and dances...and Lancelot saw Queen Genièvre.

Ezra leaned over his patient, whose heavy sleep was agitated by dreams...

When he saw Queen Genièvre, the varlet Lancelot lost his breath, and something akin to pain pierced his heart. She was tall and pale. She was the first beautiful woman that Lancelot admired, for his eyes had seen the enchantress Viviane and her companions while too young, and had become too accustomed to them. He found nothing in their faces but a courteous welcome without complaint, and the generosity that warms the heart, but nothing that surprised him.

He knew of what combats Genièvre had been the prize, and why her father Leodagan had fêted her savior Artus. For Rion of Norway, the monarch of the frosts, who dragged captive kings toward his indented coasts and held them in snowy regions to decorate his drinking-bouts and coarse feasts in his wooden palace, had wanted to curb Leodagan's pride, and the old lord had only been saved by Artus and Merlin.

The youth marveled at Genièvre, with her eyes like blue flames, her pure complexion, her perfectly rounded neck and her long ring-laden hands. And when she walked, he thought he was seeing a swan glide, and when she came near him he thought he would faint. When she spoke to him to question him about his native land, an anguish rose into Lancelot's throat; he was unable to reply and the Queen passed on. He did not see her again, but her image alone, in broad strokes, reddened beneath his eyelids.

The patient turned over again, and Ezra could almost follow his dream; he knew that he was courageous, besotted with adventure and beauty, and suspected that a similar image and a similar desire were passing within his fever.

The old woman, unquiet by her son's bed, was muttering prayers.

Ezra turned the pages...

In the plain, near the camps of Artus and Galehaut, separated by the fordable river, Queen Genièvre summoned Lancelot.

"Is it for me, then, that you have accomplished so many great deeds?"

"Yes, Lady."

"But now it will be necessary for you to remain close to us."

"Would you have loved a man without valor, Lady?"

And Queen Genièvre thought about the former valor of Artus, reliant now on the strong shoulders of his knights to sustain his power and oversee the peace of the world. She saw that the two of them were similar, and of the same race of men. Artus had doubtless been like this young man when he had brought forth Excalibur and thus had himself recognized as the designated king. Thus he had still been when he had fought the pagans in Carmelide. It was the future valor of the world that was in her presence, and Genièvre bowed to Lancelot.

And the patient woke up, and gazed at Ezra and his mother, pensively, and said: "I was dreaming."

"Yes," said Ezra, showing him the book—and the young man blushed.

"Yes, Master, I was reading the beautiful adventure."

"And do you know the ending, perhaps better told than here?"

"That the Queen died, and Lancelot languished in consequence, at about the time when Artus disappeared in the direction of Avalon."

"I know this one:

"When Artus had visited the castle of the enchantress Morgain, the room in which Lancelot was imprisoned had depicted the entire legend of his love, the hours of his pallors and those of his kisses. Artus was returning, ardent for vengeance, when he collided with Mordret's revolt, and Genièvre was Mordret's captive.

"When she firmly believed that, having been at the mercy of the traitor, she had been tarnished for Lancelot, she wanted to flee into a cloister, on the most distant cape of Gaul, to bury herself as far away as possible, among the mountainous waves. The Queen cut off her blonde hair, covered her hair with a wimple, and her body with a long black cloak and a white garment, and every day, as the Queen of Great Sorrows had, she went along the long terrace over the sea, in spite of the wind that lashed her and the arrival of the white swirls of the waves thrown pell-mell against the colossal stone balcony, with the cries of the seagulls—and the tumultuous sea seemed to her to be running like the minutes of her old love and her living love.

"Every morning, after mass, the nuns had to pass through that open corridor of rocks to get back to their cells, and the Abbess brought up the rear. Since the Queen's arrival she had taken the penultimate position in order to leave her to walk freely and remain alone on that terrace.

"Facing the nuns' cloister, some distance away on an islet, was a convent where a few monks submissive to the hardest rule were doubtless expiating excessive pleasures in prayer and contemplation. At different times from those habitual to the nuns, the monks also passed over a terrace that overlooked the sea and faced its counterpart, and the waves of that narrow strait also came to cover their narrow pathway with surf.

"One day, an extra man marched behind the file of monks, a hood over his head and a long habit around his body—and he too was allowed by the Prior to gaze at length at the enraged waves of the strait at the extremity of the terrace—those furious waves, that drew away to calm down in the sea. And Queen Genièvre saw the monk, who, perceiving her indistinctly, was struck in the heart and remained there with his back against a pillar for some time, as if incapable of movement.

"The Queen waited for him to recover, and addressed a slow nod of the head to him—and from then on, Genièvre and Lancelot, both closer together and more separate than they had been in their time of caresses, bowed to one another once a day, slowly, each following a file of faithful souls with whom they lived. And for fear of being seeing one another too closely, of discovering how many wrinkles had marked the faces orphaned on their love, they only stayed on the terrace momentarily, long enough to bow, and Lancelot never took off his hood, or Genièvre her wimple—and the immortal illusion floated between them, to the violent racket of the sea, and vibrated its extended white wings between them. There is no greater suffering than great love, no greater cold than when it is destroyed, and no greater fever than when it begins."

The sage Ezra, having poured a large dose of Lethe into a cup, held it out to the young man, who soon went back to sleep. Ezra said to the old woman: "He will be better tomorrow; send him to my house."

And he went back into the nocturnal city.

THE CITY

The city awoke. By virtue of the flight of the shadow, the tall belfries and the steeples of bell-towers seemed to stretch themselves. Hurried sailors prepared ships. Rafts towed by barges glided along. Shutters struck the walls and the wrinkled faces of old women showed momentarily; then smoke rose from high chimneys. The screens of shop-windows were raised, and people became visible cutting cloth and sewing leather. A morning song rose up, multiple and discordant, and large carts presented themselves at the bridges, fully-laden with vegetables and bellowing or bleating animals. The city's hunger awoke. Fisherman hastened, and their damp and scintillating booty quivered on marble slabs. Baskets of fruit and pitchers of milk encumbered the main square, and townspeople with voluminous cloaks circulated with difficulty in the midst of these encumbrances, augmented by the shrill cries of pigs, the screeches of poultry and the joyful yapping of dogs marveling, as always before so much nourishment. The tavern doors were already open; people were tucking into beer and salted fish. Metal clinked on the tables of restaurants and the counters of money-changers' shops.

The Sun rose above the gilded roofs and held itself motionless over that chattering multitude of sellers and buyers. Helmets and lances flashed at the entrance to the square and a file of cavaliers passed slowly by, to disappear in the direction of the bridges and the countryside. Carillons of bells rang out in chorus, and the doors of the churches soon let out processions of smiling women clad in velvet, and young men crowded around them; white greyhounds sent mastiffs packing; soft words were exchanged between the church and the square, and robust tradesmen paused to watch them pass by, and then resumed work; and impatient individuals waited in front of their shops for their distraction to conclude, on order to obtain a cloak or shoes confided a trifle rapidly to the idle obsequiousness of those artisans.

At the foot of structures of scaffolding, masons folded their arms meditatively, in the fashion of poets. Sellers of herbs and vegetables stopped to listen to the beautiful voices of public criers, proud of the riches they trumpeted from one to another. The petty merchants of hot drinks ran around everyone with their iron cauldrons, their ladles and goblets, chirping, boasting, shouting, offering and inciting everyone to take the opportunity, thanks to their pretext, of a minute of leisure.

The joyous matinal tumult was not contained by the main square; it extended through the streets, as far as the narrow side-streets, and its cheerful din penetrated as far as the narrow back-street where Rizpah, standing in the doorway next to the tanned and parchment-faced old woman were watching the departure of the young man whose fever old Ezra had calmed the previous night. And young Samuel, after having turned toward her one more time, disappeared around the first street-corner into the moving current of the crowd.

First he went past the palace of the emperors, whose roseate marble colonnade was enhanced by the gilded horses rearing up. A cambered balcony marked the place where the newly-crowned emperor showed himself to the people, the crown on his head and the cup welcoming him to the city in his hand. Facing it, surrounded by wrought-iron railings decorated with grape-clusters and roses, a fountain wept. On the cornice of the building, colossal statues symbolized strength; a high tower permitted the ruler of so many people to glimpse the sea, by which bold seekers of fortune went away and the harvests of victory returned, and the arrows of a thousand masts were beginning to gather at the quays not far away. Then he arrived in the main square, where the pinnacles of the

Town Hall and numerous stone statuettes were watching the cluttering of the market stalls, and the black enormous mass of the Market Hall facing them, from which porters emerged carrying quarters of meat and artisans carrying cloth and leather.

If the palace of the emperors was sparkling with gilded statues and richly-colored emblems, bearing on its white and roseate background a grandiose appearance of ornamented youth, and if the Town Hall, in its chiseled gray robe streaked with bands of colored écus, with its statuettes, stones strung out in a symbolic necklace, an ornamentation acquired stone by stone, resembled an opulent lady in her prime, still beautiful, content in sober dress and quiet contemplation, the Market Hall was a squat pile of brick, heaped up brick by brick, where hard work could be divined, and he gauche building with its lateral belfry had something of the appearance of the heavy gesture of a laborer accustomed to carrying his burden over his shoulder. The building suggested a durable and gathered strength, unselfconscious and limited to toying with its burdens. It was a naked building, where frescoes ought to be.

Further on, the façade of the cathedral barred the largest square, and its high towers dominated the city, higher than the palace, the Town Hall and the Market Hall. The immense mass sparkled by virtue of its stained-glass windows; the gold of the sunlight was transmuted as it passed through translucencies in enormous rare gemstones, impassive ornaments in gold, silver and rubies, fixed fires embodying the promise of marvelous lands.

In bright valleys, as green as the meadows of Heaven, luminous sages marched, where there were Perseuses slaying ancient dragons with scales of azure and light, with aureoled crowns around their helmets. Processions of maidens descended toward rivers between the grayer mass of mail-clad archers, and the bright light and the vitrified substance with the splendors of magical water increased the ecstasy in their eyes, and the saints in prayer were as handsome as pagan gods, Apollonian tresses crowning the foreheads of the Saint Michaels.

Under the three immense portals, bas-reliefs chained vanquished enemies to the church doors: cloven-hoofed Pans, devils who disguised themselves as monks and those who adopted the costumes of wise men introducing, with the familiar and usurped ostentation poured out amid the most venerable white beards, bad advice and lusts to families, abusing the daughters while the fathers are away at war, and lifting grimacing fauns by the ear in their robust hands. The beauty of foolish virgins sparkled in the granite, and the emaciated bodies of saints, their hollow eyes upraised, seemingly exorcising the memory of the ardors of those captive fauns. And the flora of contorted, curled up, simplified fields, sometimes also deformed in a thousand sculpted tentacles, garlanded that tableau of victories and captivities, which even contained the victory of the soul over death, the pure soul escaping from the boat where the bloated clawed fingers of the hairy bodyguards of sin wanted to maintain it.

The church doors opened with a slow beat and closed again soundlessly. In spite of their thick solidity, the faithful were able to perceive that there was nothing really there but a curtain to separate the palace of prayer from the outside world, momentarily occupied elsewhere; and the triple naves launched forth into a symphony of sculpted stones, columns that were tall petrified trees.

In the scintillation of the stained-glass, sometimes reminiscent of the radiant dawn, sometimes the sunset over a plain of marvels near a fabulous Jordan, the tall polychromatic columns played the part of the eternal and primitive forest, the forest of cults, the one in which fearful humans had paused to stammer a prayer and returned to listen to the exiled priest preaching generosity to them, and adopted the custom of fixing a day to come back for the sacrifice and the offering.

That primitive forest they carry with them into their cities when faiths are victorious, and reconstruct it, solid against the vicissitudes of the seasons, against the autumn that prunes the graceful roses of legend and the winter that throws refrige-rant ice beneath bare feet. It is the forest of summer with all its legendary noisiness, its simplified perfumes remade, rising from cassolettes to entertain the illusion of the warm clarity of apparitions in the clearings; and the organs restate the grave song of thickets distances, which the wind plays like instru-ments.

If faith contains a few problems, which might agitate be-tween a few philosophies, there is no trace of it here. The common man has constructed an envelope around his chimera, and alongside the god about whom he is told—the one who cries in the thunder and appears in the depths of souls in ad-vice of forbearance—he has placed all his gods, all the ancient gods to whom he still remains faithful, and with them his faith of the present moment, his desire not to die, for the long cla-rion-calls of resurrection launch forth from the arches here.

He has brought his love of candid beauty in a blue dress, with blue eyes, flaxen hair and hesitant tread, advancing through the tranquil freshness of meadows, in a cheerful and busy countryside, for here is Mary walking cautiously over the rump of the Evil One. He has brought his troubled love, em-barrassed before imperious beauty, dazzling beauty, true beau-ty, and his rancor against eyes that are too willful and authori-tative, for here is the golden-haired Mary Magdalen, humi-liated.

The common man has added to this the unexpectedness of his song, and he remembers his humble friends, the birds that sing to distract him, the turtle-dove with the swollen throat of which he dreams obscurely as a symbol of his desire, and messenger birds that bring the beloved the gratitude of the lover, for here is the white dove. If the master architect has lavished in the nave pathways cleverly disposed in the form of a cross, to recall the martyrdom, the common man scarcely perceives it, and it is to the signs of resurrection that he goes, amid the forest of pillars, beneath the somber vault where the music drones; and that music, whatever effort is made to measure its cadence severely and throw a shred of the veil of

134

mourning into the light, consists of ancient songs, those rendered in loud voices along the roads, in the sylvan solitudes and at celebrations, which would have been recognized by the models of the statues, statues of martyrs, statues of kings ancestral to the virgin—his creatures, or at least his memories, his heroes blurred by a millenary dream.

Along the walls of the church, under the horizontal tombstones, sleeping in a false humility beneath the tread of passers-by, are old counts and old dukes, and the noble splendor of their spouses laid beside them in a mendacious equality, in a mendacious humility that seemed appropriate to them, a final and solitary sacrifice made during their lives to the to the popular chimera of coming to sleep at ground level in the forest of stone without a roof-nothing but an image, like the industrious play of a few stones in a clearing indicating their presence. They are very old sepulchers.

Already, however, near the choir, in the part of the cathedral in which the organized pride of the priestly hierarchy reigns more evidently, not far from the stalls with the heads of griffins where the dignitaries sit, the high tombs appear, upright and full of pride. The carefully-hammered and retracted copper retains tints of gold in the coats-of-arms of those who are laid there on a bulwark of marble, bearing on their black marble cloaks on their broad shoulders whose carefully-lowered hoods hide their faces.

Are these forms, without any attribution of sex beneath their hard and durable drapery poverties, humilities, charities and forgivenesses, or rather the dead aspects of courages, determinations and violences of desire? In their gestures, lowered beneath the weight of the body and the bed of exhibition, ought one read the joyous submission of disciplined virtues, accompanying the body and soul that was their host, or vanquished captives, or intimidated servants? And why have those marble faces been hooded in black: for reasons of modesty, or the fear of perceiving them?

The motionless funeral procession of the sequence of tombs seems, in the maze of columns, to be a somber procession of mourners paused among the trees of the forest. They seem to be strangers among all the sculpted, painted and sung joys here bequeathed to the soul of the people; the excessive pride of armories shone over the excessive humility of the bearers of the definitive stretcher, but higher still, up toward the vaults, the most elevated of the stained-glass windows continue the colored fête of fairy-tale characters in the plains of merriment: little gods, joyful corporation mascots, almoner saints and familiar spirits deified; the entire thin and regal lineage of gods given birth in crowds by all the ages—and then the steeple rising toward the blue sky, ever-incomplete, reaching ever higher; for in every century, people have always tried to construct Babel.

And all around the cathedral wound narrow streets, profound caves beneath the Heavens: streets that were almost silent, where footfalls were muffled, shop-fronts deserted, stillnesses plastered with images in niches and little lamps burning as in obscurity—and that tortuous network resembled the tangled roots of the great popular forest, and rudimentary souls lived there silently, immured in the prodigious nursery, living the vegetative life of seeds, with all their threats and promises.

It seemed to the young man that in that rigid heap of stone flowers and bushes, with the vivid roses and scarlets of its stained glass, its sunflowers, its lilies and its columns decked in honeysuckle, perhaps there was a soul asleep, as Merlin was asleep, numbed and enlaced by some Viviane. Until when?

His footsteps had brought him as far as a quay, and on the opposite shore, beyond the boats, he saw horsemen riding past in festival armor, young and joyous.

"Oh," he thought, "in the midst of this city, and the world that the architects of the cathedral and the fathers of those gay cavaliers have made, where are the palaces of Viviane the artificer, she who draws men into her bosom and enchants them for a century with the sound of a song? Where are the palaces of Morgain, which draw them into round-dances where they sing and dance untiringly for a century for one of Morgain's kisses? Where are the portals of the high blue valleys over which trail silver bands of cloud, veiled by distance to hide the shores of departure from those who cannot be summoned? Where are the springs hidden that are the fairies' mirrors, and what harsh customs weigh upon the world as far as one can march, know and learn?

"Since Morgain's companions collected the enraptured and broken body of Artus amid the reeds, the miracles of the land of dreams have scarcely been renewed; where are the great palaces with immense terraces overlooking the blue extent of a sea without ripples, whose foam seems a fringe of eternal celebration, and whose sky smiles as it drives away its white clouds in order the that golden fruits of Avalon might flourish? Who travels the roads strewn with ambushes, guarded by wild beasts and men-at-arms, paved with marvels, toward the unexpected houses in which the truth suddenly lights up, as simple as a beautiful festival evening, imprinted with fortunate melancholy and grave music? And how many people have their eyes raised without anyone knowing whether their gaze is still following the ascension of the already-vanished Grail, or whether they are waiting for the firmament to open to show them, in the distance, more distance, more space, more festival processions dressed with pomp, so very distant that they leave them no more than the confused memory of a chimera?

"And what should one do: live like them; or live according to the strict color of things; or gild the present of that in which one has the presentiment of eternity?"

How much of that did she contain, the glimpsed princess, so white and lily-like, with her long train, a circle of dull gold around her long hair, who listened so ingenuously, her lips parted and her eyes delighted, to the songs of minstrels, and seemed particularly pleased with her own? Would she love, since she seemed less apparent, less herself in lovely candor, on hearing the grandiloquent couplets of some singer, the lull of the music of Samuel and the freshness of his long, captured

137

by the reeds of the river? Had she, perhaps, heard the frisson of the past mingled with the tremor of the future in his song, if she had really been the one to whom he wanted to sing, and if the evil magician who changes into copper the pieces of pure gold one brings out of one's purse had not transmuted them while he was arranging them?

He saw again the pride of being summoned to the elite who are the music of a race and a time, the sound of whose voice is amplified in the throats of others, and to whose cadence the world marches. Perhaps there were blue valleys in the eyes of the gentle princess, and the reformed rigging of the sacred ship of love in her hair, and the dissolving delights of Avalon in her lips—and perhaps her voice would be able, in the white palace of her arms, in the blue valley of her unfolded cloak, to charm the poet in order that he might sing as in a dream, with his entire soul, for an entire century, in a single song with infinite modulations, a true life of love, unaware of the labyrinths of power and the undergrowth of force in which he lived.

These beautiful meditations brought Samuel to old Ezra's door.

The people of the city knew almost nothing about the old man. He had arrived one day, long ago, from another capital. It was presumed, and rumored, that he was originally from the Orient, but many years ago, and his slow progress had been interrupted by sojourns, by long and patient healings. His old man's face with its long white beard and keen eyes, offered no symptoms of age among the nuances of aging. He was stern and upright; the poor people of the low quarter always had recourse to his benevolence, the cheerful and powerful aristocrats to his science. He had often been seen entering the palace of the emperors, and within its marble-paved courtyards his footsteps marched in concert with those of a powerful bishop or a valued adviser.

Special virtues were attributed to him for calming poor madmen: those who make the attics of saddened houses resound to a slow but continuous ululation; those who scamper on all fours, swinging their haggard and drooling faces; those who hide their heads under a scrap of cloth, draping the air around then, staking a staff at the clouds and seeming to command infinity with a verbose gesture. For them he put dolors and ambitions to sleep, and brought back the poor powerful sovereign, betrayed and abandoned, to lie down in his wretched bed, and sent him back to the closure and calm of dreams. People brought the poor girls him who weep inconsolably and whose souls filter through staring eyes, and he lulled those sufferers, and resolved the excessively profound and silent dolors that weighed too heavily upon their hearts into thin, refreshing tears.

When he passed through the streets of the city, invariably clad in a long brown robe with a collar and a thick bonnet, fur in winter and velvet in summer, the townspeople in their doorways took off their hats, and the gentlefolk bowed to him, for everyone owed him some recognition. Nevertheless, in spite of his ever-steady tread, his silence broken only to reply or give care, and the simple monotony of his attire, for those people who saw him every day he remained a stranger, originally from the Orient, who might go back there, either by the road to the east, going to meet a caravan stopped at one of the great fairs, or the road to the west, on a ship chartered for the long haul.

His justice and his fair-mindedness had made him the arbiter of many disputes between individuals, and even some of a more general order, but that was also because it was felt that he had no particular interest in these litigations that were addressed to his firm clear-sightedness, being detached from overly personal impressions. He seemed to be under the jurisdiction of something more permanent, more exact and more personal than everything that surrounded him; the strictest modulations of organs were less distant than his thought, and theological discussions and disputes regarding the organization of the city appeared slightly juvenile in the regard of his aphorisms. Gravity marched by his side, and the mysterious prestige of his cures accompanied it. He was treated with a hint of fearful respect, because of his immediate utility, and his near-perpetual claustration, combined with his willingness to disturb himself, without haste or urgency, to soothe someone's pain, was astonishing as his choice of friendships, careless of influence and advantages.

"You drink from a strange cup, Samuel," said Ezra to the young man. "The wine of the chimera hides a hard wall on which one might break one's head only too well. That is the whole of your malady, and your thoughts drift too freely. Take care that they do not tangle you in some knot of aquatic herbs above a whirlpool."

"Is it a malady to be young, to sing?"

"No, but it is to dream of impossible places. Where are you trying to go? You're physically weak, your eyes are not those of a conqueror but those of a contemplator. You're able to understand the fugitive moment and pick the rare flower of emotion, but do you think you have the arms and the vigor to row against the current of an avid and harsh society? You can see—don't seek to rule. There are too many petty monarchs of copper coins, wisps of straw and nutshells around you. Don't strive, work, be silent and see."

"But sage Ezra, that is my only desire and my only ambition."

"Why, then, this wasted ardor, this lacerated heart, this expectation of a dream? What possibility do you see that a princess will emerge in life, as in ancient tales, and incline toward a poet a heart that you would like to think gentle? Are you not familiar with the haughty mothers and harsh barons among her ancestors? And even if she wanted to escape the chains, the barriers and the silken bonds, where would you go with her? And your faith—don't you give that any thought?"

"I have no other than what I have glimpsed in your teachings."

"That doesn't matter—you're a Jew. Your entire race clings to you, in spite of itself. It will be forced to grip you again as you will hurl yourself toward it again, having no other route surrounded by menacing points—not swords, but instruments of torture."

"But we live contentedly under the emperor."

"A respite! Do you seriously think that the reproaches directed at the rich on the Pont des Orfèvres, at ship-owners and to the poor people in these back-street hovels really result from the participation of their forefathers in a great murder? No—but since a pretext suffices to drive them off the road, overturn their fortune or take away their power, the pretext is conserved. They are outcast, and if you, the minstrel, find concession to the extent of sometimes associating with the aristocracy, it's because your youth is attractive—and youth is only temporary. Can you heal, as I do? Don't you want to learn, in order be tolerated when you are withered?"

"I go toward the splendor of forms, the beauty of faces and clothes, the great gardens enamored of luxury and the beautiful processions in which I want to take part. Master, does your faith not lack audacity? Every day, do not the dusks in which you take pleasure anticipate the arrival of a soft night, full of attenuated lights on high, tempting for the human sun, propitious to a long, inert and sweet dream. O Master, everyday life breaks up our thoughts like the stones of an old wall, and seeds arrive there by means of the logical curves of gentle winds, and flowers are born there that are bound to come and are the perfume of the land. Why not mingle with active life, the life that smiles and creates—and weeps, I admit, but also laughs around us?

"Consider the procession at the head of which the emperor marches in his golden cloak, and his priests with gem-studded crosses behind him, and the sumptuous warriors with gem-encrusted blades, and the beautiful ladies, so high on their decorated balconies, from which they watch it pass by, so close to the music of the singer, the word of the poet; and the rich and the valiant, the former on their beautiful mules and the latter on their chargers—and can you not believe that there is a place on the borders of their route for everyone, for all those of courage, boldness, skill and honor? Isn't it true that

141

you, who dispense cures all day long and tire yourself out next to beds of fever, seek within yourself repose and pause for thought, while I, whose existence is attaining the rhythm of song and pursuing the slippery image, and the melody of the world that is coy and does not want to be captured, spend my spare moments dreaming, on the contrary, of those women whom one sees in their entirety, of mingling my fire with the flame of the world?"

"I see, on the contrary, that there exists close to you, within reach, a kind of happiness for you, and that, like everyone, you are letting go of it and turning your back on it to seek adventure. Do you think this is the first time that a cry like yours has reached my ears? That during my long years, of which you have perhaps never asked yourself the number, I have not seen the procession of which you speak approaching? But if you were to look at some of the members of that sequence of people, whom you think you see moving through the open air, with the eyes of experience, you would see that it is a solid mass, of iron or lead, of which you can see only one side, the more sumptuously decorated. The individuals within it are stuck within a matrix, each in a fixed cell, and it is always the same one who holds the same pace. This universe does not change. Fixed waves seem to break, sometimes the mass vacillates momentarily, but it requires a great many cracks for it to crumble, and for the passer-by on the road to mingle with it. Are you anything other than a passer-by? You can stop for a moment and, still numbed by your march, imagine that it is the others who are marching and not you. That's all. But you will return from your chimeras by yourself, and I wish ardently that it might be soon and that you will not be badly bruised by them."

MASTER ASVERUS

I

They were conversing in this fashion when the heavy door opened and a jovial and profound voice shouted: "Here I am, Master Ezra, back again. What a change in the fine city—in its soul, at least, for the streets and the people seem identical to me!"

The newcomer was tall, his accentuated features shadowed by an unruly graying beard. His costume was simple, like that of a traveler. All his features and his body indicated a considerable antiquity; his eyes were deep and harsh, his shoulders still square, his hands robust and muscular, the sinews as brutal as ropes.

"Be welcome Master Asverus. Here, things only change after a very long time—but you, the traveler, the pilgrim to the beautiful, and the shrewd merchant who knows all roads, what have you seen in your wandering?"

"Cities, cities, cities by the sea, cities on rivers, hanged men next to calvaries, galiots along the quays, cities preparing furs, cities collecting masses of wheat, cities in which thousands of weavers make cloth, and make canvas, so that great cities like this one might buy it, and, in many places, misers who count gold with a trembling hand. There are also sages—less wise than you, worthy Ezra—and numbskulls less stupid than you, Samuel. There are also bishops and monks who are ignorant, and savants who study, and the stewards of lords who are rich and shelter their full and indolent hands in fur gloves, and peasants who are not content. The world goes, as always, in an indifferent direction and a petty measured trot, in order to conform with the well-known expression: *That's the way of the world.* The world, at present, is in the shade of a large tree that is not very solid. No one knows the condition of its roots, there are branches with somewhat disproportionate fruits, which might one day fall off and bloody a few noses, but it's holding together quite well thus far. There are also

143

boring-beetles in the woodwork of houses, which are audible in the evening when everything falls silent after prayers, but people go to sleep contentedly and seriously, as after prayers. It's only idlers and dreamers who hear them. How is Rizpah, Samuel?"

"Well."

"That's curt. Well and what else?"

"She spins, she dreams, sometimes she sings quietly and sometimes thunderously; she plays the lute, she reads the old tales, sometimes, and hears the gossip of the century and the moment, no one knows how—from the breeze, the maidservant, for my distractions and he tales of my old mother, who still knows many things that were fresh half a century ago. She's like all young women."

"Do you think so?"

"Yes."

"What use is it to a dreamer to discern things so well? She sings, she spins, but do you know what is happening beneath that everyday appearance? She is beautiful, Rizpah?"

"Undoubtedly."

"Our young friend," said Ezra, "spins with the distaff of legends. I believe that he's besotted with Queen Genièvre; it seems to me that he has found a reflection of that vanished beauty, but he has sought her in places a little too high. It might cost him dear to love an inaccessible beauty. What can one say about a man whose life is sent contemplating the reflection of the Moon in a river, or waiting for a capricious fire-follet from which he is separated by an impassable marsh? Doubtless there are admirable reflections at night in the river and the lake, but can the melancholy heron catch one?"

Master Asverus became grave. "Samuel, you won't listen to my experience; it's extensive, however. Look twice before cracking the mirror of your life. Rizpah is beautiful; for you she is the future and the past. She's a strong woman, like the one whose name she bears; she would be able to keep the eagles away from her sons' gibbet, and keep watch in the

144

desert, her eyes dry, eating hard bread, clad in an old sack.[18] For you she will be the true magicians' lamp, the lamp with the inexhaustible drop of oil. Pay attention: there are beings that one does not have the right to offend; she is one of them. Think first of your duty and then of yourself. You have a good traveling staff; don't break it."

"I love her like a sister."

"But when she has deciphered the first pages of the book of life—soon, now, very soon—will she love you like a brother?"

"Everyone fulfils his destiny."

"Oh no—one follows one's first error, when one does not know one's destiny. And what is the reflection?"

Samuel remained silent, but Ezra said: "Princess Marie."

Master Asverus studied the young man anxiously. "Where have you seen her?"

"At the palace; I sang there with others. She thanked me in a voice so soft and said such accurate things about my art that I am still charmed by them."

"And here you are, drowned in the clear blue lake of her eyes, under the spell of that voice, which still seems to be modulating a romance. Here you are, having become quite impersonal, since you are not the only one that her beauty has ensnared. You love her because she is delicate and seems soft, all that heightened by the pomp of power—but can you hope, can you believe that she will descend from the high throne toward you, not for a minute, a minute of banal conversation, but to dream with open eyes for an entire lifetime? These slender blonde beauties are scarcely the work of old Asverus—for what can you hope? Will you sing for your entire life, arms upraised, to an image whose sapphire eyes bathe an entire room full of poets and warriors with soft light? If she is Genièvre, you are not Lancelot. Trust old Asverus: leave, and take Rizpah with you—there are other cities—or cut the dreaming part out of your heart. It isn't an honest flame that's

---

[18] cf II *Samuel* 21.

consuming you; it's only a smoky brand that it's necessary to throw away. Leave."

"Certainly not."

"When bells tinkle and glitter about your head, my friend, put on a fool's cap and go forth on the roads; cry that you are the knight of the impossible and the lover of the white phantom of the Dawn. Go stammer at the crossroads, go stammer, for what can you do, what can you learn, face to face with the portrait that you are carrying beneath your eyelids? For already, to be sure, a Princess Marie other than the true one—the one that exists, fair enough and good enough, but frail, very frail—is living in your head. A poet, a poet who has blood and sinews, who can sing as naively and frankly as a cockerel at sunrise, to an iridescent bubble of air! Beware, listen to Ezra; don't seek to scale a tower without a ladder, to open a door without a key—and look after yourself. Unoccupied dolor is the most terrible thing in the world."

"But I'm strong."

"You're weak; the strong ones are me and him; the strong are those who surpass the ages of weakness, those who live for a nurturing ideal, in a determined search. You're weak, I tell you, like all those your age, and you need to live next to the strong, and mature in their company, if you want to shore up your debility until your shoulders are firm enough. If not, go dream among the reeds; like you, they sway at the whim of the wind, and are content when it draws music from them."

"Oh, Master Asverus, you don't know—you can't know—that beauty is a game of the unexpected. It seems to me that I've known Rizpah for centuries, that my anterior soul knew her in other existences. Our souls have surely already exchanged, in previous lives, so many words and oaths of love that it doesn't seem possible to recommence them again. She's a strong woman, I don't doubt, but for how long, how many times, has my pretended debility been supported by her? Lives break, however, and existences recommence. I want a new life, without the memory, without encountering the memory in every new hour. Don't you believe that we have already lived so many times, elsewhere, differently, and that it's necessary to begin anew, no matter what—happiness, pain, torture—but something else, fresh waters."

"Dreams! But if you've lived before; if you've encountered Rizpah in anterior lives, do you not see that encountering her now, on the threshold of your existence, brought by fatality under the same roof where you live, is a sign; a superior will is giving her to you."

"It enchains me, then."

"Does impenetrable necessity manifest itself in any other way than instructions and bonds? Whatever you want, whatever you do, whatever you dream, or whatever you flee, you're the prisoner of the gracious face of your destiny. Do you think that, at your request, the songbirds of the world would chirp a different song, that the icy northern stars would dress in red robes, that the song of the church over there would resound with tender delight, that death would no longer be a miserable skeleton, that the steel-clad hearts of men would soften, that people would no longer hunt for gold with brutal actions or honeyed words, that flattering voices would cease to resound in white palaces? Can you not see in opposition to your design the file of monks, the file of priests, the file of soldiers, and the laughter of the crowd, a thousand open mouths, and two thousand hands full of stones—and can you believe that your idol will perceive your dream?"

"She has already perceived it."

"Momentarily! Can your dream, pure and radiant now, but which you will soon crumple between your angry fingers, remain radiant and new for long? Dread that you might live it all your life, in some corner of an unknown lair, alone with despair, with a parody, a withered flower, an old smile that will no longer be anything but a subject of the harshest sarcasm—that which one addresses to oneself."

"No. I've thought about it; I shall attempt the adventure of happiness. However far I might fall, my objective will have been beautiful."

"So much the worse," said Asverus.

In the little room, Rizpah is spinning; her dull face is shining, amid her broadly curled black hair, with the soft gleam of a mirror behind gauze, and her large black eyes have the soft languor of night over Eden. Her robust grace is as slender as a young tree, and her lips are roses in the heart of a flame. Her rather high forehead, the fine and proud bridge of her nose, and the genteel nostrils give that face a character of splendor that is almost august and heroic; her frank gaze is like a joyful fire, and the song of her intelligence rides a long way, a very long way, over beautiful plains of promise, toward a horizon of gilded cupolas, toward a fête of odorant flower-baskets.

She is alone, and the familiar things nearby seem to be admiring her.

Asverus comes in.

"Are you looking for Samuel?"

"No, I wanted to talk to you. What is Samuel doing?"

"Oh, he dreams, he dreams, he makes himself suffer."

"Why?"

"He searches the white clouds, he meditates, disappoints himself. He suffers, and I suffer in consequence."

"You still love him?"

"Yes."

"And what about him?"

"If he doesn't love me at present, he'll love me forever. When he has gazed at the world and the white clouds, he'll come back o me."

"He'll suffer."

"Then I'll console him."

"Suffer a great deal."

"Then I'll cure him."

And Rizpah resumes spinning, her eyes darkened, but as if words of hope are passing precipitately and silently over her delicate lips, which seem to be counting the turns of the wheel.

Chapter Two
YOUNG AND OLD VOICES

I

The days are woven with black and white threads.
The shuttle of time mingles them indifferently
beside the clock where the cadence of the hour is slow
and yet brief.

The sand on the river bank trots quickly beneath the au-
tan
and whirls like a thousand tiny fleeting sphere;
it is the same sand and the same loquacious water
that are always juxtaposed without moving a handspan
but seem nevertheless to be running.

The slow sails of ships on the blue-tinted horizon
make haste, and a hundred willful arms are braced
against the soft liquid wall of the greenish water;
the ship arrives, the ship departs. It remains
on the same droplet of water, which dies
in the same place, and swells and swirls
and also dreams of a long journey.

The fire that sputters in the hearth,
imagines climbing up
immense, to the blue-tinted ceiling
of the sky, and heaps itself on the floor of the hearth
in gray ash,
in gray ash,

As gray as my temples and my dirty hands
which leave in the morning for the maternal Earth
and return in the evening to the eternal Earth

and curl and knot like roots
that throw a gleam of gold and green into ravines
　　　　and winter arrives, hiding in the soil that they hollow out.
　　Ash, O infinite word, O eternal refrain.

Thus, in the little suburban house with the low ceiling, from the gray beams of which hung the copper lamp, next to packets of dried herbs, the serene old mother sang the old un-forgotten song in a quavering voice, and Rizpah, who was spinning beside her, took up the refrain, while the old wom-an's spindles rotated monotonously.

　　I hear the voice of my beloved,
　　He is coming down from the hills
　　His face mingles with the scarlet dawn
　　and I shall soon wipe away the dew
　　From the hair hanging over his forehead.
　　He is coming down from the nearby hills.
　　He is bringing me red roses
　　I await him with large lilies
　　and pink roses gathered
　　from the garden I keep for him.
　　I hear the voice of my beloved
　　Hastening toward my mouth

　　I hear his rapid gliding steps
　　rapid beside the water-tanks
　　where the women, to draw water,
　　incline their smooth and smiling bodies.
　　A more solar glare lights up my rings
　　for the eyes of his soul rests thereon
　　at the moment when our fingers pluck a white rose;
　　the fires of the Sun stop at my threshold
　　and amid the shade and water of the perfumed yard
　　where my desire waits for the scarlet to arrive
　　amid the white marble and scarlet pomegranates

and vines of hope and strength the color of the sea,
I shall hold him captive and joyful, and the bitter herb
of absence will wither between the stones.
    I hear my beloved coming.

And the old woman, weary and quavering, took up the refrain again, the spindles continuing their monotonous sound.

It is withered, the city that shone like a rose
in the midst of a garden of perfumed cities,
the dust stains it gray, the pearl-colored city
amid the golden sand and sapphire sky.
    The powdery road
By which long caravans once came
Laden with balms and manna
Toward the palace of your kings
    Jerusalem.

The columns of the temple lie amid the stone
and the voice of prayer is extinct
that rose up toward a lovely tree
    toward the azure,
and the doors of sanctuaries
lie, touched by the fingers of rust,
    and from the frescoes of the walls
the vultures have pecked
the verses of truth
and the lines of beauty,
and cracks run over your marbles,
    Jerusalem.

The door opened abruptly, and Samuel came in, gilded by the abrupt glare of a beam of sunlight, gleaming with youth by comparison with the somber gray room where Rizpah's beauty, facing him, was attenuated and vivid crimson colors ran over the objects.

The shadows of the room were pierced with golden streaks by an entire lacework of festival foliage, and he cried: "Mother, Jerusalem is everywhere where there is sunlight and happiness!"

But against the keen, noisy and sonorous breath that came from the city, the two women remained mute and somber.

II

On summer evenings, old Ezra admitted Master Asverus and Samuel to his garden, which descended a gentle slope toward a slow silent canal, in order that they might savor the mildness of the hour in his company. That bushy garden of broad laurels, tall linden-tress and cradles of meticulously-tailored foliage, beautiful with rare flowers, seemed a well of coolness when the rosy vapors—the reflection of the sunset—transfused the faded blue of the sky.

On a grassy bank beneath the spreading branches, whose leaves were amorously nibbled by a light wind, they listened to the silence invading the city, obliterating one by one the sounds of a soft embrace, and then, having crept up to the level of the market stalls, climb along the houses to dominate the exhausted city, formidable in its quietude, that place abandoned to dreams and so much inaction and the subtle poison of fatigue that stops the movement of the body.

One might have thought that the garden was far from any city, apart from any epoch, devoid of any neighbors, on the shore of some enigmatic infinity, and in a shadow that no other light could penetrate but that of the Moon and the stars. The three men conversed in a leisurely manner in low voices, emptying a few cups.

One evening, as calm, as fine, as perfumed and as uniform as any other fine summer evening in that enclosure of saps and meditation, it seemed to Samuel that his cup escaped from his fingers and that he was gazing with dreaming eyes at an ancient landscape familiar to him, but which he had forgotten for a long time, and which, in the long deployments of its palm-trees, its terraces and its profound thickets with golden fruits, was saying to him: do you recognize me?

In the background, endless stairways rose up toward enormous towers crowned with thick obscurity, and from that altitude of dream solemn voices were shouting: "Truth! Truth!"

And one more solemn voice replied: "The great fires are not yet lit; and one senses that numerous watchers, present and hidden, are searching the horizon."

When he turned toward someone who was nearby, at ground level like himself, to ask what the strange country was, he saw Ezra and Asverus, but not as he knew them.

Ezra wore a luminous tiara on his head; a necklace of gems scintillated over his white a tunic, bordered in scarlet, and his face was extraordinarily old, furrowed by a thousand wrinkles. His eyes were blazing with an extraordinary youth, a fire of childhood and generosity. Asverus, thinner and more tanned than Samuel had ever seen him, seemingly robust, his hair black and bushy, clad in a coarse, dark robe, was talking to him, and they were both looking toward the high towers.

A tall old man was coming down the steps, who was carrying something like a large luminous vase in his hands, and Ezra and Asverus took a few steps toward him—but in a strong gust of wind, the luminous vase went out like a lantern.

With infinite sadness, Ezra and Asverus watched a kind of opaque and murky wall veiling the stairways, the tall towers and the deep thickets full of golden fruit, and the darkness grew, becoming ominous, while in the distance—far away— denatured like a feeble echo, the voice repeated: "Truth! Truth!"

The reply was almost imperceptible, with so much weariness, its tone neutered by distance, little more than a whisper: "The great fires are not yet lit."

Samuel thought he saw himself kneeling before Ezra; it was his own face, and the rhythm of his body, but clad in a long and archaic white tunic. Ezra looked at him with a kindly expression; then the darkness invaded the last terrace of the unknown country, and it seemed to him that he woke up after a long absence of his soul.

Ezra and Asverus were beside him, mute.

Then, getting up and adjusting his long black velvet cloak, Asverus said: "Seigneur Ezra, I shall leave you; tomorrow I have to supervise the departure of one of my ships from the port."

He made his farewells, and Samuel followed him.

PRINCESS MARIE'S CASTLE

Already, as she was a little more than a child but not yet a young woman, Princess Marie often said: "I would like to have a castle like my soul, a castle made in the appearance of my soul. I'm sure that an important person, when she is rich and powerful, especially the daughter of an Emperor, can have a castle built on the model of her soul. I'm sure that the fortunate who have reached Heaven by means of martyrdom or bounty possess, beyond the clouds, in the great expanses where the earth is blue, where white clouds run instead of our springs, have castles built according to the model of their souls, entirely enveloped by marvelous flowers that are the colors of their souls. For souls have a color, like everything else in the world; is it not said that green leaves are the color of hope, and yellow ones the color of glory, violets the color of mourning and red flowers the color of love? Souls have a color, and one glimpses the color in one's soul on sleepless nights, when the feeble gleams of night-lights have, by chance, not gone out, and one sees them better in dreams, when they float above you of their own accord, in the pathways of the great infinite garden, and one knows that, at a sign from them, the roofs would open and let them escape toward the stars."

And when the women whose duty it was to augment her wisdom asked her: "What color is your soul, then, Princess?"

she replied: "You'll see when I'm grown up, and I build the castle of my soul."

The Emperor—who was a tall and solid soldier with a gray beard, who loved playing with his children between wars, and hiding in order to give them a scare and console them immediately—having also questioned her, she replied: "My castle will be similar to yours, and dissimilar; it will have neither the same form nor the same color, but I think that it will be in the same land."

Then she had run away, laughing.

When the Emperor caught up with her, he tried once again to sit her on his knees and interrogate her; she wanted to tell him the fine story of the child who found two horseshoes.

"Poor Pierre had found a horseshoe. He hung it on the wall in a corner of his little room. He had a little room because he was very small. The next year he found another horseshoe. Then he worked hard until he had made enough money to have the two horseshoes welded together. Then he worked hard until he had enough money to have his two horseshoes gilded. Then he wanted to wear them like a crown, but as his head was very small, the gilded horseshoe crown kept falling on to his shoulders, so that he no longer had a crown but a necklace.

"Every time he put his crown on his head he had the very best ideas, but when he ran to put them into action his crown fell on to his shoulders, and he stopped, all contrite, and nothing succeeded for him any longer, except that people said: 'That poor little Peter has a very fine shiny necklace—but look, just as the necklace does not seem to have been made for his neck, nor are his shoes for his feet, nor his smock for his body, nor his nose for his face.'

"Annoyed, little Peter had his horseshoes recast and made smaller, so that they became a true crown for his head. But as the horseshoe had been altered, it no longer brought good luck to everyone, but none at all, any more than any other piece of metal, and as poor Peter wore rags and a crown at the same time, everyone made fun of him, which irritated him.

It is even said that he was hanged on a great horned gibbet, by a very surly executioner, with a face covered with scars. Is that true, Father, the story of little Pierre?"

She ran away laughing, and the Emperor could not discover any more, for he was called away that day, perhaps to recommence the war.

When the wise chaplain charged with teaching her to read and write enquired in his turn about the future castle, he received this explanation: "The castle won't contain anything black that might be reminiscent of ink, nothing white that might be reminiscent of parchment, nothing gray that might be reminiscent of sand; people there will laugh, they will dance, they will sing, they will recite verses."

And the little princess left him there, half-smiling, half-groaning, mouth open, the word he had had ready abandoned before utterance.

She had lived in many palaces, little Princess Marie. She had been afraid in some, which had been located in the North, in the midst of black and bushy foliage, where one arrived by narrow roads felted with pine-cones at melancholy pools—extremely melancholy, as gray as lead—ringed by a thousand fragile lances of reeds, and which sent you back your image as if fatigued and ill, so pale and mute that you burst out laughing. In the evenings, seen from those windows, lightly latticed with lead, noisy crows passed by, and then there were owls that perched on the stone window-sills, long corridors shivering with cold between their thick walls, rare and reddish lights flickering—always flickering—throwing themselves backwards as if to push away something invisible.

She saw cheerful castles that bathed their foundations in large clear ponds, where hides had been built in order to fire arrows at ducks and wild geese. There were thick wall-hangings in the rooms, of violet and silver leather, the color of sunburn and the color of gold, in which knights passed endlessly over rearing unicorns and praying saints prayed endlessly. In those castles there were butterfly gardens, and on the ground, men of stone crowned with vines or ears of corn, scarred and eaten away by moss, and in the rounded, excessively white rooms, the hue of ivory or icy flesh grown old without wrinkles, lamps shed too harsh a light.

There were also castles whose gardens ran down to the sea. Abruptly parting the foliage, one perceived the broad white band of a beach, and the sea, as green as the leaves, and sometimes as yellow as the harvest, or as gray as wrath unleashed in the mud and surf. In spite of the splendor of the Sun, in spite of the amusements of the seabirds, whose white tribes went into exile as soon as a stranger approached to within a few strides, in spite of the gaiety of the long ribbon of surf that came to play on the sand, as glad as a thirst appeased, and disappeared laughing, laughing and laughing again, those castles were sad. The beach, as pure and white as a page of destiny, as virginal as an undeployed white sail, became sad as soon as human footsteps disturbed the solitary majesty of its silence, made of the monotony of sounds.

She had lived in many castles, little Princess Marie, but none was the one that her soul had chosen. When she grew older she lived most frequently, under her father's orders, in the palace in the city, and a castle surrounded by pleasant woods not far away.

Princess Marie loved songs. She loved all the songs she had heard; her memory of music and the longs of poets were like a well-arranged garden in which she wandered incessantly. For her, music was a mirror, songs a population of mirrors; as she was always, within a short span of time, sad, cheerful, lively, depressed, loquacious, silent, foolish and reasonable, she often ran rapidly to all her mirrors and looked at herself.

She was, fundamentally, always a tall slender individual, with a very pale complexion and very symmetrical features, with a flush of first youth and exceedingly blue eyes, which were sometimes a trifle gray, sometimes the violent blue of the southern sky—but the mirrors did not always respond to the same things, and she was much changed if she saw herself in the one that had picked out of her surroundings a poor student, whose song had suddenly sprung forth while, as a poor weary pedestrian, he was eating ripe apples in the shade of a tree, or the mirror that had been carefully opened by some great lord who sometimes leaned over her love to restate it.

She kept them all nearby, always close to her heart, songs like rural grass and songs like beautiful ostentatious roses; those that are sprigs that girls raise to their lips while walking along the road at dusk; and those of which people in velvet robes dream in the evening before the pulpit, repeating a verse that determines an unexpected echo in the high dark hall, which call forth speech in order that it might be heard again; and those of the birds in the forest; and those of goblets on the table; and those that one reads after prayers; and those that one never reads, and never listens to, but which one hears all the same, for everyone sings them.

Time had produced great bouquets of then, because people had loved a great deal, suffered a great deal, and songs had spurted from swollen hearts, perfumed by various suns, from the swimming-pools of disputed Jerusalem to the grey strands of the North, from the high towers of the church to the open entrails of the Earth where metal-miners are busy.

On the lips of the princess many songs murmured in their freshness of springs running over pearly mosses; king's sons espoused shepherdesses and king's daughters espoused captains charge with conquests and fortunes, but no one could remember having heard the tale hummed of how an emperor's daughter had given herself to a minstrel.

Princess Marie, who was tall and slender, with an undulating mantle of golden hair, circled her forehead with a narrow silver crown, exceedingly narrow and simple. She dressed in long white dresses gathered around the waist by a silver belt with a heavy clasp, and there were only a few gilded embroideries at the bottom of her long, trailing dress. On her shoulders she fastened pale blue mantles; of her necklace of gold and pearls, whether hidden by her mantle or her hair, a flood of blue or a flood of gold, one only perceived a few links on her breast, and her hands were not laden with any rings.

With the stance of a noble princess she amalgamated childish laughter, with the result that he robust emperor with the gray beard could refuse her nothing. Into her slow and measured stride she sometimes introduced an acrobatic agility, with the result that serious men—priests, soldiers and clerks—felt as benevolent toward her as to a pampered child. And since she was young and knew all the ancient songs, she wanted to know the new ones, and the poets came to sing them to her; and because she was beautiful, and she listened to all songs as if dreaming of tender morning sunlight, the poets were infatuated with her—Samuel more than any other.

How he loved that beauty; the music of so many poems dissolved in that beauty, some distant apparition amid the sumptuousness of the gardens of the palace and the pageantry of the guards, or that beauty and that power leaning down to the level of the road to listen in the hedges for whoever had the most beautiful and lively voice. What did he hope for except a choice between two tortures: to keep his love beneath all the locks of secrecy, or to hear it mocked. If some new tolerance had admitted that the princess might have a lover in the city, a sonorous and docile lute, how could that passion end?

Was he in love with her? He believed so; he was sure of it; he suffered in consequence; he knew no more than that.

He could not see clearly into his own inner depths. He did not even try, any more than the shoot that an errant seed lodges in a crack in a rock reflects on its motives. Like the blade of grass, he lived, shivered, trembled, folded beneath the rain, dried out in the Sun, knowing nothing of life but slumber and dew.

He had obtained from the learned Ezra what a man of his time was able to know, but that mass of information had passed over him without even brushing his soul. To him, his knowledge was like a bookshelf, always with arm's reach. He forgot it most of the time, but on certain days, moved by the occasion, he reached out his hand and opened one of the old tomes. To him, his knowledge was like a nearby city to which one sometimes goes under the cover of tall trees, by virtue of habit, where one amuses oneself momentarily, but without ever participating in its life. His knowledge was his, but outside of him. He was like a child burdened with heavy luggage; he liked nothing better than to set it down in the corner of some cheerful and populous square and forget about it; his whole brain was full of neglected terrains, where the bushes of hazard could grow at their leisure and produce all their leaves and berries. It was also a bare plain in which any fire might run wild and set everything alight at a stroke, beneath the vault of a low sky without enough stars.

The princess knew that she was loved, and smiled at him, for the poet, in his serious youth, seemed a poor creature not yet steady on his legs; she had been curious enough to listen to him and compliment him; since when there had been golden cupolas—sometimes, admittedly, veiled with cloud—on Samuel's horizons, in moments of effulgent hope.

THE MAY FESTIVAL

It is the day of the festival of May, the celebration of the salvation of a people by the ardent Sun—still its god, always and in spite of everything. Because the river has broken its cold white clots; because its mossy and yellow waters are no longer flowing slowly and slimily beneath a long quivery radiance, but running blue and steely as rapidly as arrows of silver and light; because the star has dried the mud on the land, from which stems, leaves and wings are springing forth everywhere, the entire City, with its citizens, its priests, its emperor, with its old men, its women, its children, its wisdom, its beauty, its hope and flying banners of duty, law and religion, is setting forth on the road of celebration, of flowers and draperies and music, to acclaim the divine Sun—which, say the ages, rotates around the Earth in the divine imponderable ether, in order to warm everything more effectively with its caress, and kiss its innumerable breasts!

The people of the city are going into the great plan, where the May Tree will be planted; the people of the coasts and the sea are coming upriver; their fanfares respond to the music of the city like the cries of gulls and the crowing of cocks. The beautiful daughters of the city line up along the river, throwing flowers to the beautiful daughters of the coast, traveling in their beribboned boats, and their gestures are so noble and beautiful that one might think one were seeing the Muses flattering the Sirens.

At the head of the procession, first of all, there were the scarlet heralds, golden eagles on their breasts, golden eagles on their tall hats, and the long staffs in their hands that protect the friends and smite the enemies of the empire. Then came the trumpets, long tubes of polished brass like the buccinas of the emperors of Rome, slightly raised toward the radiant sky, and bowing right and left according to the musicians' steps, playing the strident appeal that wakes up the soldiers in the distance of immense camps. Then came the long drums draped in scarlet, whose muffled and heavy beat is like the footsteps of the host running to answer the call of the brass conches; then a thick curtain of ironclad cavaliers, with gold on the visors on their helmets, gold on the eagles on their breastplates and gold on the head-dress of their horses, sheathed in iron coats of mail and the shafts of their long lances, like an autumnal forest; the Sun lit up the points like a pyre; red sashes the color of blood, with gold stripes, evoked the horror and the recompense of war.

Behind them came the forest of foot-soldiers, the long pikes on their shoulders decked with flowers and branches, their coarse ale-drinkers' faces, beneath large crenellated hats, smiling at the thought of the imminent libation. They passed by in broad ranks, wearying in their number—and then, on a chariot decorated with beautiful fabrics stiffened by golden thread, supplied by the Church, noble ladies and rich townspeople, a chariot moving like an enormous radiant plaque, came the May Tree, held upright by the burgers of the city clad in red velvet. And before it rode the Emperor, in helmet and armor, his charger radiant with golden armor and blue enamel.

Today, the men-at-arms, and the first among them, the Emperor, are merely vassals of May.

A folly of green branches, fleecy thyrses in the soft colors of a dawn-lit sea, transparencies, nacres, sparkling scarlets, amaranths and nacarats, around the white flesh-colored petals, blue, green and black flame-flowers, streaked with gold, glaucous amid the enamels of eyes, pinks in the candor of long white or pale yellow veils, golden tresses iridiscent with sunlight, brown tresses circled with roses and bright silver, a blaze of living gems scintillating and smiling, advancing in a bright fading charm as amid the mad kisses of the light: these were the young women of the city, the queens of the May— and among them, in a large cart overflowing with carnations, bright poppies, streaming branches of lilac, upright and blonde, dressed in white and silver, with a high crown of silver and pearls restricting the golden glow of her curls, Princess Marie.

She seemed to be guiding the white horses of the Sun, magnified by the entire swell of beauty, grace and youth following the train of her long white dress and blue mantle, by the slow and rhythmic oscillation of tresses that pressed upon her heels. She stood up, a mystic flower, a magical flower, as the elect of that gathering of soft and striking features, as if surging forth from a general beauty, ready to reproduce itself once again and forever, as immense and multiform as the light and the sea, and their unlimited play; and the swarm of laughing young women was as dense as an army.

After them, bearers of branches, all dressed in bright velvets and glittering silks, illuminating the grassy ground with a splendor of fabrics and plumes, the gleam of whose weapons had been banished for today, came the young men. For this festival, they had to choose a leader who was named the Prince of Lovers, and of their own accord, they had picked Samuel.

The young man, on horseback, followed by squires carrying lutes and guitars, was radiant with that momentary processional sovereignty: a lightning-flash between the grey of the day before and the profound darkness of the dusk that would fall when the Sun finished tearing up its scarlet and carried that brief splendor away into the far neverending west.

And in their wake came a festival march, and a masquerade of animated statues of gods, demigods and goddesses on marvelous carts: light and vibrant Fame raising the horn of joy to her lips, with agile Mercury beside her, and Night in her long robe the color of retreat and shelter, her forehead starred with twinkling gems. Fauns and Satyrs bore in their brawny and muscular arms an enormous smiling Silenus, red-faced and pot-bellied, periodically bursting into laughter, and behind him, back and grave, the majesty of Pluto and the severe mourning-dress of Proserpine, and their sober retinue of pages of Erebus.

Immediately, however, rustic flutes hymned the presence of Pan, one of the kings of the festival, crowned with roses, a long beard flowing in blond waves over his shoulders, serious and meditative, surrounded by Nymphs and Dryads, who were spreading perfumes around him and carrying curious baskets of flowers and rare fruits, brought from odorant shores by heavy galiots: golden fruits refreshed by the pale estuaries of Northern rivers. And also surrounding him, in carts drawn by white goats, were the most beautiful of the city's children.

On a high litter, as high as a terrace, carried by vigorous shoulders, was a Bacchus with a forehead circled by vine-branches and black hair that made his symmetrical face seem thinner; soft and coquettish, in a ship of white silks and doves, arrogant with her cerulean eyes and the noble curves of her face, was Venus; after laurel-bearers and living torches in the bright daylight, Apollo was dragged on a low quadriga, bow in hand; in the midst of a howling pack of hounds and mastiffs, was a light, upright and virginal Diana, and beside her, holding her hand, chosen for a strict resemblance, but older, grave and black-clad, with a star of gems that seems to be melting in

164

the daylight into glittering droplets suspended between Heaven and Earth on rival rays, the somber and grandiose Hecate.

Amid the quivering of long, undulating palm-fronds and the slow sound of cymbals and silvery bells, with bare-armed women with naked ankles dancing before her, the Queen of Sheba advanced, a tiara on her forehead, white veils embroidered with large imaginary flowers the color of sunset tumbling over the flanks of a black horse, her dull gold-tinted face the color of thirst-quenching fruits, the color of the liberating metal, the color of the bright tunics that the hours escorting the chariot of destiny wear.

That was Rizpah—for custom dictated that all young women of grace, virtue and beauty should appear in the procession—effulgent among that gilded decor, with the softness of her delicate features, her welcoming lips and her eyes, softly burning in the bright amber of her face, which seemed changed, hardened and magnified. Among the undulating palms, and the angelic salute of graceful dances, and the tall stature of guards with sparkling shields and lances made of sheaves of silky flowers, and the multicolored dwarfs capering behind the guards, and amid the slow murmur of admiration that ran through the edges of the crowd, she stood up in her own right, more than herself, as her true esthetic incarnation.

After her, after the variegated dwarfs, came the troop of chimeras, the bizarre masks in which humans dress up in their dreams, and in their knowledge—which is also a dream—of the humans of the distant past, of whom they know nothing. Moors, miscreants, black men, people of Cathay and Taprobane, Hyperboreans, Ogres, Giants from the Arabian deserts and mountains of Ethiopia, slingshot-wielders who fell mountain-demons, fishers of souls in seas of pink coral, and the black faces of those who dream for a hundred years in the hollow of a tree as vast as a forest, which is multiplied in the ground by a thousand verdant pillars—all of these masks mounted on oxen and donkeys or perched on stilts, yellow, red, green, shiny with enamel plaques, helmeted with iron saucepans: all the grotesquerie and strangeness of the distant, following, singing, crying out to the sounds of the flattest music.

Then, after an interval, as if triumphant over this gathering of peoples, intercalated between the beauties of the city, its wealth, its science and them, marching preceded by a varlet bearing a star of gold on high, and a perch garlanded with lilies, came the three mage-kings followed by the four evangelists.

In the wake of this figurative procession, after the beautiful forms and the beautiful colors of the past, after the images of strength and beauty and love, the image of number, after the emblems of the mind of the city, came the emblems of the city itself and its mighty banners, with its escutcheon of ships and lions, the banners of its guilds, borne by liveried standard-bearers, banners with the images of patron saints arranged in broad and profound lines before the populace—and before the human mass, which arrived singing and numerous, a man on horseback who was, for the day, the Prince of the People: an elected prince as ephemeral as the Prince of Lovers.

He too, that evening, after the festival and the empty pitchers, with a quotidian and negligent gesture, while fastening his ample sleeping-cloak, had to surrender his copper crown, and the scepter that was almost a mallet, and remove the plumes and decorative brasses from the horse's harness. The people, who chose him to march at their head on that day of solemn, but also slightly mocking, rejoicing—for there is mockery in all collective joy—did not mean to confer honors upon him and to put him at their head, for any other purpose than amusing ceremonies. To be sure, the Prince of the People had to be popular, but that might as easily be for a fault as a virtue, for a particularity or an eccentricity; sometimes he was a foreigner that they desired to honor.

The man who marched behind the banners that day, was primarily an object of curiosity to the people. Laurent Télice had recently arrived from afar, it was said, in a small ship decked in flags, coming upriver, with his crew singing joyfully. He had dropped anchor; he said that he would be staying in the city for a few days, and had swiftly become notorious, hunting with white Syrian falcons with golden eyes, accompanied on his excursions on the river by numerous pages emptying pint pots and filling even more for the thirsty throats of idlers in the city's taverns, taking up residence in the most beautiful palace he could find, and opening it sumptuously to the many new friends he had rapidly made among the soldiery and young layabouts. He was liked for his virile elegance, his handsome face, his long blond curls falling over the shoulders of Atlas, his dexterity as a horseman, and the bravery with which he was widely credited by virtue of his penetrative blue eyes.

Weeks went by for him in very evident enjoyment; then, for a few days, he no longer went out, his house remained closed, and all that was seen of him was the reddening the attic windows far into the night, and black smoke dissolving in the sky. After these brief withdrawals, he reappeared, renewed, rejuvenated and more prodigal. It was because he was prodigal that he was liked, and it was because he was more prodigal every time he came down from his attic rooms, that it was rumored that he was an alchemist, and that he knew how to make gold.

He was not hated for that, nor endangered, but only excited jealousy. The city loved gold more than anything else—like every city, every village, every hamlet and every paltry or enormous group of poor earth-dwellers.

Laurent, knowing what form the festival would take, brought up to date with its customs, had wanted to be the Prince of the People; he had begun with large disbursements, and had been for a few hours the god king who pours and slices for his people.

In the great meadow, at a spot which the feet of the crowd have not trampled, among the white seed-bed of golden-hearted daisies, the new May Tree has been planted, and like its neighbors, aligned along a broad esplanade overlooking a bend in the river, it will grow, a sign of one more year's prosperity, if no storms come to wither its branches with a grim blast, as happens to other trees.

The priests, emerging from a large chapel built on the esplanade for that purpose, come forward, and amid the light smoke of a little incense, terrestrial vapor rising into the vapors of the sky, they bless it, and the Emperor thanks them. He is very close to the tree, the princess by his side; the young women of her retinue hold on to the garlands of the May Tree.

It is the moment when the Prince of Lovers has to present himself and offer his homage to the May.

Hail to the new May, which laughs upon so many lips
beautiful or wise: the flowers of laughter
in all the gardens of flesh are open
   in the hands of the divine goldsmith
to Spring, a youth in a green cap
   who will grow in time to be Summer!
He has come to the Church of Gladness to predict
   a year of joy for the beautiful city.

The day has its stars; they twinkle in your eyes
in the polished gleam of your brightness,
O beauties divided by the dream of your fingers
   Slender and industrious!
In avenues of trees and flowers, welcoming trees
   show the route to kings,
   show the route to knights,
   show the route to pious travelers
who are heading directly for the Church of Gladness

Tree of the new May—one more head of hair
that the gentle evening wind will caress with kisses
while the violet night will guide toward you
corteges of balms that leave Arabia
and traverse the world to bring to you
their counsel of love, hope and adventure

and inspire your benign hands, on bended knee,
to gather joy in the shadow of the night.

Tree of the new May, when your fruits come
to crown your strong branches with heir tender freshness,
and your leaves against the ardor midday Sun
    will be the shield, solid and fragile
and fresh, to the sound of springs amid the garlic,
ready alms for the traveler, that he might rest and eat
and dream, even weary and dusty, that the Sabbath
    welcomes him to our city of hectic bells,
tree of the new May, tree with sacred roots.

Grow in the Mays of the future Sun;
my love replete, my charming and harsh pain
ended, concluding my exile far from words
in which my Lady charms her mirror, and the mad vine
of her scattered thoughts, by the scarlet and the songs,
enable my hands to plant a rival beside you,
tree of the new May: a tree scaling
the white and blue Empyrean with branches of desire
heavy with the garlands of triumphal crowns.

And may its shadow cover the distant fields,
and the tree of love be so tall, so vast,
and such a blessed retreat, such an ardent cupola,
that others who love, others whom emotion
similar to mine, pieces and devastates the heart,
might sleep at the whim of my victorious kiss,
which will make a shadow around it, in which all hearts,
might nestle in the frigid silence
and love in tranquility, in tranquil delight,
tree of my love with sacred roots!

Then, Sire, your city, the city of Gold and Passion,
will shine upon all the world's hills; the horizons
will gaze upon your great flamboyant pyre of joy

and its bloodied tiles like lips lacerated
by kisses. Behold the city with gates of love
where joy holds its lamp high night and day,
as straight and firm as the Sun,
and the marvel of your city will be built
higher than giants, towers and Babels,
piers, churches and paradises of old.
O Sire whose wisdom is served by Genius.

The hours of my life sing from ground level,
Princess, among the stones of the road, and the moss
    of sources in your forests!
The hours of my voice are those of a sparrow
which flutters and sings its pain and emotion,
outside paradises guarded with heavy bars,
rough against imprudent and overly direct leaps.

But today is the fête of leaves and blades of grass,
when nature opens its basilica
   to landings of trees, vaults of sunlight, pavements where
sheaves
    might provide bread in abundance to the starving;
    concede grace to the poem of the Prince of Lovers.
    For you he has the eyes of entire nations,
    his voice declares the love of all, and then his own,
    a love without a pledge, a prayer,
    more than a desire and more than a vow, ancient love,
    swallow of the soul, which builds its nest beneath my
eyelid.

The Emperor had listened silently, stiff and indifferent;
he evidently did not like the music, and the last verses annoyed him. Powerful as he was, at this festival, semi-
Saturnalian in the evening and popular by day, he was primarily a guest. Obviously, the poet had not strayed too far from the
canon of poems of that sort: a compliment, an homage to the
beauty of ladies of high rank were implicit therein; the imperi-

al ears had often heard cruder ones—for the Prince of Lovers was not always a poet, but sometimes a soldier or an overly humorous songmaker—but today, this young man, with the serious face, the emotional tone and the handsome appearance, had indisposed the emperor. He took himself too seriously; his commencement had had something about it that was much too sacerdotal, his conclusion had been pronounced in a very intimate, very profound tone.

Fragments of legend surfaced in the emperor's memory, trivia distractedly overheard in the conversations of poets that the princess attracted to the palace. Oh yes, Princess Marie's lover! That remained to be seen. The princess had listened too, with a very attentive expression—but that was of no importance. He looked sideways at the princess, who, according to the established ritual, her expression naïve and blank, only smiling with her eyes, was offering a red flower to the poet with her pretty and graceful hands. Immediately, and without further ado, she turned in an amicable manner to the Prince of the People, who said:

"Sire Emperor, and you, Princess of power, grace and beauty, the city of joyful life and kind hospitality had decided that on this feast-day it should be a foreigner who makes a speech to you, doubtless to furnish you with the opportunity to amuse yourselves by the manner in which he travesties your mellifluous language. Nevertheless, the opportunity is infinitely welcome that permits me to express my profound respect and arrest your attention for a moment on your humble servant. I would rather have appeared before you in a fool's cap, however, for such is my crown to me; and if such justice had been rendered to me, I would have said to the tree of May, the sovereign of this day, and to you, Sire Emperor, its vicar, everything that passed through my head, and my head produces witticisms and follies as sea-dunes produce thistles, gardens weeds, a stockbroker's purse écus and your power, Sire Emperor, the abundance of all goods and the sign of grandeur, blessed Gold—accursed Gold, as has sometimes been murmured. Perhaps…but here it is blessed Gold.

171

"It comes from distant seas on heavy ships from whose prows Neptune's horses gallop incessantly. It comes from isles with pearly shores, aromatic forests, roads who ditches produce abundant spices, profound valleys in which diamonds and carbuncles flourish, where the birds are bubbles of gems. It comes to you from forests felled at the base, whose great oaks have fallen into your river. It comes to you from broad plains, which turn green and then yellow. It comes to you, a king's ransom, under the guard of your cavaliers and a thousand chariots, bringing it to your charter. It comes to you from the Heavens, for the Heavens are witness to your piety and greatness. But above all, it comes to you from the City.

"Your city is a crucible in which everything is amalgamated to make gold; you have in the palaces that surround your noble palace a thousand Midases who change everything into gold, and to whom no mythological punishment has ever been applied. The richest veins snake through your streets, and the merchants' signs are, in truth, enormous vines entwined before their doors, which produce the grapes of the Hesperides. They extract gold from everything: from hunger, from thirst, from vanity, from love, from devotion, from gluttony, from sloth, and bring you your share scrupulously, for they fear their conscience as much as the hangman's rope. All that they lack in order to be entirely happy is this: to extract gold from nothing at all. They are weary of giving something in exchange, in fatigue or thought; they would like to possess the philosopher's stone.

"Who will give it to them? Will it be under your ephemeral reign, Tree of May? Will it be your successor, one of your successors on a day of rejoicing, who will be acclaimed as the first tree of the Golden Age of paradise marching over the Earth among torches gleaming with metal? I would like it to be in our time that this good fortune be realized for all your people.

"Hail to you, Sir Emperor, and to you, noble Princess, and hail to the city with the enormous walls and to the marvelous unknown that reveals the years of the future—and thank you to all you people whose goodwill desired my presence here, wise and sagacious people of the great city."

The Princess, with a smile that was a ray of sunlight over the ripening wheat, offered him a flower, as she had to the poet, but with more abandon, and the Emperor, who had listened smiling, thanked him with warm benevolence, and the high officers and the populace applauded and cheered, and the clergy considered him with a very indulgent curiosity.

Chapter Three
THE ASHEN TOWER

That night, Samuel had a dream.

Into the brown heaths of his soul, lit by a faint cold daylight, sad and harsh, people were coming. They were tasting the water of the river; they were turning toward the red-tinted hills that closed the horizon; they were planting the pegs of their tents and releasing horses that bounded toward the plateaux furnished with meager grass, and cooking-pots had been placed on the fires.

All these people were small, with stern bushy beards, except for one of them, with a melancholy and weary expression, who let orders fall from his lips in a very low voice; but they extended their ears at close range and carried them out quickly. The chief soon had a large fire lit, near to which he shivered until a rapid flame reddened his face, and Samuel perceived that he resembled him slightly.

The man who was warming himself—the fire twisted like a hydra in a hundred serpents of flame; then there was a bush whose scarlet branches were devoid of white and heat-sensitive flowers, and fragrances of mulberry and juniper and the rustic savor of resins—the man who rested in the warmth of that heat and light reached down and raised a trap-door at his feet; men with the same bushy beards, even smaller than the servants busy on the plain, climbed out therefrom. One by one he watched them appear, and each of them offered him a strange luminous flower, shining with scarlet, violet and orange fires, and the man dropped them disdainfully.

Finally, one of these dwarfs begged his permission, humiliated himself and, picking up the flowers of light from the ground, wove a crown out of them, and the man allowed it to be placed on his head. The crown shone with a vivid gleam, whereupon all the servants scattered in the plain came running, making signs of child-like joy.

174

Even paler and more morose, the man pointed to the open trap-door, and they soon came back up, carrying enormous blocks of raw metal. The man smiled, and then the dwarfs over all the surface of the ground threw up their hands in gestures of despair, and slipped away and disappeared—and the servants came up through the trap-door and went down again, always more heavily laden with valuable stones. Finally, the man made a weary gesture; then the servants lit another great fire. A kind of vertical blue and yellow curtain, in which points of gold were burning, rose up, and atoms of gold were leaping and rebounding from the ground in a long indented plume, and hammers made a hole in the silence, and sparks ignited tufts of grass that suddenly burst into flame with a dry crackle.

An enormous crown with a harsh and continuous glare was formed. The man threw away the one the dwarfs has given him and put it on his head, and the beautiful unknown flowers of the rejected crown went out, with a plaintive crystalline hiss. When the last one was extinct, light wisps of a black-tinted mist gradually invaded the plain, and Samuel could see no more in the brown heaths of his soul than indecisive clouds.

That shadow thinned out and became more ashen, then gray, then white, and it was no more than a brown-tinted fog—and a thin streak of dirty yellowish light appeared; then a deep red-brown gained substance, became a disk and then produced yellowing extensions on various sides. One might have thought that a spider was slowly stretching out long legs, barbed with other long and filamentous limbs, and the whole fog crackled—and through sudden fissures, Samuel perceived monstrous stained faces, moving in the jaundiced light of a distant and somnolent Moon, from which the wind was slowly stripping the last white veils away.

Then the faces became calmer, the water mobile, and, from a dolorous aurora about their cheeks, a pale aureole congealed around their faces; and the great confused eyes of a sphinx, as large as marshes with islets of vegetation, gazed at him; and the crowned man emerged from the fog, as if climbing the steps of a difficult stairway. An entire sparkling mountain abruptly appeared, sculpted from the base to the summit and guarded by a thousand sphinxes on all of its platforms.

The crowned man tried to go up; then a sphinx, with a slow and indolent movement, shifted the entirety of its leonine body, as if it were emerging from the mountain, and barred his route. The man was forced to descend into the symmetrical and ornamented stones with which the slope of the mountain was lined and then go around the sphinx and make his way laboriously toward another platform—where, with a similar feline undulation, another sphinx barred his route. Up above, on the superior platform, a great triangle of light appeared, alive with singing voices and the forms of veiled women. The crowned man gazed at them, weeping and putting his hands together, and in his fervor, he stumbled, tripped and rolled to the bottom of the mountain.

And something like a velum of bright and gilded mist, a compact sparkling wall, covered Samuel's eyes completely.

The wall gradually became a solar light. From its center, rays like immense scimitars shone more terribly red-gold on the mat gold background. Blue-tinted frissons furrowed it from end to end. It seemed to draw away slowly…slowly. It retreated…retreated, ever more resplendent, and seemed to seal the horizon.

In the foreground, blackened forms had been swarming for a few seconds—in dream time—and when the wall of light was far enough away for the eye to be able to distinguish what was standing at its base, Samuel perceived that there was a forest; its branches and trees spiraled everywhere, and it grew; one might have thought it a sheet of lace applied to the golden mask from a distance.

The crowned man was at the edge of the forest. He tried to go into it, and his arms reached out toward the bright jewel of the horizon. Stray radiance lit his face vividly, and his body was deducible in the green shadow. He climbed long banks, sometimes upright, sometimes helping himself with his hands;

brambles rose up like springs to lash his face, and thickets bristled before him, as if hurled by an abrupt gust of wind. At the crest of a slope, he perceived the solar palace, far away from him, at the end of an immense tree-lined driveway, and he raised his arms to the Heavens, his face painted with discouragement. His beard became gray in that livid moment of melancholy. He seemed to Samuel to be someone of his own race, who might have known his father.

The crowned man sat on the ground and sighed dolorously; then he got up with a gesture of sudden determination—but water splashed around his feet. Reed-beds slowly stretched their tall gladiolar stems toward the sky, and ululating black wading-birds circled overhead. He set off again alongside the reeds and skirted the barrier of water. Sometimes, a small advancement of the ground gave him the illusion that the obstacle had ended, but it began again, and in the depths of the horizon the wall of light drew away, without becoming paler. Regretfully, the man retraced his steps. He came back, he went on.

He bent down to pick flowers. The shock he gave the plant was excessive; nothing remained in his hands but exfoliated stems. He beat the air with his hands, and a butterfly with crazy colors escaped him and bounded into the bright sky. Hares sprang forth beneath his feet, and rain fell in fine leaden networks—and the man fell to the ground and sobbed. An olive-tinted mist, in which it seemed that one could make out arborescent hollows, covered everything.

Then Samuel saw the brown heath again, with reddish hills on the horizon; a pale moment, a cold midday. The crowned man was marching alone. The servants were asleep near firebrands that were going out, and the man leaned over them to wake them. With a broad gesture he showed them the entire plain, and with a straight upwardly-inclined gesture seemed to be indicating some great objective—but they remained seated on the ground, and stretched out their hands full of blisters and wounded feet. The man wrung his hands. The caravan's animals were lying down, deprived of movement, and the man went from one servant to another, ardent and anxious, pointing at the river, the animals, the ground.

Finally, one of them men stood up, painfully, and went to draw water from the river; and slowly, one by one, the others joined him. Picks and spades dug into the ground. Soon, Samuel heard through his slumber the heavy blows of hammers and the screeching of saws, and rafts came along the slow river, and a nocturnal veil enveloped them.

The somber and splendid sunset! The star's blood flowed in scarlet waves, dense and profound waves; gilded stars plunged into it, swirling as if in an eddy of the red gulf. From an immense, open heart the warm and abundant blood flowed in a thousand bubbles—from an immense and lacerated heart, in a pale torso, generally ivorine, green in places—and one might have thought that a head crowned with a ruddy brown clouds was leaning over, hanging on to a shoulder by virtue of excessive weariness.

The veins of the dying, vacillating God, unable either to stand upright or to fall, with no support within range of his wounded hands, irradiated in every direction the crimson semen of life and light, and from the terraces of distant Babels, very tiny by comparison with his stature, crowds and races watched death invade him, and the shadow prepare its hordes and somber horses for the sudden invasion of his plains.

At ground level near the river, however, by the blood-colored reflection, and in the hills where furnaces lit up, there were half-built walls of brick, wooden towers remained in framework, fragments of mosaic sank into the dusty soil, waiting in vain for a nearby paving-stone to support them, and futile flagstaffs awaited standards. There was the entire groundwork and foundations of a city—shards of wall, scattered materials, recumbent columns—but already, a curt and sterile forest of mallows and nettles was growing around them.

In the midst of scarcely-traced roads, all the servants were reloading the animals of the caravan; they were getting ready to leave. In vain, the crowned man showed them the melancholy of the deserted building-sites and skeletal scaffolding, the sadness of the abandoned materials, the sacks slit open on the ground, and the rafts run aground near pontoons full of green moss, flat tresses and violet viscosities. The servants shook their heads; they held out their hands full of blisters, their wounded feet, and while the crowned man tried to persuade one of them to stay, another, not far away, departed—and the man, discouraged, sat down at the foot of a column, and let them leave, defeated.

He raised his eyes toward the Heavens; the last rays had bled away, and the paleness of the twilight rose up like a liquor of ashes and fire. The river was the color of lead, and only the grey canvas of clouds was reflected therein. He went to the trap-door he had lifted up that morning and opened it again; he called out, he moaned, he begged; a black, level silence remained in the bowels of the Earth.

The crown that the dwarfs had offered him still lay close to the opening, still throwing off a few fires. He passed it over his arm then, and his desolate tread was kicking the sparse pebbles pensively, when he saw a bizarre individual, sprung from a heap of stones, advancing toward him. The face was that of a man; a dry bushy beard, the color of dust, framed a flat visage aged by a thousand wrinkles, with dull eyes the color of lead. The browned torso seemed to be hairy; the creature was supporting itself on the ground with two hands, splayed and enlarged toward the thumb, like the hands of a man placed on a flat surface, and its legs, folded beneath the knee, were hopping instead of walking, like the legs of a batrachian.

The crowned man spoke to it. The creature did not reply, but came toward him. The man recoiled, and saw that similar hideous beings were coming toward him from every direction. Fear gripped him, and he fled into the total silence—and the sullen chimeras followed him, silently.

Abruptly, Samuel saw him again, at the corner of one of the city streets. Pale, he was marching rapidly, murmuring words. He retreated from populous streets and went into back streets, only to withdraw from them immediately. He searched

179

among the lights of the shops at ground level; finally, he spotted a money-changer's shop. An old man with a bald head was weighing, behind a counter laden with little ingots and coins.

It seemed to Samuel that he went in behind the crowned man, in the shadow, and that he later removed the heavy forged crown from his head and the dwarfs' crown from his arm, and held out both of them: the one of solid gold and the other of luminous flowers, and he spoke. He wanted to sell the last vestige of a splendor.

The old money-changer smiled at first, and then seemed to become irritated. Gazing at the haggard aspect of his visitor, however, and the dolorous eyes and the cloak soiled with the mud of the road, he said, also in a sad tone: "But these are leaves, mere dry leaves."

And Samuel woke up.

Some distance away from the great city, toward the north, is the Ashen Tower. Its square mass emerges like an islet carved in the land by four canals, all rectilinear, which depart toward the sea and the land. Green grassy dikes, devoid of trees, extend beside these tranquil slumbering waters, and are mirrored in them. Into the motionless mirror, their slopes plunge so clearly that the canal-beds sometimes seem to be filled with a powdery green substance, of solid air or ductile earth.

A few grazing sheep, moving in flocks, are the only moving forms in these solitudes, with a few shepherds leaning on their staffs and occasional soldiers on the iron shafts of their halberds. In the plain, willow-groves surround a few buildings arranged in a regular square.

From the platform on the tower, further away, the uniform bulges and parallel lines of the sea-dunes were visible. Black hollows, green-tinted hollows, hollows bright with white dust—and beneath the clouds in the form of anvils, giant fish, monstrous dogs, the long fleece of the sea, limitless and devoid of islands, the perpetual mad arrival of long white lines that run forward to break and retreat, and rebound.

On the other side, the huddled presence of heather-clad slopes, chased by the sea-wind from the interior lands, fugitive trees twisted out of the reddish earth, and a meager terrain cut by dusty and disorderly paths, joined the dunes and the sea to encircle the sad and deserted tower. The calls of marine birds rose up from large pools covered in marine vegetation, from the gray crust of variegated mosses of the sea, streaked by the flight of herons and curlews, saddened by the approach of evening, and the crepuscular clouds lingering there in expanses of shadow.

At midday, from the platform of the tower, there was all that echoless solitude, frightened by being so vast, overwhelmed by the harsh flat light, lying low, and by the terror of so many ardent arrows, without refuge; and in the evening, the sad partitions of the night came to close all the roads, and mourning bands veil the pathways and mask the entire unknown of the networks of thorns, potholes and perfidious tall grasses.

On fine days, to be sure, the eye cheered up at the thought of departing in dream in the direction of the sea, with the ships passing by in the open water like towers with sails, and in the direction of the land, on the thin rim of the horizon, there were blurred houses near bell-towers, and the vague lines of distant towns bathed in glittering pulverulence.

On both sides there was life, distant and improbable, for the ashen tower was a sort of prison, and at close range, the sentinel's halberds, the canals serving as a moat, and the playful barking of dogs trained to chase fugitives, harshly recalled the purpose of the massive square tower, gray and dolorous—and all that Samuel knew, for days on end, of life and the horizon, was that which could be seen through a narrow loophole. He saw guards pass by over the grass, or on a circular path.

The heavy fall of colorless hours into oblivion, the duration of a time that nothing could any longer measure! A captive's minute is as long as the day, and his days are like years, and when his soul, wearied by the immobility of the body, becomes feverish and takes flight, into what rough skies it soars! And after the fatal return, what fatigue. And the gray minutes recommence their trickle from the coarse pitcher of captivity, so slow, so extensively menacing, and stalactites take root in the grottoes of ennui.

In the inactivity full of daydreams, the nightmares of the night and the clammy and tormenting apprehension of insomnia crawl, inevitable caterpillars among the weeds of thought. The mind, like a beautiful mechanism robbed of some essential movement, turns and turns in the void, while the body lies on its pallet, while the body turns in its cage, where it has yielded to so many enervating hours. Sleep is nothing but the expansion in fear of the bitterness of awakening; the captive soul folds itself up, gnawing itself for nourishment; it consumes itself, it bumps into the four overly-restrictive corners of the prisoner body, and plaques of oblivion harden in the mobile walls of the imagination.

The silence was profound. Samuel turned over on his pallet, and somnolence and dreams took told of him again...

THE SLAIN FOREST

There is a high forest. The trees are straight, dense, united by enormous tangles of florid ligaments whose leaves are almost black. The man is walking; it seems to him that there are muffled whispers all around him; when he stops, the whispering stops, fading away from the plants underfoot. The whispering seems to him a little more distant; then it propagates, and swells, is almost a voice. The man goes on, and no longer hears anything but a distant murmur, from high above. The lianas in front of him unfurl, as if frightened, retreating to more distant trees. Nearby, creepers run from right to left like fearful animals, twisting, stretching themselves out to their full length, sprawling, as if attempting awkwardly to increase their length slightly, twisting back and falling limply.

Thorny bushes flagellate his legs; when he steps back, the bushes resume their normal aspect; when he goes forward, the bushes extend toward him and direct their needles at him;

when he moves sideways and goes around them, the bushes collapse. The green grasses on which he treads turn yellow and shrivel, and as he plunges into the mobile thickness there are sighs, agonized squeals, tremors, fears.

The man speaks, and a kind of long plaintive voice exhales and replies. He arrives in front of an immense tree, from whose foliage agile lianas descend; their protruding flowers seem to be looking at him. One might think that they were suspended serpents, darting their heads toward him, but well above his own head. It seems to him that a form detaches itself from a large crevice in the heart of the tree and looks at him. He runs toward it; there is nothing but the profound black cavity. He continues going forward.

The whispering, murmurous voice resumes, analogous to the passing of the wind through the leaves. In its slow and melancholy intonation it resembles the voice of the wind, but it is not. It also resembles a human voice, by virtue of its tremulous suffering, but it is not that either; the vibration is too indecisive. It is not a animal cry; it is too sustained, too slow, too personal for that. It modulates itself, dies away, reverberates, swells, and ends up in short breaths, little sobs.

Here is a clearing; the man goes in, and it is as if faces that appeared momentarily have vanished; branches brush one another and rustle, but no noise of footsteps is perceptible, and the long sob becomes more accentuated, swells and swells and them calms down. The plants on the ground before his feet have fallen back toward the Earth along their entire length.

He breaks a branch; there is a dolorous sigh. He plunges his knife into a crevice in a tree; blood spurts, and a human form falls forward, displaying its punctured breast, and falls down in front of the tree with a loud scream—and an entire angry clamor rings out.

Frightened, the man steps back, terrified by the explosion of sound—but everything is limited to that loud noise. The being he struck is still lying at the foot of the tree. It is pale; around its face there is long hair—or, rather long green filaments like suspended blades of grass; its staring eyes are green-tinted; hair-like protrusions cover is torso and its legs are fused with the bark of the tress. The man drops the knife and runs away, fearful of having immolated a god.

But the regular cadence of sounds, like a drumbeat, leaps from tree to tree not far away, and a trenchant refrain accompanies the strenuous efforts of woodcutters. An oak falls with a dry thud, the dolor of stricken plants, and the axe-wielders march on. The man speaks to the men; he tells them his story, about the animate tree and the stricken wood-nymph—but they smile.

"We've been told already," says one of them, a robust fellow with frizzy hair, "that that's the way of things in great forests; beings live here that are neither entirely plants nor entirely people. Some priests recommend that we look after them, like poor helpless brothers; other priests order us to extirpate them, because they're people whom divine vengeance has attached to trees. Our own destiny, having been exiled from cities by poverty and driven far away from owned land by men-at-arms, is to take what remains of their land from them. So much the worse if they're brothers; so much the better if they're miscreants; too bad if they're only the souls of trees."

And the axes resumed their regular cadence.

"But haven't you heard the voice?" said the man. "The great, slow and flexible voice that rises from the stricken thickets?"

"Of course," the woodcutter replied. "We hear it as we begin our assault on the branches and leaves, but afterwards, it becomes submissive to us; woodcutters tame the voice of the forest, and teach it to repeat their own words."

He provoked an echo. He was very proud of making it repeat his words—but he did not notice, although it seemed obvious to Samuel, that it was the vanquished Echo, modulating her repetitions with the inflexions of an infinite sadness.

Samuel, or the man that he glimpsed in his stead in the dream, was marching rapidly, as if harassed, without any visible cause. He had turned his back on the vanquished forest. It seemed to him that he had escaped an ancient islet of the old world, miraculously preserved for a long time, but where new footsteps were resonating in a new triumph.

He was in the hollow of a path bordered by living hedges, where reckless grass disputed with the dust. He saw a little bent old man, who was picking wild flowers and immediately throwing them away, and asked him what he was doing.

"I'm looking for flowers," the little old man replied. "Once, there were many of them, they were everywhere, in all the paths and all the fields—the whole Earth was a garden. Then it became more difficult; one only found them in the market, but one could still find them. In every city, the most beautiful square was selected. A fountain marked the center, like the angular pillar of a temple to the open sky; care was taken that all the houses around the designated square were beautiful and neat and uniform, in order not to spoil the beauty of the flowers, and the rare ornaments that were allowed there were made of wood, and imitation foliage, in order that the flowers might find themselves in their preferred environment—and then every city, every village, had its temple to flowers, and the perfumes sang to the music of the colors. It's all over now; there are no longer any to be found anywhere; all the flowers are hardened; all the flowers are false; they're unperfumed wax, even on these unknown roads. They're modified like that in all their transitions. Everything that they carried, everything that comes near them, becomes that colorless substance. What are they? Only women—everything has changed since this new religion of womanhood."

Suddenly, Princess Marie stood up before Samuel's dream, high on the great silver cart drowned in white roses, and the pain woke him up.

THE TWO EPHEMERAL PRINCES

In a single instant, he relived the most painful moments of his life.

The evening after the festival, when the Emperor and Princess Marie had emerged from their palace to walk among the crowds in the main square, neither one had paid any heed to his religious bow; both were still talking, at length, about his rival, Prince of the People, dressed that day entirely in red and surrounded by quivering buffoons. The latter quit the large elm beneath which he was drinking, cup still in hand, in order to joke and laugh with the sovereigns and the high officials.

The curiosity of the princess was satisfied on hearing that Prince of Fools tell stories of his arrivals in distant lands, and his search for happiness in all lands—and the Princess's eyes, at that moment, during the banal narrative, were no less candidly pensive, her mouth no less subdued by silence, and her clear face no less calmed by profound meditation, than when listening to songs awaken in timeless reveries.

What did he know about banal narratives? Did not the entire city listen—more willingly than to his songs, which only young lovers, and only in moments of passion, picked out—to the brief stories of the voyager who had come, had seen and had left to see something else, his gaze and his speech ever victorious, and his hands always open. Oh, they were not the flowers of the old man in his dream, who fell upon them at every occasion, during every pause, brief or long, but the Gold of various and different effigies, the gold of the princes of the Earth, the gold of wages, the gold of powers, the word ambition ductilized, desire simplified, one of the currencies of Force.

In the large square, shadowed by beeches, which advanced in a triangle of coolness and light upon the mildness of the river, where Laurent Télice, the Prince of the People, was speaking and laughing, he had seen Old Ezra. Ezra had come over to him briefly, then had led him closer to Laurent. They had listened momentarily, and then resumed their walk.

Before Ezra's gaze, it was as if all the people there were projected on a screen, in judgment before the eternal—but

Master Ahasver was sitting not far from Laurent, chatting with him gaily.

Samuel had questioned Ezra about that; the latter had told him: "Asverus is a sage; it's because he is a sage that he keeps company with fools of that sort, who are only fools for some, and seem perfectly reasonable to the majority of people. They know that life is short; we know that it is not—but we are both right, and logical, according to our point of departure."

In Samuel's eyes, the city was oscillating with the scarlet rumor of fires of joy. In every back-street, light sprang from open doors, illuminated windows and lanterns perched on strong beams, producing a whole strip of artificial daylight with rare shadowy corners. Only the points of the roofs reached the night. Around fountains of wine and beer, in the vicinity straw-padded clowns, eyes raised toward scintillating acrobats, the crowds laughed at their ease. Outside taverns decorated with green branches they delighted in storyteller's tales, soldiers' bluster, the charades of wits and the merry clucking of singers.

A physical wellbeing and material ease fanned the imaginations of the host. Everyone was cheerful and happy. Next to men whose eyes were closing slightly with fatigue and good cheer, women walked slowly, in groups, with a slightly shrill gaiety, dissolving into excessive laughter beneath their calm, enervated and expectant expressions, as if they were still only watching the prologue of the Comedy. The simplest beggars lit up an entire crossroads with joy. In the large squares, chains of dancers of both sexes swirled around, and in the delightful and fertile cool of the evening and the earth, embalmed serenity departed from the plain, the river and gardens to drift over the city.

Weary, Samuel had headed for a garden beside the river, planted with old chestnut trees, in order to shelter his solitary sadness from all that tinkling pleasure. He leaned on the wall; a few bright-lit boats were already drawing away toward the villages. The wind, messenger of the bright folly in the distance, brought him bursts of musical notes; then only the sounds of the water and the foliage lapped within his melancholy.

Black clouds gathered together to immure the stars; on the quay that bordered the other side of the river the smoky ruddy light of torches picked out running pink fauns. A flash of lightning sprang from a cloud, splitting the black curtain, and the city appeared to him as a dismal series of white cubes.

In the triple flash of another lightning-strike he perceived a chariot of violence launched into an avenue of tombs.

The distant scraps of music, the stars that allowed themselves to fall into the immense net of shadow, the sparks of torches that extended along the quay to fade away in the city, the bright squares of light in the houses that closed one by one like drowsy eyes, the still-distant rumbling of thunder and the dull din of the distant agitation, placed themselves within his mind at the extreme limit of the apprehension of misfortune. Under the whiplash of the lightning he saw the entire city again, and its towers and domes, and then the pale furnace of its lights—and it was a colossal and multiple hypogea, in which people were still stirring before the ultimate sleep.

Under the whiplash of the lightning, it was a city beside a river descending to the sea, its hands abandoning the lives of men and cargoes to the sinuous banks: warehouses without end, the good news contained descending slowly toward the loading-docks, the perspectives of harbors and havens, toward the islands and continents beyond the sea, toward other huddled phantoms welcoming the haste of the specters from here, conversing with them, inanely, about trivia, exchanging their insipid chimeras.

It was a cage in which a thousand fireflies were buzzing around the torches in whose gold they were doomed to die, bringing their bodies of snow and sackcloth and their blazing eyes—dots as brilliant as the fire, but which could not see the fire—to the cage whose form modeled all the flights of Ephemerae; and those which did not perish entirely in the flame crawled on the ground, or ended up on the viscous bank.

And the insufficient warning-light of the Moon fled into the clouds, as if masked, a mediocre adviser or a witness to everything, forever pale—and with what fatigue, or what ennui, if it has only to wander over the same cakes of wax, so regularly honeycombed, with the same passion, the same tedium, the same destiny, in the depths of all those little gulfs?

The stormy Night appeared to him, over the pale city, like a threat, and the minutes charged with malaise passed over his tense nerves.

"O City," he thought, "where a few sounds of harps have sown necklaces of blonde pearls, in exiling themselves to infinity, City where beautiful faces have gazed at the Wanderer, which is forever renewed and marches on, from their windows garlanded with emblems of hope, you can offer a man a crystal cup and draw from your cellars the wine of love and duration, but you hold nothing in your hands but a copper plate covered with coarse aliments.

"O City, your hands ought to be those of a beautiful and robust woman scarcely entered into her prime, and the savor of your aspect would make the thin soup that your present to the guest pleasant—but your hands are stiff and wrinkled, those of an old woman, harassed and plastered.

"City, your sons ought to be densely gathered around you, attentive in the evening to music and strength, smiling and moved by the beauty and truth they are able to perceive—but you have no sons any longer; you have only guests, and when you open your threshold to them, it is in a banal whitewashed chamber, without effigies on the walls, without palms at the doors, without beauty in the lamp, that you direct them to an empty corner ,and a cloak with which to warp themselves and await the dream.

"And the dream, in your home, which could descend in a light veil of perfume and grace from the crowns of cedars, to refresh with the broad waters of pure springs, comes to our sleep timid and dwarfed, as if emerging painfully from a gray cell in which a spider extends interminable webs.

"When you sing, it is not with the large and free voice of someone summarizing your land, your sky and your temples; you repeat old counsels and judgments. You do not walk in the great foliage of a park; you sit down and crouch in the depths of a meager garden, near a shallow well in which you sometimes see your image—you and a few branches of the petty tree that shades it—and your guest becomes breathless and chokes between your bushy borders, if he is a poet, if he is the messenger for whom you seem to be waiting.

"When he is close to you, you raise your eyes to the Heavens and you wait…in an irritating silence you pretend to be unaware of his presence and the fact that his hands are extended toward the folds of your dress, and you interrogate the luminous and empty sky with the blue vacuity of your pupils—and if he persists, if his cry has been loud enough, piercing enough, violent enough to disturb the slothful harmony of your vague reverie, you call the priests and the doctors, those whom you adorn with the heavy embroideries of your winter nights, and ask them whether a new truth is shining, and what has been discovered beneath the peristyles of the palace of the stars.

"It is your bleak science to interrogate the truth when the guest has summoned it, when the guest so soon misunderstood arrives charged with nothing but wonder for beauty, and your balances have judged him insufficient. When he turns away, dolorously, when he has departed once again by hard pathways into your plain, you reopen the gymnasia in which our learned men trace equal squares in the sand, in order to ask where beauty is.

"I know full well that large kitchens extend behind that gray house, and that huge quarters of meat are roasting over the enormous forces that you can light, and the glory of your skill as a housekeeper and farmer's wife, storing enormous amounts of grain; I know that—and also your harvesters' dances, and the brim-full glasses that your cooks drink; and every evening, after the crimson mantle of the Sun has unraveled, you dream momentarily, and from your balustrades you follow with a little sadness the dull vintagers of light disappearing over the horizon.

"Melancholy! Melancholy! Vain custom, vain habit! When you lean on your elbows and wait, if nothing that moves you is profiled on the black screen of night, you know that nothing will arrive, and that is what your serene majesty of expectations contrives. No light comes in the night, nothing rises at dusk, nothing can match your moment, O queen of futile and servile fatigue.

"And if you are genuinely pleased by the jewels of the evening, the mobile pink pools that it paints on the glass rooftops of your pavilions, do you not have at that very moment the certainty that you will not fail to forget them before the last glow-worm expires? And you go up to your terraces, with the confident and dignified gesture of someone who can look without being smitten, and you are already thinking about being firm and grave and robust in the dawn, an active overseers of labors in which you take pride, to make sure that all the debris of butterflies come from who knows where to your veridical, fateful and destructive torch is swept away.

"If the servants show you a body in the current of the river that washes the dependencies of your great gray house, which is descending slowly among the clumps of grass, you will not recognize the guest of yesterday, the man who spoke to you about beauty, and whom you did not want to hear."

Samuel's sadness was eased by the accuracy of his thoughts. He was alone in the empty place, under the old somber chestnut-trees, beside the murmur of the water, whose tenuousness is associated for humans with the idea of gentleness, before the city that had been brutally sonorous a little while before, but was now unfastening its necklaces of light with weary fingers.

The tiaras and lofty diadems of the city, its towers and its domes, were gradually attained by the devouring shadow, and

191

the lamps that were going out, having flickered, were being touched one by one by a finger of ash.

The sadness of terminated festivals is like an unexpected solitude and an ineluctable destruction. That ascendant shadow increased the opaque horizons of the young man's soul, already so sad, and his sadness became dolor—perhaps mistakenly, for every festival comes to an end; none is ever a festival of happiness, and today's dolor was no more acute, and ought not to have been any more profound, than yesterday's because he was alone, because it was the palace he had chosen as the threshold that he wanted to cross. But what did that matter? Is not a man who is dying by virtue of his own fault suffering as much as one struck down by destiny, in the logical and habitual course of affairs? All agony remains agony.

Samuel became weary of the bland silence and went back toward the city. The quays were still enlivened by cordial farewells; at ground level the sights of shining taverns and the sound of tankards and voices rang out; dark back-streets were languishing. In the smaller squares, like reddening embers of the fête, there were joyous encounters under the branches, murmured songs and words of love as people gradually got a grip on themselves after the noise and general merriment, and tardy children picked up crowns from the ground.

The acridity of Samuel's dolor increased. Did all those contended people, all those wheedling women, not understand that tomorrow, hard labor would again unroll its oily waves? Had all of them accepted servitude and the imprisonment of their dreams in exchange for one day of merriment? The laborer would take up the plough in the same place; the weavers would recommence the squirrel-play of the shuttle in their cellars, their sad uninterrupted song repeating like the threads of their fabric:

The days are woven with black and white threads.
The shuttle of time mingles them indifferently.

All of them would be marching to their sentry-boxes, their shops, their palaces, to their courtyards and workshops, with the same mechanical step, to the same refrain, very nearly, as the night-watchman who announces the inevitable march of the hours.

As for Samuel, it was as if a distant beacon-light in his life, until then sufficient, had gone out; as if a cord of love, a solid fiber of his being, had broken inside him.

"Oh, City, sleep monotonously in your network of ennui: I shall be like you, sad and grave, and go mad for one day of the year. I shall be like you, monotonous and bored; the shuttle of my life will bound like a squirrel in a low, closed room, and if I should see a ray of sunlight filtering through the ventilation shaft, I shall cry, like them: 'Oh! The enormous disk that warms me and burns me!' And if some child should throw a poor dandelion flower down the ventilation shaft, I shall cry: Greetings Sun, the color of God; greetings, color of gold, reflection of the solar fire; greetings, perfumed gardens, circuses of flowers, festive mountains, delight of all ringing bells! Ha ha!'"

And he laughed, somewhat dolorously.

A shrill fanfare of fifes, lively Basque drums and little bells rang out; a procession emerged, and there, amid the dancing clowns and madly singing girls, solid and enormous in his one-day scarlet, was that hearty fellow, the gay Prince of the People, red and breathless from singing and shouting, with a mallet in his hand. Samuel could not avoid them, and amid the laughter, a beautiful girl shouted: "Here's the Prince of Lovers, all alone!"

And laughter bust forth—not hostile, but drunken.

"It is, Seigneur," a buffoon cried, "a grave infraction of our laws for the Prince of Lovers to be encountered, at the Festival of May, so solitary, brooding like a catafalque, and so poorly lit by the reflections of good wine."

A beautiful girl came toward him. "O timid Prince of Lovers, you have missed all your rendezvous with the joys of this evening..."

"That's true," said others. "We've lost sight of you..."

"Poets seek pools of shadow in brought daylight, and the Sun by night," said the other.

"Truce! Peace, even!" cried Laurent. "Our two majesties will drink together; at the hour of our eclipse, let us be united, so that out two natures might stumble into obscurity together. Come to my palace, Seigneur Samuel, which will soon be full of cups, jokes, and all these beauties."

"Thank you, Seigneur, but I'm tired and want to go home."

"At least, Seigneur, you'll do us justice here; here's my majesty's tankard, borne by my trusty follower." And a man approached, carrying a tankard and a cup.

"Thank you, Seigneur," Samuel relied, firmly, "but I won't drink and I won't go with you—I'm tired."

"It's just come back to me," cried Laurent, "that you're an acrimonious seigneur, discontented that the world is not in step with you. The mildest of men would be offended this evening by your dark expression around my pardonable and legitimate gaiety. That might cause grief between us, but if it pleases you, let's drown the dispute, so that we'll have forgotten it tomorrow."

"Neither promises of pleasure nor threats can prevent me from retiring, Seigneur."

"You'll doubtless find yourself in worse company; my buffoons are certainly worth as much as your reciter of familiar nonsense."

"That's enough, Seigneur."

"I think so too—we'll see one another again tomorrow."

"Now! Now!" cried a female voice. "Now—and we'll laugh afterwards!"

"I have no desire to laugh, I assure you," said Samuel. "Let me be."

A buffoon had taken Laurent aside to calm him down, and everyone had started to dance around Samuel, laughing and singing, when Samuel, addressing Laurent, cried: "Messire, it's insolent and cowardly to make a fool of me by means of your valets, instead of drawing your sword..."

And Laurent came forward, sword in hand.

Their combat frightened the women, who began screaming. Their blades clashed, and their animosity increased at the unexpected contact of the weapons. Anger mounted within them. Undoubtedly, they were obscurely aware of their fatal enmity, of the latent hatred between the poor poet, reflective, all mind and passion, and the agile adventurer, all nerve, movement, ambition and egotism. It was no longer the hostility of two men, one of whom had been greeted more kindly by a princess admired by both; they were no longer merely rivals of a day, but enemies of all time, the man of intellect and the man of action—and their swords clashed.

Loud noises brought people running, and before they were able to wound one another grievously, the men-at-arms of the watch had surrounded them and taken them prisoner.

The officer of the watch, embarrassed because of the importance—at least for the day—of the two captives, took them to the palace, in order to refer the matter to the emperor. They were each locked in a room. A short time afterwards, men came into Samuel's room, put him in chains and blindfolded him.

He was not able to see again until he was in his cell.

A loud noise of chains and the cry of a slaughtered animal tore Samuel from his reverie. An atrocious, inarticulate clamor had just terrified him.

"People are killed here, then," he murmured. "So be it—but why?"

Footsteps were heard, jailers opened his door, set down a ladle and a pitcher in a corner without saying a word, and went out again.

"It's not just for today, at any rate," he said to himself, "But where am I, then? In what singular prison, so dismal and tragic?"

Chapter Four
THE COURTYARD

A jailer shoved Samuel into a large courtyard and said to him: "You can go until someone calls you back. You're in the open air and good company here."

The latter hesitated momentarily before the meager sunlight; his legs, only just released from their chains, were unsteady. Then he went forward, slowly and confusedly. A few ragged individuals with overly large eyes considered him. Samuel went to a bench and sat down.

The fresh air, even parsimoniously poured between high grey walls, dilated his lungs. A man sidled over, and said: "One and one make two, and two makes four, and four makes eight, and eight makes sixteen, and sixteen makes thirty-two. Ha!" Then he sat down. "Tending my meager vines near the seashore, I earned ten ducats. I put fifteen years into it; I was a serf; I needed strong vine-stocks, energetic vine-stocks, patient vine-stocks, heaped up like this—even higher than this—to glean ten ducats. They came in helmets, armor and strong boots and took everything, you know. One day, I released Silenus, who had been beaten with a beanpole; he blessed my efforts, and for nearly a century, my ducats grew like beautiful trees; here's my accounts, you see"—he took out some sheets of paper—"you see, I'm going to buy the Empire. I'm waiting for the right moment, when that door opens. You look like a good man—you can be the seneschal. Would you like that? Would you? You look tired; I'll buy you a horse."

He got up and tiptoed away, turning round and making urgent signals.

Another man approached. "Seigneur, that merchant has doubtless wearied you; he abounds in strange words; one is obliged to shut him up. I'm locked up myself, though: Fritt, divine counselor. I'm the pupil of the famous Syracusan Megacles, who has discovered that the Sun is an enormous animal, a sort of chameleon, but with wings of a membranous sort, like those of a bat. It flies perpetually above our heads; the Sun is its only eye; the Moon is the same eye, whose light we perceive attenuated by its lowered eyelid. But here's my enemy..."

And with a piercing voice and an ardent eye, a little man bounded toward him.

"Is the world still sand, and more sand, with brambles and lizards? Where do you come from, stranger? From far away? Then you've seen the sand, yet more sand, accumulate; worlds appear and disappear; the wind models them during the night; the Earth is never the same two dawns running; but every day, as perhaps you know, the old demon Habitude, our enemy, works to bring it back to a conventional form. Oh, how beautiful and varied the world would be, if the demon Habitude no longer existed!

"Listen, but don't say anything. They hope to capture him and chain him up here; perhaps it will take thousands of years, and I'll be very old, very old, when he comes. He'll be so big that we'll all be relegated to the attics; we'll only be able to see the Enemy cast down and chained through narrow windows, like cracks, and perhaps I'll be blind. Oh, what misfortune, what misfortune!"

And he bellowed in anguish.

A young man was hopping frantically around the courtyard; he passed by swiftly, hurriedly, murmuring: "Throw men-at-arms at me, pikemen; march, march...victory!"

An old man, weeping with laughter, imitated him ineptly. He addressed himself to Samuel: "There goes Alexander of Macedon and Caesar the Roman. He has wings on his feet, he runs after his shadow."

But the pupil of Megacles chased him away, uttering squeals.

"That old man," he said, "has been a swineherd; he annoys everyone with the bestial odor he retains about him; he was put here for annoying everyone. He's a coarse emanation of the universe; he was introduced here as a measure of persecution, to disturb our serene discussions—but permit me to leave you. I have to meditate."

Samuel got up and started walking. He understood. Prison would have been less harsh than this madhouse. But why this vengeance, and who could have anything to avenge upon him?

A voice sang:

From the distant tower,
one can see the sea, the ship, the devil
and the girl combing her long hair.
To the distant tower
the evil king has exiled me
because my timid confession
reached the ears of the queen.
Destiny overwhelms me,
they have put me in chains.
One can see the sea, the ship, the devil.

The priest of Saint Martin
has exorcised this morning
the girl who combs her long hair
in the window of the distant tower
and the soldiers with hollow bellies
have killed and eaten everything.
The beech that sang has been split
and the leaves have been dispersed.
One can see the sea, the ship, the devil.

My poor soul is sorely wounded,
crows laugh, for it is all white
in its skipping gentleness;
from the distant tower
one can see fields of snow,
fields of foam, fields of sand,
and here is my procession,
my great pain with lowered eyes.

From the distant tower
one can see the sea, the ship, the devil.

It was a pale young man who was singing. Next to him, another young man was weeping and repeating; "Here, to fill the pool of my distress, are tears, more tears; they're as red as my blood. Oh, when will she return? Oh, when will she return? I'm already nearly blind. I'll never see her again."

Another prisoner, powerfully-built, approached Samuel. "Is that you, traitor?"

"What? What do you want?"

"I recognize you, although never having seen you; today you are the man who marches in my shadow."

"Eh? Certainly not."

"Yes, every day the evil one creates a new enemy; no one would dare to touch my brain; they know the world is born there; it would be too dangerous to try to touch it; I carry it safely in this left hand, and the right is here to defend it; but since they have discovered that the ideas develop and ripen by passing through the shadow that is our simplified portrait, the portrait of our soul awaiting the man we built of ourselves and within us, they train the executioner's servants to chase our shadow and intercept the progress of truths—but I take hold of them, and you shall not escape me."

He was already raising his right hand when howling burst forth. Two captives had hurled themselves at one another and were rolling on the ground, bloodied and foaming at the mouth. The guards arrived, armed with whips, and struck the unfortunates. Beneath their blows, amid loud fearful squealing, the courtyard emptied, and the prisoners were taken back to their cells.

Samuel threw himself on his pallet, irritated, mortally sad and bloody—for he had been struck, and had defended himself.

THE VISIONS

He begged that he not be taken out again. Fever ate away at him, and he was no longer able to touch the coarse prison food. He waited, lying down, for some miracle no less unexpected and bizarre than his imprisonment to render him respirable life—and in his oppressed mind, the strange and perverse enchantment of vision, consolatory and tyrannical, unfurled its long ribbons of anguish or fury...

There was a short paunchy old man, trotting along, mumbling and whispering. He ran along and immense terrace, raising his hands to the Heavens.

"Eternal, Eternal," he cried, "when shall I see anything new under your Sun? Always the waves and always the wind, and the umbels of plants, which open and close in your hands, dewy in the morning, igneous at midday, bloody in the evening, black by night, as with some fatiguing and filthy work.

"Eternal, you have made me, I am your fault, your very great fault. Why, with colossal tortoises, immense plants, long serpents that sleep after swallowing prey, and spiteful dragons, and the beasts of the dens, the burrows and the mire, did you create a being with consciousness? Why did you set him upright, on two legs? Was it to let him know that one cannot look your solar palaces in the face?

"Eternal, Eternal, what did you want from us when you woke us up in the mute chain of dreams? We stood up, our hands feeling that they were tearing themselves from an embrace; we had neighbors, whom you had allowed to sleep. What were they? Why did you choose us, mosses marching on the Earth, and nourish us with sap, if we were to be ignorant, if we were to turn on one another, suffering for suffering, forgetting nothing and knowing nothing?

"Behold your son, too, at the foot of this wall, scraping his ulcers with a potsherd, and asking himself why he is this pestilent dot in your avenues of indifference. Behold your son, his limbs rent upon a cross, and why that dot of agony in the avenues of your indifference? Behold your son, torn apart by furious women, and why that pale head rolled by the rivers of your indifference?[19]

"Why are the great pyres of the mountains replying, and the herdsmen there flinging oaks, saying: 'we are waiting for the new,' and the priests in the sanctuaries saying: 'so they say.' I am old, I am tired; why have you given me, in this weary and ugly body in the form of a calabash, in this body adherent to the rugose Earth, this unknown desire, this desire to see your face other than veiled by the archangel's blade? Or at least, if you are only the elastic and deceptive fire before the real face, to which worlds want to weep, why has Job not finished suffering…?"

"Man, the hair-shirt is on my back. You're heavy and turn around and around, and complain of not knowing how to get out of yourself. Me, I'm strewn at crossroads with torture-victims on the cross. In traveling, I plough the infinite route of miseries. The man will never come who will break the padlock of dolor and undo the seals of the shackles compressing our limbs. The horse Aquilon[20] leaps from North to South, and from East to West without finding anything but women wringing their hands beside bruised and careworn men, who remain seated in order to make them stand up! They lied, the voices of the annunciation, or it's an ancient dotard's dream transmitted to us by our ancestors..."

And in the Heavens, the Eternal, hearing these plaints, said to Azrael: "We have to do something."

Azrael's great wings darkened the air; his lance touched the two old men who were complaining; his palms seized their fluttering souls, and from the two spirits of discontent he fashioned a single soul. It was habituated both to wealth and poverty, to desire and contrition, to power and misfortune. It

---

[19] Presumably a reference to Orpheus.
[20] The classical god of the north wind, sometimes imagined to be riding a horse of thunder.

had already groaned a great deal; the décor of palaces and visions of the desert were already painted therein in violent strokes; it had already grown old in pleasure and suffering.

Azrael's wings beat and rose up. His broad wings brought momentary night to the noble palaces of Sion; beasts bellowed as if a storm were approaching; a heavy sleep invaded the grand palace. Azrael passed overhead; the little prince Solomon was asleep. Azrael touched him with his lance and collected his soul; he kneaded it with the one he was carrying and woke the little prince, who gazed at the enormous figure, the enormous wings, and especially the soft and calm eyes, like a beautiful harbor full of ships at rest at the approach of dusk, with which the angel bathed him.

"Who are you?" asked the child. "I seem to remember icy spaces."

"You have not budged from here; I am the oldest of your brothers; you shall see me again." And he put the child to sleep again by caressing him with one hand.

"You now have all of the human soul," he said, "the impatience and the ennui, and the unquiet desire to extract from his own clay a statue of the unknown man, of the man who slips through crowds, and the profound grief and bitterness of the most ancient sufferer, the man who has not been spared any thorn—and also your infant candor, and all of your future strength. You shall hurl yourself at all objectives; you shall burn, that the statue sculpted in your soul will shine with divine fire on the vastest platform and the highest mountain, and you shall have the strength to desire little—but all the glories and pleasures will doubtless have, for you, the bitter taste of ashes, for your new soul is already old, and no power can create an entirely innocent soul."

Azrael's flight carried him away into limitless deserts. He soared like an immense eagle. In the sandy immensity, scarcely studded with a few hillocks, he touched a large stone slab with his lance. "Eve, Hagar, Mobed!" he exclaimed. "Get up—the messenger is here."

The stone slab rose up, and a tall form freed itself from the folds of a shroud. "Here I am! It's really you! Am I not safe here?"

And the angel said: "It is necessary for you to return to Earth once more; you must bring about the rebirth of the Eden that you have carried for so long in your hollow eyes; your lips shall smile, your supple hips shall sway over the world; you shall recreate the great perfumes of voluptuousness. The Creator has need of you. Come—you shall be called Balkis."

The tall form had emerged from the tomb where she had been asleep for Centuries.

"You are no longer the mother; you are becoming the woman again."

And the long grey hair fell away, and the severe and angular lines of the body softened, and Eve reappeared in her candor of the world's first day. The angel carried her to the terraces of an immense temple; at the impact of his lance the priests came running and veiled their eyes with their hands.

"Here is your queen," said Azrael." And the priests led her away to crown her and announce to the people of Sheba that the prophetess was revealed.

Near the temple, a palace abruptly rose up, as if it had been there all the time and the sudden dissipation of a fog had suddenly revealed it to the gaze, in response to the smile of Balkis; palm-trees sprang from the ground and crowned themselves with their acclamatory palms; Balkis' fingers touched bushes, and there was a forest of rose-bushes praising all the violent, dominating or hidden nuances of flesh; a smile passed over her lips and the whiteness of her teeth appeared, and that was the signal for an immense florescence of lilies; and the Sun came to light the flesh of her cheeks and a population of gilded flowers appeared in the corners of the garden.

She walked, and the springs murmured; she ran over transparent beds of white marble in order that an agile mirror might exist in consequence. She raised a branch to her lips and heavy ripe pomegranates were born, and vines extended, clusters of red and white grapes swelling in order to be sweet to her lips; she picked up a pebble and enormous gems gleamed between her fingers, and outside the gates of the great marvelous garden, the priests massed guards with golden shields; she sang, and a thousand birds replied, and a thousand birds arrived from every corner of the sky, and cherubim descended from the Heavens to bring her veils and robes in the purest colors of the clouds.

She threw a great saffron-colored veil around herself and went back up the steps of the palace, and on all the terraces of the city people gathered to acclaim Eternal beauty.

In the evening, the stars trembled on the lake; a perfect sweetness emanated from the drowsy languor of flowers. Souls in repose learned down from the Heavens to watch the valleys of Sheba fill with violet light, brighter than the night, softer than the day. Lunar gleams silvered the fronds and extended a candid ribbon of slightly roseate snow over the palace. Large swans cleaved the waves beside boats. One perfumed boat carried the queen's repose over the lake, and on the colonnades that bathed in the calm water, choirs of men and women with voices of delight responded. One might have thought the white cadences of a dance were visible in the sky.

It seemed to Samuel that he heard his own voice resonating among the choirs.

CHOIR

O purity,
your softness spreads in infinite candors
over the bosom of the Earth. She awaits your kiss;
the Earth has been dreaming all day
and labors have split her with their nourishing plowshares
and her forehead is furrowed with wrinkles.
She dreamed that in arid lands
her children were suffering and cursing.
O purity, in your white smile you appeared

and you pass your dewy fingers over your weary forehead
O purity.

OTHER CHOIR

Behold, with the evening, the blessed herb is sprouting,
O dream, transport me, all day long I have toiled
against the agile smoke in which my soul hangs
and instants were flowing that I could not collect
and like the spark, living and flying away;
O dream transport me, that I might become
between your fingers of the dawn;
shall I see your heavy golden gates open
on countries where I awoke
before, or will the wicker cradle
of yesteryear, render me my soul
in order that I may listen?
O dream, your palm and your solace,
blessed herb of dream I want to respire.

CHOIR

Her smile awakes in the roses
of hope, and emerald is her palace,
her lips the calyx that sprinkles
the honeyed water of Heaven and the milk of stars;
one reads in the book of her life
her eternal footsteps among the forests of stars.
She lives. I forget the customary disaster
of the hours of the enchained Earth:
O to nestle in the immense tresses
that fall in rays of immaterial purity
from the Empyrean to the crowns of these forests
and sleep in the perfume that endures
in the flower-baskets of her beauty.

OTHER CHOIR

Seek among the lilies, seek among the dawns,
behold the towers spraying forth fires of hope
as beautiful as crowns, and calm.
The sea polishes her own immense mirror.
Behold the galleys returning from afar,
behold the old pilots leaping on to jetties,
the Astarte of the prow laughs at the sea
as calm as a green-tinted mirror;
one sees large spongy plants afloat,
and little narwhals playing around the galleys.

CHOIR

We raise to our lips the eternal cups,
the cups of yore, the cups of forever,
the great birds of the dusk bring us lilies
plucked from the lakes of Eden, the isles of delight
that the Lord's right still hides from our eyes,
but already our souls are equipped,
the oars of our senses star the first wave
and the younger Sun will spring from the clouds,
there, on the horizon, the benevolent mirages
that deploy great beds in which golden dreams sleep,
the trees of youth spread voices of shade
beneath the clouds of all the saps of the Earth
and amid the flight of clouds with white wings
love laughs, love waits, love is strong!

OTHER CHOIR

The hymn of your servants, the hymn of your slaves,
O queen, among the fresh nocturnal mists
fly toward your grace; listen, O queen,
to those who break the silence and enchant the Earth
and the voice to feeble to declare your beauty

the pale voices, the vanquished voices, will fall silent
so the instruments may tell how Nature
throws at your victorious feet her flowers and crowns,
all her perfumes and her beauty, which she gives to you.

And a benevolent calm spread through Samuel's feverish sleep. It seemed to him that years had passed, that a wall of grey cloud covered the horizon, and that he was marching in constant shadow. He sensed himself marching, but he could not see anything, and the shadow was both hot and heavy.

Finally, the clouds parted.

In a high-ceilinged hall—so high that the cupola becomes uncertain in the smoky torchlight, King Solomon seems to be meditating next to a bed of rest on which a corpse is lying. The rigidity of the final sleep is weighing upon that form, and the king is dreaming aloud:

"Bathsheba, mother, they are closed, those eyes which conquered the kingdom, cold, those hands which, posed upon my father's arm, calmed the lions of his wrath. You can no longer move that finger, which a little while ago, raised to our lips, commanded a silence in which you could have heard the sound of a thought. A reaping-hook has passed, and the stubble of your life is scattered—your will and your regrets, and the soft inflection of your voice. And if you are undertaking your last dream, if, nearby, your spirit is contemplating that which was your matrix, what do you love now? Where are you going, if you still exist? But if your immobility maintains your entirety, what good was your life? If the same cold will soon invade me, what good is my life?

"I have seen her eyes die like an opal. What use to you now is your life's past? I know its story, and that Uriah died for the excessively beautiful jewel that he possessed.[21] That was your goal. The serene and tragic beauty in which the glorious Sun slept that King David glimpsed on the terrace and the distant forests has become like the vertical carpet on which

---

[21] cf II *Samuel* 11.

your body lies, unable to belong to anyone but the King. How much, disdainful of an obscure rank and blushing at an unmerited birth, you desired to mount the steps of the throne—which doubtless gave you the destiny marked out in your regal stride. At any rate, good or bad, you had a goal: the crown; and afterwards, the same objective continued in me.

"And my father, who was the conqueror and the proscribed, who departed from his own father's field rich in ambition and valor—I understand his relentless struggle, and his dolorous but love-strewn wanderings. The eyes of heroines were drawn to his vigorous arm. Victory led him to this palace, to your beauty. After the exiles and the pain, he had the softest pillow. The hard Earth in the solitude of companions-in-arms had told him of its divine luxury. To be the greatest was his goal; and then that was to continue in me—to continue, and also to be perpetuated. A challenge! What is perpetual beneath these mute skies, save perhaps for the appearance of the river in which all lives are renewed at every instant, and the high mountains, the dense cadavers of fire.

"How weary I am already of omnipotence! Where shall I send armies that I take no joy in guiding? Something akin to the slow lassitude of advanced age is already filing my limbs, and my strength, whose surge no desire commands, is no use to me. I was born on the calm summit, to which one can no longer ascend, and at the top of the citadel that anterior foresights had built for me, in the midst of archers they had gathered; I live monotonously and the royal headband almost weighs upon me, even though I cannot envisage without terror a life in which I would be stripped of it—not because of the lost power, but because of the terror of rubbing shoulders with the crowd, whose members will then become aware of how different I am from them, a lazy and sedentary traveler on a road on which everyone is running and hastening. I believe that I was born with an old soul, a soul from the earliest days of the world, and I regret Eden because it was empty, and I shall never love an oasis hidden in a desert without travelers.

"Bathsheba, mother, what will you leave behind you? If, as I believe, the soul dies at the same instant that the organs cease to be its servants, if it is extinguished like a lamp in the wind, what will remain of so much beauty? A memory…smoke. And what, then, will remain of Solomon? A name among names, a stele among steles, a rumor that the pedant will evoke momentarily among other rumors, when he opens the slender casket of human memory. The wine of life is heavy and the cup is crude…"

Abruptly, Samuel saw Solomon again.

He is seated, upper body upright, on a golden throne. Among the thick and regular curls of his hair and his black beard, his face is immobile and his eyes are staring. The calm stasis of autumnal things is imprinted in his dull splendor. His precious robe is embroidered with red roses and pomegranate flowers, the emblems of his opulent power. His white hands are motionless on his knees. With him are the high officials and the sages, the golden breastplates and the white linen robes, the white tiara of a black-skinned magician next to the ephod of a priest, and draped in their white burnooses, bending their knees before him, the Ishmaelite ambassadors.

Coiffed in gilded miters, clad in long red robes, leaning on long scepters, the Tyrians wait for the sovereign to deign to address himself to them, and afterwards for the royal ear to listen; and that immobile mask will see the dwellers on the banks of the Euphrates, the horsemen with legs bound by leather laces ornamented with metal fasteners, who are begging for the shelter of the reflection of his law.

Soon, when the affairs of state are terminated, difficult disputes between his subjects will be submitted to the king's arbitration, for the king sometimes comes to life in the study of various and somber souls. He is just, for passion has never disturbed his clear vision; he is clement, for his indifference is profound.

When the king listens, words are reflected in his mind like an image in water devoid of any other ripple. When he speaks, his voice is distant, and yet as strong as the wind that comes from the Liban and has wearied itself running over the expanse...

The grey mist comes to invade Samuel's eyes, and suddenly there is an expanse of gold; there is a silvery Sun at ground level; bubbles of ardent metal race over the tips of the grass and the reeds; there is a blue canopy of triumphal light; there is, in an ardent midday, an unlimited light brown splendor that extends without limit to a horizon of blue mountains: the plain near Jordan.

And the Queen of Sheba's cortege of surged forth in a blaze of scarlet, perfect whiteness and streams of amber and gold.

Her face was an admirable April; a golden thread lost itself in her black hair, and gemstones emerged like multicolored birds among leaves. A profound and innocent generosity emanated from her large dark eyes. Her white, polished, elevated forehead was the peristyle of a temple. A pale melancholy was resident in the line of her face, and the slightly large mouth that presaged gentle speech. She smiled, the ardent gleam filtering at first light.

She came forward upright, guiding the white horses with the fine manes like spun silver herself; her chariot of odorant wood, embellished with gilded plaques, skimmed the ground. A young slave by her side held a large long-handled fan of white plumes, and all around her the great horsemen of the desert made the most spirited horses prance, and after them came the equivalent of an entire army encampment, packed up on camels swaying their long necks and on laden mules, with people on foot accompanying the beasts of burden.

And on the parvis of the great palace, Solomon waited for the beautiful and wise Queen.

The palace resounds with noises of celebration, and the splendid halls are like enamel plates that pleasure holds up to the sky. The king and the queen are alone on a large terrace that winds around the palace. From one of its extremities they can see all the rejoicing in the city; every street is a torch, every courtyard a lake of light, and instruments color the soul of the city. Its smoke is incense. At the other extremity, the terrace overlooks the gardens. And between the halls of joy, dazzling topazes of life, and that profound and seductive density of darkness and repose, they talk.

"Queen Balkis, you have come to remove with your fingers of splendor a kind of mantle of darkness that enveloped me, and through my tunic I can see my heart. It seems to me that I am beginning to be born. On how many evenings like this one I have questioned the silence and expectation of the Earth. They sent me back nothing but indecisive gleams, troubled images and perfumes, reflections of fugitive illusions, an all those signs signified the slight, the undulating and the ephemeral. You come, and your bountiful fingers touch my forehead, and it is circled by a tranquil crown of certainty. This is the first moment to which I would like to say: Stop!"

"Why, King Solomon? Why has the voyager, if you are telling the truth, already built her wing in your palace? Do you not fear that it is only the unexpectedness of my arrival as your guest might be dazzling you? Are you not embellishing my face with all the attractions of hazard?"

"What a hazard it was that brought you, beauty of all beauties, as wise as temples, from the distant depths of your country. Yesterday or tomorrow, hazard might perhaps have evoked in you the desire to meet me, but could hazard direct your march toward the moment when the tents of my desire were ready and waiting? For you, my thoughts have returned from exile. The agile servants of my sensuality are filling the jars and the foundation that will quench or thirst; my patience is recalling from afar the marvelous flowers embroidered on these carpets. My memory is effacing all its engraved stones, purifying itself and preparing itself for the most beautiful of effigies. The singing moments that were familiar to me are disposing attenuated lanterns, whose light ought only to be rivaled by the milky gleam of the pearl that will soon be knotted in our blaze. But how beautiful and tall you are, and how proud and enamored your peoples must be! Captives and slaves undoubtedly serve them, and their entire lives flow in happy meditation that rises toward you envelops you with innumerable individual gazes."

"No," said the Queen, laughing. "But I have not come for you to admire my beauty; I have come to understand your wisdom."

"Do not call Wisdom that which was, until you, the disguise of my soul, and which I believed to be—how foolish and ignorant pretended sages are!—my very essence. My erstwhile wisdom? The Heavens are empty, no one holds the sword of justice, generosity is merely the cool of the evening. Beauty is the reflection of ourselves made sublime, having embellished us, which we seek in all the fragile impetuosity and debility of our knowledge—but what does it matter? Your beauty has dissolved my memory."

"King Solomon, I am as old as the world."

"What does it matter? I too have seen myself in the depths of dreams, as in the depths of dark cellars..."

"King Solomon, I am, in reality, as old as the world."

"Like the youth that has been flowing for so many thousands of years, then, and the dawn whose arms are always fresh, and the exquisite gentleness of favorable sleep."

"Would you love me, King Solomon, if you believed that I am as old as the world?"

"What, then, is the minute of duration that has vanquished Azrael?"

"Me," she said—and she seemed to the king to be enlarged and transfigured.

"Who are you?" he asked.

"All that is capable of fecundity, the mother of death, and all the grandeur of appearance, and all the flowers on the edge of oblivion."

"I shall pick you, then."

As if in the dazzling heart of a colossal lotus, with sat-colored petals blazing in the night, the two lovers lie down. The queen's long hair is loosened, and entwines around her lover's body, and everywhere the tresses rest, a kiss awakens. The triumphal lotus grows with their happiness and rises up into the depths of the sky, and the stars, like orbs of gold and ice and fiery wheels, form an escort for the slow ascent. The king's head rests on the queen's shoulder; lips parted, neck swollen, one might think him a placid child. She has absolute majesty in all the curves of her body; the amplitude of her gaze occupies the broad vaults of worlds; one might think that something new were about to be born in the endless lands of being, that a totality is about to spring forth and illuminate.

Balkis' voice softens again. "King Solomon, I fainted just now. Creature issued from the profound desires of humankind, you have embraced in your arms the very objective of its desires. The voluptuousness that I can give you, however, is so transient that you will only have the memory of it tomorrow, and within you, it will be like a beautiful idea that has germinated, and will arrive at the plenitude of its essence. And yet, I have ornamented your slumber for a long time. From this night on, the barges of memory will descend toward you, and today's happiness will be a cherished wound tomorrow. I have ornamented the empty depths of your horizon with an image—and since I am a phantom, no trace will remain of our embrace. From old souls, no power can create a new soul. Our embrace will remain sterile, but within you, at tender moments, springs will gush forth; you will lean over to listen to their sound; you will get up in order to repeat their music to others."

The vision retreated and faded away; it seemed to the dreamer that he was Solomon; that before him was the queen, no longer brilliant but afflicted, bathed by a calm beauty.

He saw once again the little house in the city, and Rizpah, who murmured: "Poor boy! Poor boy!"

A mirror reflected his face. Ah! It was certainly not that of King Solomon, but a pale and hollow face of dolor.

He opened his eyes again. There were familiar objects around him, and Rizpah, weeping, who wiped her eyes and took his hands.

Samuel fell back into a delirious sleep.

Chapter Five
THE SECRET

Trumpets had traveled through the city. They preceded a herald who announced the imminent betrothal of Princess Marie and the King of Scania, a valiant warrior returned with honors from the oriental wars, and that to mark the occasion, imperial munificence would stream through the city. In the meantime, amnesties were extended and the prisons opened—and that was how Samuel had been returned to his home, ill.

During that interval, the Emperor had also received, with ostentation, the envoys of the King of Hibernia. Among other matters, the latter had asked His Most Serene Highness if he would permit Laurent Télice, one of their master's subjects, to return with them; they hoped that the Emperor would put his supreme persuasion at the service of this desire, and, if necessary, a parcel of his strength. Without overmuch explanation, and making it known that Télice was not a criminal, but merely that his refusal to return to the lands of his king would assume the appearance of rebellion, the King, not wanting to unleash a bloody litigation—no threat intended, lest there be any misunderstanding—insisted in the name of the ancient alliance and a sequence of services mutually rendered between the two powers.

Consulted, Télice asked for a little more time to make preparations and to free himself from an obligation that he believed he had contracted with regard to the great welcome that the Emperor and the city had given him. He wanted the princess's betrothal to give him an opportunity to offer the city a perfect product of his art, and that the moment of happiness for the princess, before being acclaimed by bells and artillery, might chime from the frame of a marvelous clock that he wanted to offer to the palace of which the city was proud.

Anxiety about not wanting to appear to accept anything from a vassal, and also a slight disdain, led the Emperor to indicate that the cathedral seemed to him to be a more appropriate place, in order that everyone might enjoy the beautiful work of art, and Télice acquiesced, saying: "Then I shall fashion it differently."

For long days, his house was closed, as it had been before for brief periods. In the evenings, the windows were ardently ablaze. Only the merchants of precious materials were welcomed into the ground-floor rooms, and he sculptors and ornamentalists were not allowed to see the whole of the work in which there were participating. No curiosity-seeker or courier was able to get into the sealed house. A lateral wing of the cathedral, near the choir, was abandoned to Télice, and the pieces were secretly transported there. Before the celebration of any ceremony, however, the Emperor wanted to see for himself what Télice's labor had produced.

Against a polychromatic wall, red strewn with gilded passion-flowers, the somber body of the clock massed its precious woods and the gold of its polyphony. At the base lay an old man crowned with laurels with a long beard, as pagans had once been accustomed to represent venerable rivers. His urn was empty, and metal children pressed around him; the forms of branches and garland emerged from their hands, which climbed up the case made of black wood, over which beautiful reflections ran and quivered as on the lustrous pelt of a beast in bright sunlight.

Along one side of the case was a tall gray form, the color of iron, holding a staff; his arm rose up under the slow pressure of a spring, and struck the central panel. In order to extend the arm it rotated slightly; only the iron-colored folds of its robe were perceptible, and its monkish hood, which covered its head and its extended arm.

The panel opened; two enamel birds sung, over which two hands clapped, and a ballerina appeared from a little door, bowed and disappeared. Death followed, carrying a scythe, but a richly-gemmed enamel robe covered the skeleton, falling in small heavy folds, and apart from the hollow face, the only other bones that could be see were those of the hands and feet.

Halter in hand, Death was leading the twelve apostles, which followed him, then a pope, a crowned emperor, a young woman and a soldier, and behind them, almost crouching, ran a bent old woman making the gesture of picking something up and nibbling it—and then a carillon of bells tolled, slowly and funereally. But the old woman turned round, abruptly stood up, and touched a door with her finger.

Then, on a higher balcony, a man dressed in red with a gilded head emerged and dropped into a metal basin, loudly, a dozen pieces of gold, whose ringing signified the hour of noon; and the entire summit of the clock was garnished with enamel heralds, and the notes of the carillon sounded like a golden fanfare of triumph. Above them, a large eagle shook its wings, until the large form the color of iron touched its staff once again to the flap that had opened, and the entire clock returned to silence and immobility.

"What do you mean by that?" asked the Emperor, brusquely.

"Nothing, Seigneur—it's only a mechanical toy. If you care to, however, you might admit that an obscure creative power emanates from the living forces of Nature—of her rivers, her flowers and her branches in your realm. Here is this statue, made of ordinary metal because it is the everyday labor of your subjects—but that robust labor opens the entrails of time. Death passes, taking away saints, apostles, popes, the Emperor himself, and goes back behind them to make sure that everything has been properly scythed down; and everything that can be gleaned, he carried away in his bosom—but as soon as he disappears, with his cortege of calamities, Gold arrives, whose power and dominion he has been unable to take, and Gold awakens with its joyful ringing the bells of your power, and the eagle of the Empire beats its wings, and everything is resuscitated."

"But I say," suggested a cleric, who bowed to the Emperor, "that this is a carefully-meditated, carefully-accomplished blasphemy and an insult to Your Imperial Majesty, as to that of the Church, your mother, your guide and your support. This river, according to the forms of the ignorant pagans, indicates the forces that lie in the Earth or the demons forging the golden boughs in the treasure-mines of the Evil One that are the branches of his power. That iron-gray form, whose features cannot be seen, is what philosophers worthy of pyres call Nature; careless of the power of God, they imagine her as a tall blind form, and her mantle is colorless because it is, in their view, within the power of humans to enamel it with the richest colors, at their whim. But to those rich adornments, they prefer the emblem of Death, the Death that is fruitful for hem, which has scythed down so many just individuals, including popes, emperors and kings. And behind that brilliant cortege, Sire Emperor, is their patience, long bent low, creeping along and picking up everything—their image of themselves, perturbers of power and faith—and that man, the golden idol, whose costume parodies the scarlet that comes of counting gold, their god, and then the heralds of the Empire's rebirth, for after a dead Emperor comes a new living Emperor, and the eagle spreads its wings, the indecisive statue of Nature and the Future come to close the hour with its iron wand and the last hour of power has sounded.

"That is what this symbol, in your capital, in our Church, recounts. A just presentiment has led you to remove it from your palace. We do not want it in our Church, where the people would read its dangerous exhortation. We refuse the gift of the Evil One, and accuse Laurent Télice of being his accomplice, with all his soul, and we demand that you deliver him to our justice."

The Emperor reflected. "Get that out of here." He pointed to the clock.

"You're according the man to our justice, Seigneur?"

"No," said the Empire. "He's subject to mine."

In the palace prison, where Télice's hands and feet are enchained, and his midriff fixed to the wall, the Emperor has entered.

"Télice, if the accusation brought against you is true, will you not have to defend yourself against it before me? I have removed you from the vindictiveness of the clerics; it might be mainly your skill that offends them—but the meaning that you have put into your work is also obscure to me."

"Sire Emperor, there is none. It's merely a mechanism, dressed with the most appropriate and amusing sculptures and ornaments I could find."

"They tell me that the little old woman who follows the powers, if she is not, as they have said, the patience of the ambitious who want to put an end to God-given rights, is even more blasphemous—the image of a second and more total death, which accumulates souls in the colorless networks of oblivion."

"I didn't think of that."

"And what does the man in red signify, who chimes midday with the ring of his gold coins?"

"Isn't it a simple and new way of sounding twelve strokes, striking a metal disk with twelve balls?"

"Don't lie to me, Télice. I know what people say about you, and perhaps those who spy on you are right. If you will put your power in my service, I'll save you from the arms of the Church."

"What power? It's very small. I'm skillful in all the arts..."

"Télice, your soul is not our own and you know how to make Gold. It's that power that you wanted to affirm. I sense it; I divine it. I want to confiscate it, or you'll die. Make gold for me, or you'll die."

"You can put me to death, but I can't make gold."

"Be careful—torture is harsh. You'll make gold for me or you'll die. It's not without reason that the King of Hibernia is claiming you. He knows your power. How did you get here?"

"By going straight ahead, at my pleasure; I can't make gold."

"Be careful, my torture is severe." He called out, and men came in with a brazier and nailed boots.

"I can't."

The Emperor reflected. He sent the torturers away with a gesture.

"Don't be stubborn, Télice. I know that you're the Master of Gold; I'd dearly like to suspend your torture, but your bones will crack, be sure of it."

"Oh, Sire, perhaps I said that I was the Master of Gold; whoever has a little of it is its master, can go right or left, north or south and remain free and proud; he gives and does not ask. By means of the mechanical arts I've obtained enough to remain free and idle for long hours, having worked for a long time, and perhaps I shall find secrets by means of which river-boats will travel more rapidly or workmen labor more nimbly and more happily. But all that's a problem of divination. The gold you seek, Sire Emperor, and which lies nowhere in the entrails of the Earth within your realm, is in the brains of your subjects, their fingers and their rapidity..."

"But then they will become, thanks to their activity, Masters of Gold, and more powerful than me."

"You are their Master and they love you."

"Let's sing," said the Emperor. He recalled the torturers.

Dolorous screams echoed from the somber vaults; the fire of the brazier colored the Emperor's breastplate with blood. Fingers cracked; there were groans.

The torture was interrupted.

"Well?" said the Emperor.

"Oh, Sire Emperor, I'm cruelly punished. Oh, for having juggled with words, for having been specious, droll, witty, oh, for having summarized thoughts, for having said long things briefly! Everyone is the Master of Gold who knows how to fabricate it with his labor, but I have none, I cannot make it..."

"You shall reflect," said the Emperor. "Good torturers will reckon with this brutal stubbornness. In the meantime, you'll guard my prison—or rather, it will guard you. Powerful as you are, and in spite of the diabolical auxiliaries you possess, you'll talk; you'll be mine, you and your power, or you'll rot."

And Télice remained alone and bloody in his dungeon.

The Emperor had gone back to the Palace. He summoned his wisest advisers and said to them: "Am I right to act thus? And give me the reasons that prove that I am right."

The oldest of the old men spoke.

"Sire, everything that exists, until the irrespirable region of the sky, within the limits of the Empire, is, by rights delegated by God, and transmitted by inheritance, Imperial property. First and foremost, it is incontestable that the land is yours—that what the land produces, above all—the crops, the earthly bread that you distribute on God's behalf, the flowers that velvet the Earth, the thick forests, the enormous granaries of winter food-supplies, and the rivers and streams, the roads through our domain, and the gushing springs—is yours. The beasts of the air, the waters and the forests, necessary nourishments, are also yours. This is sanctioned by the most ancient laws; Bounty, which is one face of Authority, deigns that domestic animals appear to be the property of those who raise them, as vegetables belong to those who water them with their sweat, but your possession, if it exercised all its rights, would be entire, and the tribute that everyone owes you is the sign of that, and the ever-evoked truth. Everything adherent to the ground—the houses, the palaces in which you lodge your faithful subjects, as well as the fields with which you nourish them—is yours. Everything on the land is yours.

"The people who live in your Empire, who lodge there and nourish themselves there, are therefore full of your substances—for which, in spite of all rents, they owe you recognition. They owe you their service and their affection. As thoughts cannot be born without the permission of God, of whom you are the perpetual legate, without the fortunate accord in the human body of the food that your broad reserves provide, their thoughts must be yours. Thus, Laurent Télice, who lives under your domination, in the immense enclosure of your property, if he is solvent—and the means for that are unlimited in your hands—ought to pay you tribute, in silver, for that patch of ground and wall that he occupies, and mentally, for the thoughts that exist within him, under your protective right. Thus, if he possesses some marvelous secret, he is in your debt, unless you dispense him of it and return possession of it to him, in return for a reasonable tithe, while he has usage of all inventions in Your city and lives in your lands. Moreover, in order that an evaluation of the tax on this idea and its accomplishments should be possible, it is necessary that he communicates it to you. You are therefore retaining him in your prison justly."

"You're forgetting that, immemorially," another old man objected, "hidden treasures can only be revealed on the condition that the Sovereign's property is increased by the largest share. In your list of the wealth of which the Crown may make the luxurious and beneficent display, have you not omitted to include the mines and the fortunate veins that run through the Earth? By analogy, one may deduce from the prerogative of the Emperor in respect of such treasures abruptly brought to light, an incontestable right to treasures discovered by skill and experience. This does not undermine what you say, but fortifies it with another reason. I agree that the thoughts hatched in this expanse of land, falling under the same authority, are vassals of this authority, and that Télice's invention is subject to the imperial will, and that he is obliged to render to Caesar that which is Caesar's."

"Yes, but can the clerics say so? Will they not attempt to prove to you that the Spiritual domain is theirs? To that, Sire Emperor, we submit that you should reply that this is not purely the Spiritual domain. Doubtless Caesar, vicar of God on Earth, may hand over to the power of the Church, to its strong and frail hands, the blasphemer and the unbeliever, but there is no proof, and can be no proof, if the door of the dungeon remained solidly bolted and if one does not listen to any solicitation by the captive, who might desire the presence of a chaplain, that Télice is a blasphemer. He is, at this moment, like a pirate's ship traversing the estuary of your river laden with a rich booty. If you seized it, would you give a share to the clergy, or let them claim a right, on the grounds that the pirate was probably a miscreant? No, Sire, the Church is in charge of souls, and has no power over bodies. It is you who has jurisdiction over Télice's rebellion, if he remains mute, or the benefit of his speech, if you induce him to tell you everything."

"What if they're not content? I don't like having interminable difficulties with them."

"Then, Sire Emperor, abandon something else to them, which quite clearly concerns the Kingdom of the Heavens."

"But what?" said the Emperor, thoughtfully. "Who's that? What does he want?"

"It was an officer from the prison, Sire Emperor; we have, according to your orders, requisitioned the most experienced of your city's physicians—it appeared to us that the man in question must be old Ezra. Summoned, he came in haste, but when informed of the situation and introduced into the dungeon, he limited himself to zealously applying unguent to the captive's wounds. He refused to assist in the questioning. 'Call me,' he said, 'to cure the harm that you have done; it will be my duty to tend this unfortunate and soothe him, but I will not lend myself to the task of giving strength to calibrate the instant of weakness in which his soul will belong to you, and in which your hands might collect the red and wounded bird of his secret from his heart.' He laid his hands on the sick man, who went to sleep, and he left."

"What—you let such a rebel escape?"

"He had such a grandiose air about him, such an aspect of venerable strength, that it was as if our hands were nailed down. No one dared make a move against the old man."

"Find him and bring him back. Your head..."

The officer bowed and went out.

"Sire Emperor," said one of the counselors, "this is the fruit of the great generosity of your law, and the suavity of your welcome. The city is a paradise for these people of another race, for these people of another land, who come here to live as in their native land, and do not like you and do not like us. They are scarcely ever seen frequenting the Church; on the other hand, they are a strong presence in the markets, on the bridges of commercial barges and the profound storehouses that border the river. Undoubtedly, they pay Caesar's denier, but what is that denier by comparison with the mass of gold that their hands ought to be pouring into your coffers? I do not know whether Laurent Télice's secret will bring you any great profit. Certainly, if the rumor is true...and the person is enigmatic, and I believe that he does indeed possesses marvelous secrets...but these foreigners, Sire Emperor...you have them in your hand, you have only to press and the wine of wealth will flow into your vats. For that, there's no need of tortures; let your heralds touch their rods to the doors of their palaces, let your soldiers take possession of their warehouses and their ships, and I warrant that you'll be twice as rich as you are now."

"My right is certain?"

"Certain? Most certain. What are they doing in your land? Like trees brought from elsewhere, they have put down roots here, they produce fruits. Pick them—pick them without dread."

"I wouldn't like to deprive so many people; I'd dread seeing their pale and sad faces looking at me at the festivals, accusing me of having caused bitter weeds to grow where once a beautiful fruit-tree prospered."

"Banish them. You won't see them any more—but only banish their persons, so that their wealth can continue to decorate our fatherland. Or deliver them to the Church; it will be able to discover their crime and punish their thought, while you will have taken care of their body."

"Thank you, my sages, my faithful followers, but will I not become a man cited as avaricious. Will not men attribute to me the color of gold amassed instead of the color of gold conquered and won from the enemy?"

"Gold is the color of the Empire, Sire Emperor, the gold of the land is the property of Caesar."

"I'll think about this. Go and question Télice for me again, and make sure that old Ezra is sent to me." He rose to his feet.

The counselors went out, offering one another mutual encouragement and congratulating one another.

The Emperor walked back and forth in a vast gallery adjacent to the hall.

"Sire Emperor, Sire Emperor, don't you want to hold your true counsel now, with a true sage?" And the fool Thrasylle, clad in red and yellow, with little bells on his belt and the bracelets around his wrists and ankles, and cowbells on his cap and bat, pug-nosed and deformed, with a child-like face, enormous eyes and a decrepit gait, advanced toward him with all the rapidity of his short twisted legs.

"Hold counsel with you—oh, undoubtedly! To whom ought gold belong Messire Fool?"

"To everyone."

"Why?"

"In order that all might give it. Oh, if it belonged to one alone, to you, you wouldn't be able to leave your palace. All the people of the city would lie down in the path of your horse, crying: 'Crush us, Sire Emperor, but give us gold.' If it were yours alone, you'd have to provide dowries for all the maidens of the city, who would lose the better part of their beauty if you confiscated the lot, and you'd also have to occupy yourself with all the courtesans who proliferate here, according to rumor, for you would be the dispenser of all joy to your subjects. But if you take all the gold, Thrasylle will be more prosperous, for you would give him a great deal of it; you'd be fatigued by our burden, and that which you had taken from reasonable folk, you would be reasonable enough to give to a fool."

"And if you had all the gold, Thrasylle, what would you do with it?"

"I'd take écus and plant them in the ground, to see if they'd grow. That's never been tried. There's be too much risk that they'd go astray and that salamanders might devour them.

"I'd enclose up in hiding-places and have it announced mysteriously that near an alder not far from two willows there's a hidden treasure; then all the men would take the place of the good women who go to consult sorcerers, and I'd have a book of questions and answers compiled in order to have the funniest estimates in the world.

"I'd have a gold piece placed in every tavern opposite the barrels, and whoever took the one couldn't touch the other, and would have to spend a long time watching others drink, in order to put your subjects between two tortures.

"And I'd instruct the sergeants to lose some of them, in order that people unhappy at dawn should be happy all day.

"And on those days, it would be necessary to lock up all the misers and keep them at home, in order that they'd acquire beautiful yellow complexions, and possess the reflection if not the thing itself.

"Those are a few of the thousand sage measures that I'd take."

"You're joking, joker—that's your job."

"As counselors counsel. Sire Emperor, why are all the counselors old men?"

"It's because one only asks advice from those who possess experience."

"And how does one acquire experience?"

"By making mistakes, correcting oneself, and meditating on one's errors and those of others."

"Then it's by virtue of committing errors and seeing them committed that one becomes capable of giving good advice?"

"You're boring me, Thrasylle. Go away."

"I'll go away, and I'll go advise the Princess to furnish herself with very old men, those who have bumped into wisdom most awkwardly, in order to take them away and study the lumps they have on their heads."

Old Ezra, led by a palace officer, was awaiting the pleasure of the Sovereign.

"Well, old man, until now I believed you were wise, or at least prudent. Do you realize that, under the pretext of humanity, you're simply censuring me?"

"I would scarcely censure the guardian of your prison."

"Why did you refuse the service expected of you?"

"There are many other physicians in the city capable of killing in concert with executioners. Let me go."

"Where do you come from, Ezra? It's a long time since you disembarked in our port. You must have amassed some wealth here; people often come to your door to buy health, and I understand that you're an honest merchant. Gratitude is a meager treasurer, but the fear of death speaks abundantly, and brings ducats in large number to the altar of sacrifice. I swear to you, Ezra, that you will march straight along your cherished route if you obey my orders."

"Which are?"

"To assist in the questioning."

"To assist in a man's death?"

"In his death, certainly not! Stop placing a bloody mirror before my actions. No, not his death; but benefits will gild him more than ever before, more than his art could, if he tells me what I want to know. If Télice concedes that his secret becomes mine, there's nothing I'll refuse him. But admit that, if he persists in his silence, how can he profit from his gold? Would he be able to deploy the luxury that he certainly desires without fear of indiscreet and pressing interrogations? It's not for nothing, for knowledge alone, that he has researched the opulent secret. What does he want? I can't imagine that he's thinking of making criminal attempts on the rights of crowns by the power of gold; if that were the case the axe would cut his secret in two. What he desires, undoubtedly, is luxury, and freedom, displayed in the open air. I'll give him a fine position in the Empire. Go, tell him that, and bring him here, repentant and convinced."

"He can't come; his ankles are broken."

"Let him be carried."

"Futile. He won't say anything."

"Why not?"

"Because he doesn't know anything."

"You're defying us, old man."

"Alas, no, Sire Emperor. Télice won't reveal his secrets because his secrets don't exist."

"He's in thrall to the Devil!"

"There are no demons but the ones in your heart. What furnace of desire has been inappropriately ignited in you? What chimerical appetites are soliciting you—you, sated with everything? The most senile of old wives' tales have got into you, and have exacerbated your cruelty. Infantile notions are leading you to tarnish your good name with blood. What does the Emperor believe? The words of old herb-sellers, when a man in velvet passes by? Have you not yet been advised to mistrust poor folk in general, or is it the fattest that your counselors indicate to you as explicit enemies?"

"Are you Télice's friend?"

"No; I've already criticized him for making his happiness consist entirely of masquerades, droplets of pleasure and emptied tankards. I've criticized him for believing that everything in this world is a game of skill, and I didn't like his triumph. I mourn him now that his skill and triumph are killing him. How wise they are who invest their wellbeing in the ungraspable word!"

"You are one of those?"

"Perhaps, Sire Emperor."

Where did you come from when, already old, you settled in my city? Strange legends also circulate on your account. Old men say that they have always seen you, and that your appearance has always been the same, venerable without being decrepit. It's claimed that, if you don't possess the philosopher's stone, you know philters, and that your face is merely a mask veiling some dark unknown. It displeases me that my Empire should be haunted, but all in all, out of respect for your noble beard and your attitude, which resembles that of the saints in stained glass windows, I won't disturb you if you obey. I'm not even asking for you to assist in Télice's torture any longer. You're a kind man; I'll allow you to act kindly. Go to the prisoner. You, who are knowledgeable, tell him irrefutable things; tell him that if he doesn't give us his secret, you've been promised many honors to research it, and that you're going to begin the marvelous quest, and that the secret will no longer be worth anything. Persuade him. Make use of threats, employ terror, and, as you understand it, torture. It's no longer an order to which I'm bending you, it's a prayer that your benevolent Sovereign is addressing to you. You have, in this affair, my powers. Go."

"Sire Emperor, it's futile. Télice has no secret."

"Oh, wretched old man! Vile infidel, vile rebel, my force will tame you. Hola! Guards, let him be Télice's companion. Take him away."

"May the shadow descend upon you," said Ezra.

"Here are my orders," said the Emperor to the commander of the guards, while two men led Ezra away. "Tonight, torture; I shall be there. Tomorrow, if pain has remained mute, death. Let the city gates be closed, let these men's friends be imprisoned. Let the clerics be warned that they will have consciences to judge. The Empire will resume, under my will, a tight hair-shirt. I have been defied; I shall be harsh, until time has enabled me to forget this disagreeable hour. Yes, I shall be harsh—but not to you, Princess Marie."

The princess had just come in.

"What's happening, Father? I saw old Ezra being led away by guards; people are saying that Télice is in prison. These people have hardened your face; you're anxious. Will my father no longer be the good Emperor whose kindness is revered as much as his courage is feared? I've come explicitly to ask you for a favor."

"What?"

"Seigneur Father, all these people who are annoying you, give them to me. I'll take them to Scania. I'll have so much need of fools in my kingdom—fools of all sorts, who'll tell me the most amusing tales. They're the only ones who are good authors. Tell me, father, will you do that?"

"No, my daughter. The respect that we have for our rights comes before our tenderness—but if you want a fool, I'll give you Thrasylle. Anyway, there's no longer a place here for a fool, nor even a jester."

"No, Father, I refuse Thrasylle—he doesn't say reasonable things."

"Then be content with your fiancé; if he's a fiancé like all the others, he'll tell you a thousand foolish things, and the ones that you love. You've entertained passably hot heads in this palace, Princess, and it's partly your fault that they're now in gehenna. Your songbirds coloring the hours will go a little red, which will be a lesson for you. 'It is a great love, very great indeed, that subjects have for their Emperor,' is the beginning of one of your songs. How does it go on?"

"I daren't tell you—you'll be angry."

"Speak."

"They are weeping, they are weeping/Streams of blood/While his body is placed in the ground/And his soul, with slow paces/Goes away, goes away to Hell—but that's an old children's song; it's about the Emperor of gold écus who had a magician for his first minister, a gravedigger for the second and a shoemaker for the third."

"Why?"

"Because he had very large feet, in order to walk better through the blood. Sire Emperor, I'm no longer laughing, no longer laughing. You're scaring me—be merciful."

"You have nothing to fear."

"Oh, you're not playing, you're not joking. Have I, then, already so much to fear from you that you want to reassure me?"

"You have nothing to fear, I tell you."

"Father, father, I want mercy for everyone—and then I'll tell you a long story of springtime, the heroine of which is me, who loves, the hero of which is your son-in-law from Scania, the *deus ex machina* of which is a good Emperor, very good, very good."

"Go away, madwoman. Go to your apartment, and don't come out again. Don't put your eyes or your ears to your window; what will happen this evening, in the palace and the city, doesn't concern little girls. You, commander of the guards, come with me, and send someone to fetch the captains. I can see clearly; I shall act directly. Commander of the guards, go to the prison of Ezra and Télice."

"Sire, I've come to tell you that the dungeon is empty."

"Empty? How?"

"The doors are still closed and the windows bolted."

"I swear by my scepter that all these treasons will be punished. Come with me."

THE REVOLT

The city resonates to the heavy tread of patrols. In the houses, rough soldiers tear beds apart, empty cupboards, drink the contents of the cellars while exploring the corners with smoky torches, climb up into the grain-lofts torches in hand to look for hiding-places—and women weep on the doorsteps, and men are chased from their homes so that they will not hinder the fist-shaking searchers. Drums beat; the heavy tread of halberdiers plow through the city. They go to the gates to reinforce the guard-posts; chains are extended between the quarters—but what it is all about no one among the trampled and jostled crowd knows.

What is going on?

"Someone has tried to kill the Emperor!" someone shouts in the Market Place—and the fearful populace, becoming indignant, cries out and heads for the palace. The trumpet sounds; among the cavaliers, stiff and proud, the emperor is seen passing by. Whatever it is, therefore, it is not a popular riot. As people are over-abundant in certain places, however, the men at arms launch their horses at the groups, and the hands of inoffensive passers-by go to their daggers.

The cathedral bell rings; it is the lugubrious tocsin warning of unfortunate fires, and the city becomes noisy. People run around; they interrogate one another. The gallop of cavalry detachments cuts through the streets.

Here come the heralds; the people are ordered to return to their homes; the good will be spared, the traitors punished. Here, however, is the home of an inoffensive citizen filled with light and screams. A butcher uses his cleaver to fell a lansquenet who has touched him with his pike, laughing. The lansquenets kill him, and after a brief horrified silence, the call to arms goes up, and men run through the streets shouting: "Laurent Télice has been imprisoned and tortured!"

A grave royal counselor harangues the people. Télice has been imprisoned; he possesses the secret of gold; he has refused it to the Emperor; he has escaped from prison; those who know where he is must denounce him and show themselves to be faithful subjects. The city has been poisoned and perverted by the foreigners; let them be expelled. The Emperor permits that they be pillaged.

Lansquenets and men of the people enter pell-mell into the houses of the rich. Neighbors insult one another, and now the tocsin is no longer sounding without pretext, for red flames are climbing up one of the city's houses. Blood is running.

Here comes Master Asverus; he is rich; he has businesses and ships; let's stab him—but a lansquenet falls, then another, and battle is unleashed. Master Asverus and his associates have passed on, along a bloody street. The tocsin sounds; the red standards of fire cry out and answer one another from place to place.

People kill while arguing and seeking information, and the horrible fanfare of murder, with its screams, its drums, its heavy and numerous footfalls, its cries of rage, its cries of distress, is unleashed over the city. It is a continuous, incoherent, unconscious clamor. People look out of their windows while arming themselves, others fall on their doorsteps, sometimes struck down by their partisans, and in the tumult of ignorance, people cut one another's throats without knowing why.

A substantial part of the crowd heads for the palace, howling, and bloody, shouting "Télice! Télice!" and engage the men-at-arms in battle. Some people are fighting for the Emperor, others for the frights of the city, others simply defending themselves in that immense riot—and the sound of trumpets the trumpets of war persists, frighteningly, unleashing combat in every soul.

Why, no one knows. One man wants Télice free, another wants the Emperor all-powerful. Old women see the exterminating angels passing beneath the stars, and pale white forms flee through the as-yet-dark back-streets, and people attack one another by the river, in the vicinity of the barges.

The Emperor and his escort had gone straight to Ezra's house. The noise had not yet penetrated the deserted street. The house was brightly lit, the door open. The Emperor rushed in.

Ezra was standing in the main room. Télice was lying nearby, and Samuel and Rizpah were at the back of the room. Ezra advanced toward the Emperor. A red light was filtering from a wooden vessel on a table, which filled the entire room, and it was that light which extended brightly through the entire house, soft and miraculous, like a beautiful sunset.

"I've been waiting for you, Sire Emperor. Have you gone mad, murdering your city to punish imaginary enemies? Sit down with us, and listen."

A kind of invisible force weighed down on the Emperor.

"Here," Ezra said to him, "is the blood of Jesus, the man who was unjustly killed. It was in your city; it brought benediction here. It is shining this evening for you, as a final warning, for there is still time to stop the blood that is flowing and the fire that is spreading. In the name of the one you revere, who died alone and afflicted in atrocious tortures, abandon the bloody path. The Grail is Heaven's counsel to force. Oh, since Joseph of Arimathea put it in my hands, I have searched the surface of the Earth for the pure and upright man, his hands exempt from blood, the sovereign elect, in order to confer the benefit on him. It is not a talisman, Sire Emperor; its contact does not cure the sick; it does not discover hidden treasures; it does not reveal the secret of gold; it informs us that happiness for every individual lies in the reign of dolor and peace for all.

"Emperor, human as you are, do you not know that to-morrow, death will place its dry finger-bones on your forehead, and that you will crumble, and that your sepulcher in the cathedral will be nothing but a sumptuous box in which nothing will be enclosed! What does the secret of gold matter to you, who are the guardian of several thousand lives? Your power gives you the right to leave tranquil or quickly conclude the transitory movement of humans from birth to death. You are the Emperor, but where are your virtues of intelligence, where are your spiritual godsends, which will construct in your frail palace of muscles the eternal being that will survive you?

"You are nothing but a rumor. Listen to the counsel of this mute clarity. It corresponds to the learning that your infancy collected. Be human—a forgiving man if you believe yourself to have been offended, a man of common sense and intelligence if you take account of the fact that, in being disobeyed, you are being served—be worthy to approach the blood of the Savior. It signifies, I tell you, that any torture inflicted is the only inexpiable crime. Withdraw, and revoke your orders of carnage. What is happening here, Caesar, is not of your domain."

"I have listened; I like to hear these old men rambling on. Guards, seize him!"

At that precise moment, the light went out—and when the Emperor and his men had succeeded in lighting torches, the entire house was empty and plunged in silence. Everything had disappeared; no trace remained either of the Grail or its priest and his guests.

The crowd was howling "Télice! Télice!" in front of the palace. People were fighting. The Emperor was only able to reenter sword in hand. He instructed his herald to tell the people that Télice was no longer in his hands.

"But where is he?"

"We don't know."

"But he's no longer in our hands."

"You're being deceived, people!" cried a voice. "Télice is lying in some oubliette, where he has been murdered. Let us avenge him."

And again, the riot seized the throats of the people and soldiers with an iron hand.

Long, agile curtains of flame mocked the somber and sad tone of the tocsin. People murdered one another in the streets.

In the meantime, a barge was slowly making its way downriver.

"Sire King," said Asverus to Ezra, "I shall come back to this unfortunate city; tomorrow, it will have need of pity. King Balthazar, is this the last time that you will evoke the ship of Solomon? Where is your castle in Sheba, and how many times must we witness dolor?"

And King Balthazar replied: "Dolor and Folly are eternal."

The Grail illuminated the prow of the ship with a soft light; a tall female form stood at the helm.

PART THREE

Chapter One
THE RETURNS

I

Long years had snowed. They had settled one by one, slowly and majestically, on the desert strand of the world, like sea-birds informed by their scouts that a peaceful sojourn was possible between the sand and the Sun.

After a brief pause, all of them headed for the inhabited Earth, toward vegetation and distant bell-towers, and the white butterfly swarm of the hours rose around them, numerous and icy at first, then sparse and contaminated by dust, until they were lost on the horizon.

The Earth had often changed its four mantles: green, yellow, brown and white. There was always a little old woman trotting alongside time, in spite of the follies of spring and summer, the proud abdications of autumn and the senile and negligent despairs of winter. She always trotted alongside time with equal strides, while despairing of being able to keep up, and ever-ready to faint.

Fashions had often changed. Armor had become lighter, women's costumes had become more flexible. Armchairs were not as hard. People complained about the decadence of art, and an ever-greater liberty in mores. By way of compensation, philosophers had never had a better mastery of the rapid course of truth. This time, in spite of its subterfuges and volte-faces and the thousand other ruses it employed to escape the hunters, it had come to be clearly mirrored, and the tight mesh of the net of research had fallen upon it. People were often discontented with vintages but always content with wine. Bold

235

ships had deciphered the seas and noted new territories, in which the customs of ancient kingdoms had been immediately and unreservedly implanted.

The Sun shone for everyone. There were still rich and poor, but the nourishment of the poor had been ameliorated by scientific discoveries. It was more expensive, it is true, but that was only temporary—like everything, alas: the mantle of summer, the truth, and even the Sun, which was weary of shining for everyone.

Master Asverus arrived from a distant land, heading for the City. He had crossed the estuary; where he had left a bare bank, he found a quay, and congratulated himself. He got down from his ship—slightly archaic by comparison with the slender masts and elegant hulls he perceived in the harbors of the port. He hesitated among new streets. He had not changed much himself; he was still tall, very stern, very upright, his hair streaked with silver.

He headed toward a palace on the river. Having arrived, he asked to see Comte Télice.

Moments later, in a vastly extended hall hung with decorated shoemaking leather, a lively old man hastened toward him and cried: "It's you! It's you! I knew I wouldn't die without seeing you again, but where have you come from?"

"From far away and everywhere."

"Good, good, you can tell me all about it. How glad I am to have followed your advice and not left the Empire forever. You told me that life changes, wounds scar over. You know that after that formidable upheaval when the Emperor was searching violently for an imaginary windfall, when the people tried to take possession of an empty prison—blood and flame were expended for nothing on that occasion!—several years of terror weighed upon the land. The Emperor did not recover his composure. 'I have always been good; people have been hard and secretive with me. I don't deserve it.' And he was very cruel, but at the same time vacillating, indecisive and bad-tempered.

"His daughter, Princess Marie, now the Empress, benefited from that in the love of the people. At first she was perfect for the father—who had, we firmly believed, gone astray momentarily. He had been truly good before becoming truly evil. And if you knew what the chroniclers don't know, the Princess played a role relative to the old despot rather like a new David relative to a resuscitated Saul. When she came from Scania with her husband the king, to watch over the failing health of her husband, he imagined at first that she was coming to take over her future wealth in advance It was known that he had sometimes prepared poison for her, without ever daring to carry it through.

"It's curious, but the scarcely triumphant escapade of which I was the subject—the pretext, if you will, for his mind, luminous until then, darkened, and if it hadn't been that occasion, another would have provided a deed—that escapade, as I was saying, that evil victory and, at the same time, if you like, that ridiculous defeat—for he was victorious in the streets by did not triumph in his desire—could not fulfill the inanity of his objective. It rendered him adventurous toward evil, in spirit, but very timid in the application of his projects. I'm sure that he ground his teeth inside, and that people who seem quite well are often on the point of disappearing at that very moment. It was a cruel shame. But I'm rambling, and perhaps you know all this already, for you've come back."

"Yes, among the smoking ruins; but I'll stay for a little while—long enough, at any rate, to hear about some fine follies."

"And to do some good, also, I know that—but when your barge carried me away, I was very weak, although cured by Master Ezra. Do you know what's become of him?"

"No, not for a long time. He left for the Orient, that's all I know."

"Well, I was carried to that ship of yours, of whose commercial wanderings I kept track for a while, but fever is a bizarre architect. Guess..."

"It seemed to you that old Ezra, dressed in white, with a large silver necklace of pearls on his breast, mitered in silver and white diamonds, took the tiller from the hands of a tall shadow, or a form with features similar to, but more beautiful than, those of Rizpah, and that the shadow vanished?"

"So you had the same hallucination?"

"Or the same vision—or it was the same true phenomenon that appeared to our eyes."

"You see, it's mysterious, very mysterious…fever, fatigue, you were certainly overexcited too…

"In brief, when the Emperor died…I told you that before then, the Princess was the only one who could charm his black moods, by singing him sings and telling him charming little tales full of what we call primal innocence; it was a nasty end. When the Emperor died, the new Empress declared a general pardon, a plea to all those whom the ill-humor and insecurity of the previous reign had banished to return and to work with her, each according to his rank—in his slot, I might say—for the splendor of the Empire.

"I came back, and was well-received. Her Majesty's grace had the effect of making me forget the old wrongs that had been done to me and which had been largely, generously compensated. I am, as perhaps you now, ennobled, grown in fortune and honor, a chamberlain."

"Do you still make things as admirable as that clock?"

"Oh no, little things, little things; human wisdom has taught me only to make little things, but very fine, very accomplished, with a grain of surprise in every new creation. They're toys, beautiful toys. Oh, let's not go too quickly toward perfection; our great-nephews will be resentful of it; we shall not see them, but at the end of the day, I'd rather dream of creating points of departure for them, hypotheses, instead of bequeathing them perfect things. I hope they'll be very ingenious. Here and now, we pluck the days that hang in gilded clusters on our vines. If you're going to the Palace, I'll show you some beautiful things, alongside our rough sketches."

"But how are things in the Empire?"

"People laugh a little here, chatter a great deal, and most of all sing. They play a great deal of comedy, and also noble tragedy. We don't act much, but we adore watching acting. For the people, we have marvelous fabricators of tears and also sculptors of laughter, people who know how to grasp that gross good humor of good vintages, and tread it for our populace, and our city also honors the precious artisans of fine language; it's at their comedy that the palace smiles. The life of the Palace is very distant from that of the City and the Empire. A kind of thick and well-guarded wall defends us from the great cares of State. There are ministers for that. At the palace there are only concerts and masquerades, and admirable songs. I have a certain reputation in dancing performances."

"And our poets?"

"Excellent—a cheerful tenderness and an amiable sadness that doesn't go as far as melancholy, charming things! Anacreon[22] is their model."

"All that is perfect!" exclaimed Asverus. "Perhaps I'll become your fellow citizen again."

"That's it, that's it—stay with us. Come on, come with me to the palace. There are superb new gardens; we'll walk there, and then I'll ask for an audience with the Empress—who'll receive you I'm sure, with all benevolence."

"I don't doubt it, my dear friend, but that will be for another excursion, very soon. I have to take care of some business matters, and my ship will bring me back to you. Until then."

"Until then, my one-time savior, and always my friend."

And Comte Télice accompanied Asverus to the door with perfect amity.

"There's a rare courtier," said Asverus to himself, as he returned to his ship. "Everything slides over people of that sort: men of action, delicate politicians, rare courtiers; wounds

---

[22] A Greek lyric poet whose works (most of which were lost, although later imitations survive in profusion) celebrated pleasure and the joys of living.

scar over quickly. They have a little lively sap, like his city; they age themselves and the city flirtatiously; love of gold and power and good grace in a wise equilibrium!"

"Still savages, these old businessmen," Comte Télice said to himself. "To come here and not to go immediately to the Palace, the cradle of the arts. He's always had something extraordinary about him—a visionary, a utopian!"

II

Asverus left the city. His horse followed a narrow path along one of the small tributaries of the river. The waters of the rivulet ran broad and shallow; one might have thought it a large stream. The water rippled over large stones and against branches. Then it spread out into pools; seabirds and herons rose up with plaintive cries. He went through a village. A herd of cattle passed along the road; children fled, laughing. The diners at an inn saluted him. He left the village and pushed the lattice-work gate to a hose set back from the road. He tethered his horse to the inside of the hedge. A short aspen-lined path led to the house. He went along it. The house seemed to be empty. Master Asverus sat down on a bench beside the door, and enjoyed a moment of immense silence.

The silence was almost total; it was heightened by the insignificance of the few perceptible sounds: the heavy tick-tock of some large clock behind the wall to which it had its back; the buzz of insects; the rustle of leaves; a cloud of dancing flies; swallows passing by with a flicker of wings. The house, a few thousand paces distant from the city, seemed lost in some little frequented islet. A lawn of wild grass and herbs extended away from Asverus' feet. A fawn emerged from one of the corners of the house, looked around and sniffed, as if nervous. Asverus made a movement toward it; the animal leapt away. He followed it for a few paces; it jumped over a small hedge. There as a scintillation of red roses behind the hedge; the fawn went to nestle a woman who advanced briskly toward the visitor.

"It's you, Master Asverus. Samuel will be very happy to see you again. Look at my roses. They're as beautiful as the radiant past..."

"Or the flowery future."

"A future of one summer—we won't reach another. Look at my hair—it's white. Winter's approaching, and its ice. I've lived."

"But you're still upright, and still beautiful, Rizpah."

"I'm alive; I'm no longer Rizpah, but someone else. Here's my garden, here's my house. Sit down on this veran-dah. Samuel won't be long. It's the time when he wanders for a while along the sunken paths, and watches the butterflies go by. He's still Samuel."

"For you and for him."

"For me most of all, I think."

"Beautiful flowers," said Asverus, and his fingers drew a basket of fresh colors toward him."

"They're heavy," Rizpah said. "Their heads bow down beneath pearls of water. They're lives of a day."

"You're happy, Rizpah."

"Very happy, Master Asverus, but I was even more so in that distant garden where you left us when we departed the city. The dawns were fresher and the sunsets calmer, and I was still Rizpah."

"And now?"

"I still have the same soul, but the sharp scissors of the years have cut the flowers of my life. I'm an old woman."

"But Samuel must have aged too."

"Yes, but I'm less aware of it."

"And how does he see you?"

"As I am—but here he is. I'll leave you to talk to him."

He was all old age—not that his tall stature was more than slightly stooped; his face did not have too many wrinkles, his hair was only silver. Nothing about him was decrepit. But on his vast forehead and in the depths of his large brown eyes, lassitude reigned entire; his hand was devoid of vigor, and his arm discouraged. When he sat down next to Asverus, the latter seemed a young man.

"You're sad," Asverus said to him.

"Yes. I've been waiting for you; the Earth is slipping away from me; I knew I'd see you before escaping. Yes, my desire is to slip out of his existence as one leaves the room of a cherished invalid on tiptoe. And that anxiety not to wake the invalid up arises from the fact that one feels slightly guilty about her suffering. The anxiety also arises from the fear of bringing her back from a fortunate vision of the land of dreams and offering her nothing but the ingrate face of a tired man, a terminated man. I'd rather flee with muffled footsteps, Asverus, from that brightly-lit house, into the darkness I sense out there, since I can make no response to an awakening. An awakening is a fire of hope that is just catching alight, and I have no branch to throw on to it.

"O Master Asverus, the old man who is beside you knows less than the child at whom you once smiled, in the city on the river. I've seen the myriads of infinity escape without knowing their form, without knowing their route. I don't know any longer what the Spirit is. Doubtless I've never known, and have mistaken for its invasion within me moments of obscurity and semi-sleep. Oh, when did my error begin? Was I a child, was I an old man? I don't know. If the Spirit has left me, I never heard it depart. If it never came, in what shadow have I lived? Who has dictated me? Have you brought me the answer?

"Why have I echoed the creation of the reign of Speech to such an extent that I no longer recognize the reign of Silence? Alone and dead, I no longer think. It sometimes seems to me that it has not always been thus, but just now I'm no longer sure of it. Why have I been given a life, in which I have seen misfortune, in which I have penetrated happiness, in which I have been unable to see the clarity of the Spirit—and without that, everything is shadow, everything is...perhaps Death, if death is only the absence of life.

"I don't understand the gesture of other old men, who cross their arms, content, before the full barn in which they've amassed the minutes of their past, and I don't understand their smile of joy before the beehives they have planted. And yet, once I understood everything; Asverus, I shall exit this world feebler than I entered it, more uncertain. That's not what saddens me, though, but the racket of my departure."

"Why?"

"Firstly because, if I die, Rizpah's tears will flow, and her dolor will thunder within her; I shall repay the hospitality of her love, the consolation of her arms, the salvation that her lips have poured over me, and her belief in me, or the appearance of her belief in me...oh, no, I'm not mistaken, and I know the full extent of her generosity...I shall bring down as I fall a temple in her heart, and the falling stones will surely wound her, and profoundly. A temple to the genius that she believed me to be, and that perhaps I appeared, a temple to herself, to the belief that she had in the energy invested in me—what does it matter? It will be nothing but ruins and rubble when I'm gone.

"Secondly for myself. Oh, when the ice begins to expand within my memory, and I see the last leaves of my soul fall at my feet, and my trembling fingers and my entire agitated body strive in vain to serve them, unable any longer to pick them up, and my eyes will search, and no longer distinguish anything in a mist projected everywhere, where there will be nothing but themselves, as I fear the supreme moment, the flame behind knowledge.

"And to begin with—can you see them?—my old futile ambitions, all the childish desires of my life, my immense indolences, file before me, as sad as the vanquished, and after them, that laughter, or those outbursts of grief, that were the strengths that I never awakened, which, on the contrary, I bathed in narcotics. And at the most bitter turning of that last terrestrial dream, I shall see the city of my dreams surge forth: the one I ought to have built, the one whose palaces would have been made in my image; and there will be laughter…whose, I don't know, but someone's…that of forces, for there must be witnesses to so much human cowardice, and there will be laughter, as that décor that I possessed and was never able to see slips through my mortal fingers to go toward some new soul; but there will also be weeping, if that city was uniquely mine, if its towers collapse with my strength, if its gardens fade beyond my sight, if its streets and squares sink and dissolve into the darkness, because my fingers have not counted then, my voice has not named them.

"Tell me, Asverus—you're an ancient of days, I'm certain of that—tell me: when a man plunges into oblivion, is he an assemblage that disaggregates, is he a whole that goes to sleep forever? If I die, will I be a distraction that vanishes, will I be a murderer that has killed a dream? Asverus, I can still see, no longer my dream and its many details—all of that is within me, in a hard gray matrix that I have allowed to set hard and can no longer break—I can still see my life, and I see my hand striking my soul with dagger-thrusts. I see my soul palpitating in a corner, without granting it a glance. I see that in my life there has only been one beautiful and harmonious minute, and that it is not me who put it there but Rizpah. I'm already dead; I'd prefer to escape slowly and silently, and that the door should close behind me silently."

"But why, Samuel, did you want to come back so near to the city? I had placed you in the most beautiful place—almost an Eden."

"Yes," said Samuel, "Almost an Eden, and with the primitive and virginal happiness of an Eden. I read the book of joy there; I deciphered love here—not that of poems, not the troubling anticipation that I once believed to be love, and which is merely an occasional portico. But Love breaks when force disaggregates it; Love is a good companion until the Autumn. In the winter of days, the guide, salvation—call it what you will—is no longer called Love.

"Love is not a child archer, as the Hellenes imagined it. It is a strong and robust woman, and yet with the movements of a child; she bears a lantern of solar brightness. She comes

244

from the edge of forests through tree-lined avenues; she enters a garden full of sunflowers and red roses; she opens the door of a house; the lamp that she sets down shines brighter than daylight, and golden gleams play around divans; and the man gets up stronger, an adorable caress still adhering to his lips, when the beautiful form has drawn a few steps away from him.

"And the man who captures the eternal Eve and retains her in his house forgets the mists and the cool breezes of spring; he traverses Summer on a blazing river, seeing nothing of the sky but gleams on flowers, and sparks of splendor melt and dance everywhere around him. He traverses autumn with the lover at a slower pace, a more earnest pace, and the days declining amid the crimson and the gold of leaves seems slower to him, and the Sun set the entire day to melt in curtains of fire and flakes of snow among the porphyries of the palace of infinity.

"But in winter, Asverus, the beautiful and strong woman that you saw after dawn no longer comes, solar lamp in hand, through the avenues of frost and ice! She would be a poor shivering and dolorous woman, her light flickering. In winter, a woman in love is a mother, and a man in love a chilly child whom she coddles and warms up; perhaps that is salvation, but it is no longer victorious Amour, and that is one more defeat.

"One knows that, instead of entering the Palace of the Word and the Kingdom of the Future, one has simply whispered the tale of Speech, a vain tale, punctuated by interruptions, with bizarre tones and eccentric cadences; one has whispered; one has talked nonsense, and in what tale does the poem of Love end? Why does the power of Love die in a man before he does? Why has the Love that is illusion hidden the precipices from us for so long, suddenly to reveal them to us? Why does it lead two beings, who have traveled the entire road, laughing and singing beneath the benediction of the fires of midday and the caresses of the enchantment of the setting Sun, suddenly to leave them empty and shivering on the most somber of esplanades before the gulfs of shadow and infinity?

Would it not be better that no cup of joy were brought to us than that that the only one given to us must run dry? Why that beautiful dream amid our nightmare, and that attenuation of all the simple horror to which we are dedicated?"

"You're complaining, Samuel, Rizpah isn't complaining."

"Asverus, taking to you is causing me to suffer—submitting my momentary soliloquy to your temporal attention. You know, and I don't, but am I any less delivered to myself alone and forced to learn all alone? For Rizpah, I'm the end; it seems to me that she has loved me. She has embellished the desert, she has garlanded the inanity and set vases of flowers in the margin of the void. If I am gone, she is gone; she has no goal—but did I not have a goal, myself? To resonate, to resonate so high that the promulgated swords would be laws, reflections of true laws. All Rizpah's love and all her pity have fled, poured out into my hands. She has lived; she has been, if not happy, existent and complete; she has filled her phantom, and me—where is mine, which was an appearance external to me?"

"I asked you why you came here."

"When I sensed my soul becoming drowsy, I wanted to come close to the place where I was happy and unhappy, where actions touched me brutally, but gave me by their blows the sensation of my existence. I can no longer do anything but dream; I would like to dream of action.

"Since I've been here, though, I haven't headed toward the city; I remain a long way away from it, and from the Eden where I experienced love, and from the Garden of the Hesperides where I might see again...what triumphs? I take a hundred paces to the right and a hundred paces to the left. The horizon is, for me, a little less limited than the tomb, but every day it shrinks. I don't even dream any longer about the dawn of my life. I hold myself ready, near the place to which it flows, in order better to relive my entire life in a minute between all my pasts, those of dolor and those of joy. I no longer dream about anything but the desire to dream."

Rizpah came toward them. Asverus considered her long gaze, in which lamps burned directly; he saw her gaze embrace Samuel anxiously, and her tenderness sit down beside him full of mute interrogation.

"Rizpah," he said, "if a long voyage would be a considerable source of felicity for Samuel, would the things of this world—your house and the sky—hold you back?"

"Not at all, Master Asverus, but is it truly a happiness that I can give him, thanks you?"

"Thanks to you only—but it will be necessary to see old Ezra again."

"We'll leave tomorrow, if you wish."

"But Rizpah," said Samuel, "I have no need of any happiness."

"We'll leave tomorrow," she affirmed.

Chapter Two
THE CIRCUMNAVIGATION

Asverus' ship has taken to the sea again. It is drawing away from the low and sandy coast, going toward the wall of mist on the horizon, as white as a snowdrift, which melts as it approaches. White birds keep it company. Great green plains are painted on the thick glaucous cloud, and yellow expanses like fields of wheat. Large green hollow cups are sculpted among the waves, and in the distance, it is as if large white flocks are huddling together and colliding. Occasional moving sails pass, hastily. On board, mariners are singing. The Sun's glare is like a universal cupola.

The sea is populated by figurines in silver-hemmed robes. Enormous surges originated far away reach the hull, bending, breaking and licking as they arrive. A transparent plain looms up before the prow and the castles of the chimera superimpose their thousand terraces of red-streaked marble upon the sea. Shreds of the dawn are imprisoned in the blue of the sky.

The wind get up then, and plays, swelling the sails, running over the ship's deck and moaning slightly, as if slightly fatigued by its race, and the majesty of the evening sends its pale, calm heralds in advance, which unify the bright colors of the waves and the sky as if with the slow movement of a scepter, and the Sun makes it way toward its retreat at a gentle pace.

On the lowest terrace of its occidental city it pauses, and blood flows from its breast, in a slow gesture of its arms which raises crimsons in the altitudes that it has just quit. And the wind, freed from a master, sensing that the king of the day is retiring before its moment of power, shrieks and moans more loudly, and begins its threat—and the great forces of oblivion drive black expanses with crests of foam to break upon the hull and licks the flanks of black wood.

It is as if an item of news were passing from hand to hand at the ends of a thousand arms, arriving from the vast sea, which is not communicated to wandering ships. The pale disk of the Moon appears, and for some moments—long moments—it dispenses with its veils before showing its pale round face. The sailors' voices are melancholy.

It is now that the vessel senses that it is alone between the waves and the clouds; the urn of the stars is poured out over the sky, and here is the infinity of the torches of space; it is the immense domain of the unknown, which is, at this moment, a colossal city with densely-packed streets, lit by numerous torches; it is on the restricted earth that the desert of shadow and darkness extends.

Everyone on board falls silent, the pilots and watchmen go about with muffled footsteps; tomorrow there will be dawn.

And every day, the dawn that welcomes the ship is brighter, and the waves are bluer, running beneath a more beautiful sky, and the priests of the rising Sun stand up rosier above the clouds every day; and every evening, the sheets of scarlet raised by the blessed arms of the Sun become more imperiously dazzling, as violet nights surge forth, which coax and lull the waves, which dream rather than sleep. Forms allow long white robes to trail over the expanse of the swell, and sometimes the sea lights up. All the waves are ornamented with green gleams like meadows of tender grass.

Islets of florid spring and the gay dances of goddesses run over the crests of the waves, and from the immensity that plays and swirls perfumes travel, which pass over the ship and go toward distant coasts to fade away. Cool fingers caress the human foreheads. It is no longer a moaning wind but a whispering breeze, amusing itself, and total calm extends across the whole sky. The white sash of the clouds offers glimpses of profound plains strewn with sparks.

Now the ship is sailing on a blue mirror; the waves flex beneath its prow and close again gently, as if scarcely disturbed in a siesta. Enormous dolphins escort it, leaping joyfully. The ship has entered into a complete solar contentment.

Softness flows from the tranquil sky, from the honest Sun, from the calm horizon, from the infinite plain of liquid azure. Perfumes blossom abruptly like enormous flowers.

The ship that bounded over northern seas glides over this lake of repose, rocked by the sweetest dreams. The sea is hospitable to the desire to live; the light reclothes the mind in a festival mantle, and happy pilots allow the serene contemplation of the voyagers to drift silently.

The pilgrims of dolor are borne away by the waves of a physical sensuality, and the cool of the evenings is tender, almost amorous—and after long days, the ship comes to shore, docking gently at the base of a stairway that descends into the sea, where droplets of the dying waves shine on marble steps.

IN THE CASTLE OF SILENCE

"Sire King," said Asverus, "here are the pilgrims of life, vases of dolor. We have chartered them, to dwell among men; here are those who are returning to us, laden with all the sadnesses. Would you care to receive them in your palace, and, since they have not found their land in this world, would you care to resorb them here, in order that calm might penetrate them and prepare them for new thoughts, if destiny still keeps them captive in its eternal march?"

"Sire King," Rizpah added, "I have often seen your serene splendor in my dreams, when you were the good Ezra. It's true that we are a trifle weary. A few days will suffice for us to recover our strength. Outside the world, we shall revive more fully, and if new aspects come to flourish in our minds, which have suffered so long in looking through the monotonous windows of mediocre existence, we shall become young again in spirit and in vigor."

"At least," added Samuel, "We have turned our backs on the flat Earth, where I have suffered so much, where every object that my eyes encountered sufficed to evoke a cluster of bad memories. Oh, if I could renew myself, if the lustral night of refuge wished to cover me with its forgetfulness, if I could be reborn another..."

"Live here," said King Balthazar—and he guided them toward the large terrace overlooking the sea. "Do you remember, Asverus, the day when you came here for the first time? The walls were ornamented with such ancient frescoes. They were destroyed; I didn't find them here on my return. Immortality rolls many corpses in the equal waves of its minutes. Are we not as exhausted as them, as far as ever from the end and the goal? What are we, Asverus? Perhaps the frisson of a dream that is finding it hard to end, the thoughts of a colossal dreamer turning over in tormented sleep.

"Rizpah, Samuel, live here. You believe yourselves to be sorely wounded, worn out, very old; compared with us, you are perhaps still children, whose ages have scarcely begun. You entered into life by virtue of a little pain; who knows what is reserved for your souls in the long circumnavigation that they still have to travel, when the chains of our bodies are loosened?"

They went into a high-ceilinged room. On an altar, a wooden vessel shone with a soft light, and Rizpah—who recognized it—bowed.

"It's really him," said Balthazar. "The prophecies said that white hosts of innocence would rise up on his candor. I've shown him to the peoples of the Occident, and no one recognized him, and my spiritual sons, in the iron life of seekers of gold, have been reeds. Who will come now to reveal the old rite, which is vanishing from memory as our ship vanished over the horizon—who will come? Will anyone ever return to the castle lost in the light, as others are swallowed up in perpetual mists? Come on, rest, live here, let yourselves live. The unknown will speak to you here, and you will doubtless comprehend. Collect yourselves in the Castle of Silence, sleep beneath the cool and pacifying palms of Silence."

Samuel woke up light and lively, almost fluid. A ray of sunlight threw mobile flowers into the room; physical wellbeing and moral lissomness generated happy laughter, so youthful that Rizpah got up from her sleeping-mats and put sandals on her feet in order to run to his arms—but he exclaimed: "Rizpah! Rizpah! The mirror! Look at yourself!" And he leapt to her side, and picked her up.

In the large metal mirror, raised up by an iron claw, Rizpah admired the past—the already-distant past. It was her at twenty, the eyes smiling with a generosity in which a hint of dolor had left a kind of spark, like a minuscule drop of dew on a leaf; the forehead was pure and pretty; the cheeks fresh beside the mouth of hope and love, and especially the ebony eyes and the moonlight of the unbound hair, flexibly curled as if in friendly struggles; and the straight, round neck, a proud and solid channel of life and thought. It was her, her at twenty years of age!

"O mirror of marvel and of derision, dolor evoked..." But she interrupted herself and uttered an exclamation: "Samuel, your youth!" For he had placed his head on her shoulder, and she perceived his black hair, his solid forehead, his bushy black beard of yesteryear.

"But the mirror does not lie for you, Rizpah; here are your snows melted, winter vanquished amid the bushes of summer."

"No more for you, Samuel, since I see you again as in the hours of childhood dreams, when you came home and your smile filled the little house; here you are, young—shall we be immortal?

"Oh, whether this is eternal youth, or merely the reflection of a past happiness, or a mirage that has gripped our two souls, let us not waste the Edenic moment. We arrive here refreshed from former suffering; it appears to us more beautiful for all the distance that separates us from a similar vision of ourselves. Rizpah, I love you, and blessed be the man who had regilded that avowal with all our youth."

"Samuel, my soul as well as my body is hanging on your lips, O blissful mirage."

"This is no more a mirage than were the hours when my fingers untied your tresses," Samuel said, "when my lips respired your love on your forehead, and the petals of its flowers in your thoughts. This is no more a mirage than your moment of awakening in my arms, when you perceived that there was something other than songs and words. This is no more a mirage than our expectation of a renewal of spring, and since the fatigued, gasping Earth produces flowers every year in its blood-stained harvests, why can't we, the witnesses of the world, also flower again, flower again eternally? And who knows whether the limit is true that age obstinately raises up before our will? Oh, I have prayed so often to the gods of youth that perhaps they have granted my prayer."

"And I have begged them too, for my child, for you, my child, whom I cradled on my shoulder. O fountains once frozen, in which I saw my shadow quiver, the formidable fist of our desires has broken your ice, and your crests of white frost are no longer anything but diamond ornaments and luminous bracelets on our wrists. The horses of the dawn are galloping unbridled, O my wealth, O my law."

"And life is only serene and just in being durable. Come toward the Sun, beneath the pavilions of summer."

"Sun, master of destinies, profound nurse, total matrix, Sun of young years replanted on the summits, on the snowy summits where you still smile."

"Sun king, Sun god, philter of forces, clarity supreme."

"Sun that I drink at dawn."

"Sun whose evening fall bears me away and causes me to vanish."

"Kind Sun, terrible Sun, Priapic Sun."

"O gentle master whose force makes languor, and resuscitates force from reawakened languors, benign Sun."

"Divine Sun, solar altar, I burn in your heart and die."

"Sun, your guiding hands return us to wakefulness."

"O Rizpah, your hectic curls fall on the nape of your neck, and the Sun amuses itself; it has its milky way in the white span of our shoulders."

"O Samuel, the lotus grows and blossoms with all its pistils of love."

"O master Sun, O divine Sun, the color of love and the scepter."

"Crazy avalanches of joy and worlds of mist are swept away by my two hands, and I stand directly before you and contemplate you."

"And the white immortality of the gulf grips me momentarily."

"Yes, Samuel, for an instant, telling me, however, that I love you, I love you."

"For all the mourning of the past, for the happiness of the present, for the enchantment of the future, for all the caprice of my soul."

"Yes, for all the caprice of my soul and all the permanent dream of your soul, and your hands, and your forehead, and your ivory caress and for your forgetful eyes."

"Forgetful of what?"

"Oh, if we're immortal, we have only to forget; by virtue of all the beliefs of the past and future, I love you."

"Good, I love you too; you shall tell the world that Samuel loved you, in the world that is here, in the world in rebirth or remembering, in the world that might give back a moment of youth."

"I'm going away, Samuel; I can feel the snow in my hair."

"Illusion, Rizpah—you're imagining it. Oh my beloved, my caresses are doing you harm."

"No, Samuel, but that wasn't immortality, at least for me. Be calm, listen to another kiss."

"This life is criminal if the black hair of a moment ago was only a mirage."

"It was a gift. Stay here—oh, I see cruelty in your eyes, and you believe that the magicians of that moment are due some vengeance. On the contrary; they were good. Without them, could we have expected that happiness of a minute's rebirth? For myself, I thank them.

"Listen, very closely, listen—do you want me to laugh in your eyes? No, you're afraid of the vitrified dawn rising in my eyes; listen with your ears.

"There was for me a moment of happiness, before you would admit all that you loved in me, and over what pyres of dead flowers I rose to your fire of joy. I have cradled you, wounded, I have caressed you, convalescent; you have loved me with life, you shall love me all alone.

"This is the night that is coming within me, more gently because I sense that the Sun is turning around us; this is the night which is overtaking my caressing hands; they are dying entirely, and the night is rising over my eyes, which are dying entirely.

"Now I'm leaning over; a mist is spreading over my valley, where my kisses flower as white daises; I'm holding your fingers like the iron ring on the quay where a barge bearing perfumes shelters; I have given them the slowest and most distant countries of flesh and memory.

"Friend, this is death that is throwing its cloak over my valley. Oh, it's not the hard chisel that you dread, Samuel; one might think that a soul more beautiful than me is holding out a cup, and I am drinking from it."

And a marble languor settled over her face.

"Rizpah, Rizpah—I'll follow you."

Then a large form, taller the living Rizpah, all white and white-clad, the eyes ardent in the bloodless face haunted by every sadness, seized Samuel's hands. "I am still Rizpah," she said.

"Who are you?" dreamed Samuel.

"Mobed the benevolent, color of your dreams and your eyes."

And she led him, like a child, into the next room, laid him down, and with a gesture of her hand over his eyes, put him to sleep.

"Oh yes, the crazy story of Palamedes,[23] a grain of wheat, from one grain four, eight, sixteen, and forests in the granaries, all human sweat and divine fecundity gradually put in store."

"Ah, wise words, Master Asverus; a determination, added to a determination, and obscure worlds grow."

"And the luminous worlds decrease."

"According to other doctrines."

"No, by contrast in the same doctrine."

"Humans sow the seed of their belief, and one day reap harvests of tares full of flowers, the seed of that tare having been nourishing wheat."

"I've scarcely seen anything but tares, Sire King since I've been roaming the world and the world has been chattering in my ears. By dint of wandering, Sire King, my soul has taken on the color of the world. It is uncertain, it gives birth to versatile images; the background remains as solid as the rocks of the sea's gulfs, but the play of light passes over it. Perhaps the principles of life and the world are fixed, but the appearances are variegated and transient."

"There's their house, Asverus, behind those trees; they haven't lived according to that view, they've long expended all their strength of passion. They've felt the festival of renaissance pass. Perhaps they've seen the man who will serve the new truth, the truth stripped of its languages; perhaps He will make it known."

"I'd like nothing better, Sire King, but I have been traveling the world for a long time now, and the only thing that

---

[23] Palamedes is not mentioned by Homer but was said by other writers to have been one of the heroes who joined the Greeks in the Trojan War—only to be betrayed by Odysseus, in revenge for having devised the trick that forced him into the war, and treacherously killed. Palamedes had a considerable reputation as a sage, and was traditionally credited with the invention of arithmetic and all its wonders.

has changed—often, admittedly—is fashion in capes and hats."

"We shall see. You are doubt, Asverus."

"Because I am the witness, Sire King."

And they went around the clump of trees; the house was cheerful among the carob-trees and pomegranates, and the thrust of a vine embraced the whole.

"Let's not go any further," said Balthazar. "I can see her sitting on the threshold, her head between her hands."

"She's weeping," said Asverus. "She weeps as the embodiment of Birth, or Love. She has become that of Death."

"Let's go back. Let's go back quietly, so our footsteps won't be heard. Death has triumphed over Love; the terrible principle of Mobed has triumphed over her principal of joy and florescence. We are old children, Asverus, feeble in her hands, and she is not the mistress of the work of her hands. Mobed the benevolent is the force that kills. Let's go home, Asverus, let's go home. Oh, that she might remember us, and embrace us as she has done for them."

"No, Sire King," said Asverus. "I want to get closer. I want to see; I want to hear."

"But my friend, even if you get close to her, you'll only perceive her reflection."

Asverus launched himself forward, but the white, sad form was already thinning out, dissolving into the trees.

On the terrace overlooking the sea, the Sun blazes brutally; the slow blue waves fold up near the ship; the direct white fire of the marble steps is blinding.

The pilasters of the colonnade retained their proud altitude, but as if a disastrous wind had passed by, tearing away the small ornaments, and vases lay in pieces. The place of the frescoes was empty and bristling, fragments of mosaic scattered. Within the resistant frame of the palace, one walked upon the dust of memories. The Halt threatened ruin, before the broad road to elsewhere, ever open, ever monotonous, ever enigmatic.

And Balthazar cried: "Where are the kings who once tra-veled the world with me in search of marvels, of the flowers that grow unexpectedly between the stones of the village street or near the parvis of temples? We went from the Orient to the Occident, from the South to the North. Our orchestras have murmured, our poets have sung, and all the divine flowers have withered. We are more immortal than wisdom. Instinct, the need to seek, the thirst for spiritual adventure, the appetite of the human-god, curiosity regarding the well that sleeps in our soul and into which we can descend, the mines of our thoughts with intersecting corridors, the irreducible desire to see our souls come into the world and blossom, you were ante-rior to us. You traverse us, you prolong our weary and fasti-dious existence, and if our wish to die were granted, you would still endure: the quest for knowledge, the attempt to embrace us that is our self."

"But why die, Sire King, if you must be reborn the same, with the same desire, less rich in our experiences?"

"Yes, die, Asverus, in order to recover the freshness of the search, which does not grow weary in a human lifetime, since it only lasts through one of the monotonous phases that we have accumulated. Are you not, Asverus, a man who would like to lie down in no matter what cradle, hear indistinct murmurs, songs that never end, and then sense the matrices of silence closing in?"

"Silence, Sire King, is the arduous mountain that you have climbed in order to contemplate the calvaries of the world from its summit. Look, little florets are growing here. They remain upright because the wind of the world stops res-pectfully here. This is the field of ideas, the garden of the songs of poets."

"It's meager; this heath is sterile and cold. Oh, Asverus, who will warn us up at this altitude, from which the world agitated in juxtaposed scenes, fables that have been repeating for such a long time. And why would it change?"

"And why wouldn't it change, Sire King? Perhaps it isn't intelligence that created the world. If there are no new flowers of wisdom, perhaps we should search for something else in the world and the sky."

"But what, Asverus?"

"I don't know, Sire King—but come with me. We'll travel the world again, and ask for another light."

"Of whom, Asverus? To be the vassals of Gold and Force?"

"The vassals, or the masters."

"In the name of what, and with what objective? No, Asverus, there is nothing supreme but intelligence and its effort to know. Contemplation is everything; the rest is nothing. The rest is the road of futile turnings. I shall remain here with the Grail and the frescoes of goddesses.

"The Grail is extinct and the frescoes shattered."

"When we traveled the world, we three kings, we had chosen those goddesses; our hearts carried them with us. We took a great deal of trouble creating them. They enclosed the contours of our wisdom. For us, they were the matrices of the world. The women who resembled them were fecund with prophets. Why have their reflections only created ephemeral mortals? Why have the goddesses not been able to take form? Is it not true, then, that a thought can give rise to a being?

"Thoughts doubtless die—after a life longer than a human being's, but they do die; they're remembered as shadows. Is that what will become of us, Asverus?"

"Not me! I'm ready to sail, Sire King. I'm going down the steps of the Castle of Silence; my vessel will take me back among the shadows that are humans. Devoted to amassing gold, they won't see me, any more than they saw me in the past. I shall be amid their vague and futile chatter, shall see them get up, lose their breath and die. And among them, I shall be the Silence. And if some unexpected flower should spring up, a sail will bring me back to you."

"You won't come back; there is nothing unexpected; go, son of men, prepare to sail, and go toward the sunrise, toward the promises of the Sun; go, the golden mists are calling you. I shall envelop myself in the mists of the sunset."

And on the departing ship, the coarse voice of a sailor sang:

Fly, agile ship, over the seas.

It has seen the thousand palaces
mirrored in the face of the waves
and the thousand minarets
which rise above the profound sea.
Its gaze is fixed again
on the little cloud
fleecy in a corner of the sky,
and its gaze grows wings.

It comes back discouraged,
there is still a little cloud,
amusing itself at the world's masque;
it has seen the hundred thousand years
it has seen rope-makers' fingers twist
long threads of years, and the withered stems
of centuries-old plants,
its gaze has not gripped again.

Fly, agile ship, over the seas.

And from the prow, as the ship turned slowly toward the open sea, Asverus bowed to King Balthazar, whose gesture blessed him.

THE WINGS OF SILENCE

"Azrael, Azrael!" cried King Balthazar. "I appeal to you—here I am alone, and no lamp any longer burns in the castle! Open the night to me, the eternal night. I reenter it more alone and slighter than in the morning of days; I am less rich in the hope of an objective. Answer my prayer; lead me into death, gather cherished shades around me. Animate my goddesses and my prophets amid my song. I have cried from the depths of years, I have cured wounds and despairs, and I have cured hopes; I have diverted the hunger of a few humans. I have held out cups; some have died with the certainty that they would see blazing tabernacles; others, thanks to me, have vanished over lips. In the circumnavigation of time, our hands are open; I have spread the manna that I believed to be certainty. Have I done well? Infinity, Unknown, have I done well?"

Infinity remained mute. Asverus' ship bounded over the waves; the Sun sank toward the horizon.

"Unknown, Infinity, Uncertainty or Certainty which hides you from me, is Azrael, then, no longer your messenger? Let me see the fingernail that will strike me down. I want to die before time does. Oh, even if the radiant face of belief will rise up one single day from the depths of this vague multiformity, I'd prefer not to wait, for I'm so tired!

"Bounty, is that not the key to your enigma, Universe? Then may the waves of the air, the sea and the sand bury me, and if you are God, O Unknown, O Infinity, kill me now; kill my ambitious and curious soul, in order that it will not be born again in a human form. Don't leave me to live, my presence compounded of misfortunes. Perhaps the science of Oblivion will escape from this unknown desert refuge, this palace so long-forgotten, as contagious as the plague, and pollens of misery will fly away to the four corners of the flora. Universe, if you are merely a décor, do not let the anxiety of souls live on. O Infinity, do you exist?"

Asverus' ship disappeared in the distance. The heroes of the Sun descended toward the sea on sumptuous scarlet stairways.

"Mountains of silence, crush me forever. Let my quest end; it has been so futile. It seems to me that I collected a rose one day, and that I have spent the time remembering its perfume. Oblivion is all the routes that I have followed. An old king shivering on a deserted terrace is begging Infinity in vain, begging whatever there might be to appear, to listen, to reply. An old king weary of being himself, who wishes to see the vessel bearing his thirst for adventure—which is the human soul, which is all souls, since I am one of them and they are all equal—depart for the last time. Free me, Azrael!"

Dusk invaded the sea and the palace, and the long robe of evening extended over the world.

"O external powers, your negation is proof of your non-existence!

"O interior power, my soul, awake, awake for the supreme slumber, awake in Silence! I want to haunt, alone, this castle that is sinking slowly, stone by stone, with the sound of drops of molten lead, into an interminable lake. I want to haunt it with myself and my shadows. I want to walk here amid my creation, or sleep here. Silence, extreme and total word; Silence, which is the totality of God; Silence, my father, Silence, O arm of the embrace in which I shall awake the phantoms that will render me life."

Momentarily, moving in the violet shadow in the indecisive corners of the terrace, Balthazar saw the tall forms of Mobed, Theano, Glyphtis, fecundity, death and certainty, and of unjust torture, beauty and unconsciousness.

The Grail lit up again, and old Joseph was holding it in his hands.

Dares glided forward, holding his iron lamp.

"Yes," Balthazar said to himself, "it's them, the shadows of yore. I can't see Asverus, nor Samuel, nor Rizpah, those whose were true phantoms in life. Here are the characters of my soul coming to life again; we're going to live."

Summoning them to follow him with a gesture, he went inside the Palace.

Night extended over the world, and the pale disk of the Moon unswathed itself of its clouds.

The Silence was eternal.

SF & FANTASY

Henri Allorge. *The Great Cataclysm*
Guy d'Armen. *Doc Ardan: The City of Gold and Lepers*
G.-J. Arnaud. *The Ice Company*
Cyprien Bérard. *The Vampire Lord Ruthwen*
Aloysius Bertrand. *Gaspard de la Nuit*
Richard Bessière. *The Gardens of the Apocalypse*
Albert Bleunard. *Ever Smaller*
Félix Bodin. *The Novel of the Future*
Alphonse Brown. *City of Glass*
André Caroff. *The Terror of Madame Atomos; Miss Atomos; The Return of Madame Atomos*
Félicien Champsaur. *The Human Arrow*
Didier de Chousy. *Ignis*
Captain Danrit. *Undersea Odyssey*
C. I. Defontenay. *Star (Psi Cassiopeia)*
Charles Derennes. *The People of the Pole*
Georges Dodds (anthologist). *The Missing Link*
Harry Dickson. *The Heir of Dracula*
Jules Dornay. *Lord Ruthven Begins*
Sâr Dubnotal *vs. Jack the Ripper*
Alexandre Dumas. *The Return of Lord Ruthven*
Renée Dunan. *Baal*
J.-C. Dunyach. *The Night Orchid; The Thieves of Silence*
Henri Duvernois. *The Man Who Found Himself*
Achille Eyraud. *Voyage to Venus*
Henri Falk. *The Age of Lead*
Paul Féval. *Anne of the Isles; Knightshade; Revenants; Vampire City; The Vampire Countess; The Wandering Jew's Daughter*
Paul Féval, *fils. Felifax, the Tiger-Man*
Charles de Fieux. *Lamékis*
Arnould Galopin. *Doctor Omega; Doctor Omega & The Shadowmen*
G.L. Gick. *Harry Dickson and the Werewolf of Rutherford Grange*

Nathalie Henneberg. *The Green Gods*
V. Hugo, P. Foucher & P. Meurice. *The Hunchback of Notre-Dame*
Michel Jeury. *Chronolysis*
Octave Joncquel & Théo Varlet. *The Martian Epic*
Gustave Kahn. *The Tale of Gold and Silence*
Gérard Klein. *The Mote in Time's Eye*
Jean de La Hire. *Enter the Nyctalope; The Nyctalope on Mars; The Nyctalope vs. Lucifer; The Nyctalope Steps In*
Etienne-Léon de Lamothe-Langon. *The Virgin Vampire*
André Laurie. *Spiridon*
Gabriel de Lautrec. *The Vengeance of the Oval Portrait*
Georges Le Faure & Henri de Graffigny. *The Extraordinary Adventures of a Russian Scientist Across the Solar System* (2 vols.)
Gustave Le Rouge. *The Vampires of Mars*
Jules Lermina. *Mysteryville; Panic in Paris; To-Ho and the Gold Destroyers; The Secret of Zippelius*
Jean-Marc & Randy Lofficier. *Edgar Allan Poe on Mars; The Katrina Protocol; Pacifica; Robonocchio; Tales of the Shadowmen 1-7*
Xavier Mauméjean. *The League of Heroes*
José Moselli. *Illa's End*
John-Antoine Nau. *Enemy Force*
Marie Nizet. *Captain Vampire*
C. Nodier, A. Beraud & Toussaint-Merle. *Frankenstein*
Henri de Parville. *An Inhabitant of the Planet Mars*
Georges Pellerin. *The World in 2000 Years*
J. Polidori, C. Nodier, E. Scribe. *Lord Ruthven the Vampire*
P.-A. Ponson du Terrail. *The Vampire and the Devil's Son*
Maurice Renard. *The Blue Peril; Doctor Lerne; The Doctored Man; A Man Among the Microbes; The Master of Light*
Jean Richepin. *The Wing*
Albert Robida. *The Adventures of Saturnin Farandoul; The Clock of the Centuries; Chalet in the Sky*

J.-H. Rosny Aîné. *Helgvor of the Blue River; The Givreuse Enigma; The Mysterious Force; The Navigators of Space; Vamireh; The World of the Variants; The Young Vampire*
Marcel Rouff. *Journey to the Inverted World*
Han Ryner. *The Superhumans*
Brian Stableford. *The New Faust at the Tragicomique;The Empire of the Necromancers (The Shadow of Frankenstein; Frankenstein and the Vampire Countess; Frankenstein in London); Sherlock Holmes & The Vampires of Eternity; The Stones of Camelot; The Wayward Muse.* (anthologist) *The Germans on Venus; News from the Moon; The Supreme Progress; The World Above the World*
Jacques Spitz. *The Eye of Purgatory*
Kurt Steiner. *Ortog*
Eugène Thébault. *Radio-Terror*
C.-F. Tiphaigne de La Roche. *Amilec*
Théo Varlet. *The Xenobiotic Invasion*
Paul Vibert. *The Mysterious Fluid*
Villiers de l'Isle-Adam. *The Scaffold; The Vampire Soul*
Philippe Ward. *Artahe*
Philippe Ward & Sylvie Miller. *The Song of Montségur*

MYSTERIES & THRILLERS

M. Allain & P. Souvestre. *The Daughter of Fantômas*
A. Anicet-Bourgeois, Lucien Dabril. *Rocambole*
A. Bisson & G. Livet. *Nick Carter vs. Fantômas*
V. Darlay & H. de Gorsse. *Lupin vs. Holmes: The Stage Play*
Paul Féval. *Gentlemen of the Night; John Devil; The Black Coats ('Salem Street; The Invisible Weapon; The Parisian Jungle; The Companions of the Treasure; Heart of Steel; The Cadet Gang; The Sword-Swallower)*
Emile Gaboriau. *Monsieur Lecoq*
Steve Leadley. *Sherlock Holmes: The Circle of Blood*
Maurice Leblanc. *Arsène Lupin vs. Countess Cagliostro; Lupin vs. Holmes (The Blonde Phantom; The Hollow Needle)*

Gaston Leroux. *Chéri-Bibi; The Phantom of the Opera; Rouletabille & the Mystery of the Yellow Room*
William Patrick Maynard. *The Terror of Fu Manchu*
Frank J. Morlock. *Sherlock Holmes: The Grand Horizontals; Sherlock Holmes vs Jack the Ripper*
P. de Wattyne & Y. Walter. *Sherlock Holmes vs. Fantômas*
David White. *Fantômas in America*

SCREENPLAYS

Mike Baron. *The Iron Triangle*
Emma Bull & Will Shetterly. *Nightspeeder; War for the Oaks*
Gerry Conway & Roy Thomas. *Doc Dynamo*
Steve Englehart. *Majorca*
James Hudnall. *The Devastator*
Jean-Marc & Randy Lofficier. *Royal Flush*
J.-M. & R. Lofficier & Marc Agapit. *Despair*
Andrew Paquette. *Peripheral Vision*
R. Thomas, J. Hendler & L. Sprague de Camp. *Rivers of Time*

NON-FICTION

Stephen R. Bissette. *Blur 1-5; Green Mountain Cinema 1; Teen Angels & New Mutants*
Win Scott Eckert. *Crossovers* (2 vols.)
Jean-Marc & Randy Lofficier. *Shadowmen* (2 vols.)
Randy Lofficier. *Over Here*

HEXAGON COMICS

Franco Frescura & Luciano Bernasconi. *Wampus*
Franco Frescura & Giorgio Trevisan. *CLASH*
L. Bernasconi, J.-M. Lofficier & Juan Roncagliolo Berger. *Phenix*
Claude Legrand, J.-M. Lofficier & L. Bernasconi. *Kabur*
Franco Oneta. *Zembla*

L. Buffolente, Lofficier & J.-J. Dzialowski. *Strangers: Homicron*
Danilo Grossi. *Strangers: Jaydee*
Claude Legrand & Luciano Bernasconi. *Strangers: Starlock*

ART BOOKS

Jean-Pierre Normand. *Science Fiction Illustrations*
Raven Okeefe. *Raven's L'il Critters*
Randy Lofficier & Raven OKeefe. *If Your Possum Go Daylight...*
Daniele Serra. *Illusions*